THE MOON LAMP

THE
MOON
LAMP

MARK SMITH

ALFRED A. KNOPF NEW YORK 1976

THIS IS A BORZOI BOOK
PUBLISHED BY ALFRED A. KNOPF, INC.

LIBRARY OF CONGRESS CATALOGING IN PUBLICATION DATA
Smith, Mark, [date] The moon lamp.
I. Title.
PZ4.S653Mo   [PS3569.M53766]   813'.5'4   75-37688
ISBN 0-394-49888-7

Manufactured in the United States of America

First Edition

For Anthea

6208

The moon has raised her lamp above,
To light the way to thee, my love,
Her rays upon the waters play,
To tell me eyes more bright than they
Are watching thro' the night,
I come, I come, my heart's delight!

On hill and dale the moonbeams fall,
And spread their silver light o'er all;
But those bright eyes I soon shall see
Reserve their purest light for me.
Methinks they now invite;
I come, I come, my heart's delight!

—*The Moon Has Raised Her Lamp Above*,
TRADITIONAL IRISH BALLAD

THE MOON LAMP

CHAPTER 1

WE ALL KNEW the same thing about the Linquists. Said the same thing, too. "One thing for sure," Maurice Dube said, "it had something to do with the ghosts." Said it—oh, could have said it anywhere, but said it then—on a late-summer evening as he stood beneath the lone outdoor light on the porch of Roscoe's store, wearing, as he always did, the green pants and shirt of the New Hampshire workingman, with the two cans of beer he liked to call "cold soup for supper" and the box of doughnuts that would be his only breakfast managed, football-fashion, beneath a single arm. He had paused to take his nightly place among those big blue Hubbards and bushes of McIntosh and Prince Edward Island blues and new straw brooms in a bundle and cans of motor oil that Roscoe had set out to face the road, and beneath that old-fashioned lettered store sign and the rack of moose antlers that had hung above the door for thirty years, taking care to plant himself between the porch steps and the screen door. Here we also paused, each man in his turn, preferring as we do to give and take our local news while on our feet: over a counter or, better yet, just about in passing, while on the threshold of going in or coming out a door.

"Maybe ghosts," Bob Cressman said, "and maybe Linquists —maybe nothing more extraordinary than themselves." Saying this, he struck a match to his pipe—a silver metal gadget that resembled a tin whistle—and glanced at the front page of our evening paper that seems to print more superpatriotic Letters to the Editor than it does the news, looking in his baggy overalls like the dirt farmer he had never really been.

Such a remark from a man who had been a selectman of our town for almost forty years had to put at least a temporary end to the matter, and we settled into a weighty but satisfying silence, listening to the tree toads and crickets in the darkness across the quiet road. These days it was already dark before eight o'clock, and a good dark it was, too, this earlier and cooler dark, darker somehow than it ever was in summer. Well, Roscoe would soon return to winter hours and close up the store before six, someone—anyone—might have said about then, had he been willing to leave the subject of the Linquists for something else. Already a warning in the starry sky and heavy dew that we would be close to frost by morning. Too bad men no longer had to work like squirrels, someone had said earlier, getting in the wood and garden for the winter. The best time of year, this time, we always said—didn't we always say that, though? And wasn't it a good thing to have the summer people gone again? And weren't we a special people, though, staying on in the good, healthy place, dwelling all together in this old-time world of lakes and wooded mountains where the outsider and the newcomer is not at home, or—best of all—does not exist? Why, for all the good feelings we felt on Roscoe's porch, we could have floated under the cover of this dark night several hundred miles north of where we were, and a hundred miles farther from the nearest big, mill-saddened town.

Then: "You don't think, do you, Bob, that they could have had a special talent for seeing ghosts?" Maurice Dube said.

Just then Roscoe came out of the store and, ringing off his

lone gas pump, bent over to do the job of filling Maurice's pickup.

"Ghosts," Bob Cressman repeated, and he appeared to spit.

Roscoe said, "Now, boys, you know you don't believe in them things."

"Don't matter what we believe in," Cressman said. "It's what they believed in out there that mattered—to them, anyway. Believe me, it's not half the ghosts as it is their talking about the things."

"That was bad enough," Maurice agreed. "All that talking."

Roscoe hung up the hose and said, "I guess you boys know the latest, too?"

I guess we do, we said.

And we all did. We all knew. Said the same things, too. To refresh any dim memory, we said, "You know, that couple out the Old Crown Road that is always telling us about their ghosts." And if we were ourselves the dim memory, we all came to the truth suddenly with the same "Oh, you don't mean those people at the old Hoitt place who told Gardner Slim [or somebody else] about their ghosts?" Maybe in the beginning we knew them for something else. Maybe in their first years up here we identified Gene with no more remarkable a reference than as that fellow who helped out last winter with the high school play. And to Winnie—as what?—as that fellow's wife, we supposed. We didn't doubt but that we would still refer to them in such a way if it weren't for the convenient tag they had given us with all their talk of ghosts. Believe me, before they moved up here, we had never claimed so much as a haunted graveyard, never mind somebody's lived-in house. At least as far back as any of us could recall. Nor, except in church, were we given much to contemplations of the spirit world. And a good many would maintain, not even there.

Not so the Linquists, though. Why, you would have thought they were Old World Scots, or Yankees of some older, darker age, the way they could go on about those ghosts. They mused over them as we would the weather, suspected them in every unswept, murky corner, drop in temperature, sudden draft of chilly air. And when they claimed they found them, what did they do but drag them out into the half-light of their lamps where they pumped them up into their ghastly shapes, then set them loose among us in anything from an offhand anecdote to the first chapters of what promised to be a full-blown Gothic-style romance? That is not to say they talked of nothing else. Or that whole evenings at their place were completely given over to the supernatural. But even if the subject did not come up, it often seemed that it was about to. And then God help us, we often said, when it did come up, for there was no getting rid of it except by putting on your hat and coat and standing in the doorway and trying to make them hear your repeated shoutings of "Thanks for the lovely dinner, and good night!" Some evenings we even wondered if our invitations were no better than their excuse to gain themselves an audience, and the drinks, dinner, and exchange of gossip no more than the appropriate preamble for the introduction of this terrifying theme. Not that we weren't often entertained. Nor put properly in the mood ourselves.

What a powerful force, too, this mood. Put together from many pieces. Even the drive over to their place had its role to play in the conspiracy. All those house trailers, little ranch houses, and jerry-built summer camps that had begun to dot the paved roads in our area of the state were not only put out of sight on the drive over but out of mind. In some places we could have traveled back two hundred years for all we saw along those roads. The car seemed an anachronism, a sacrilege; and, darkness or no, far better had we walked, or gone on horseback, or in a small buggy, if such were to be had nowadays. Macadam roads that were no more than lanes, leading finally to a remote crossroad called Crazy Corner where our headlights reflected on the oily windows of a frame building that had been an inn and then a store and was now abandoned, its

porchlike overhang leaning over the single gasoline pump—
unused for forty years—as though it might collapse at any moment into the road. Thereafter the way was all dirt roads, the
shoulders of which were overgrown with grape and creeper
vines in summer, while the high snowbanks made them resemble a bobsled course in winter. You were to go past the
house of a family that had not lived in it for fifty years, turn at
a sawmill no sign of which remained except the race, and that
hidden by a patch of elder, turn again at a crossroad the name
of which was on no map—that was how you would get the way
from here to there from us. No, you had to be shown yourself,
and it was no good going there in the daylight and then expect
to find your way again at night. Even the Linquists' road,
which we still called "the Old Crown Road," as our ancestors
had these two centuries past, was not so much a road as a signal
for city people to stop, think twice, and then turn back. It
cut along hillsides of white pines and hemlock, passing only
two houses along the way, both small Cape Cods, one upright
but abandoned, the other falling down.

If you came at night, as we did, you could tell the house in
the landscape only by its lights, which at Halloween and
Christmas meant an electric candle burning in each window
of the dozen rooms. But if there were no lights, you would
miss it, and God help you on that road that was no better
than a stony run-off for the snowmelt in the wilderness that
lay ahead. In daylight, though, you couldn't miss it—how
could you? An early-eighteenth-century saltbox with attached
Cape Cod ell and barn, all painted a leathery oxblood red,
standing away from the road and among pastures you would
have thought were the first to have been cleared from the surrounding forest, rather than the last to hold out against its
coming back. You might have thought the house was freshly
built, too, the pride of the first successful settler in the town-
ship—it was that authentically restored. Narrow clapboards
showing little to the weather, eight-over-six windows, a six-
paneled door, even wooden shingles on the roof—all the good

taste and hard work of the Linquists. It was a property we had always called "the old Hoitt place," and we called it that still, and to the Linquists, too; called their place someone else's place, and it seemed it was just as they wanted us to call it, too. No doubt we would call it that for years to come.

And inside the house?—As true to the period as the outside. Overdone—too much researched—might have been the opinion of those who believed the last two centuries must have counted for something. It could have passed for a museum, or an antique shop, and you would not have been surprised to find tags bearing lot numbers or prices stuck to the bottoms of vases and beneath the arms of chairs. To the Linquists, such furnishings were necessary for their authentic re-creation of a setting from the past. And, as an afterthought, as the props for that spectral atmosphere they used in calling up their ghosts.

To this end, they used the parlor most of all. Once the coffee and the cognac had been finished, we would be ordered to resettle there among those slat-backs and banister-backs, sausage turnings and turnip feet, braided rugs and settles that awaited us before the log fire blazing in that mighty fireplace of hand-made clay bricks. The only other lighting besides this fire: the black wrought-iron candelabra floor stand, with its three burning candles tipped this way and that and dripping wax upon the floor, a thing on which a raven ought to perch; and the Revere lantern suspended from a timber that sent out its shivering splatter of light in which we saw each other in bits and pieces that were always changing, and which, more than anything else, returned us to the gloomy evenings of our ancestors. Here, too, the timbers were exposed overhead, although no white had been put up between them. (Not authentic, our hosts had said.) While the walls of feathered paneling, painted in a high-gloss eggplant our hosts had researched and mixed themselves, were just as dark, except in the reflection of the firelight, when they shone purple, red, or blue. Now consider also the glasses of Scotch or sherry—which, although never the best, were always the best buys—that were warming in our hands, and the nar-

cotic glow such liquor cast upon the dinner of cordon-bleu or
Swedish cooking that had finished up with blueberry and rhu-
barb pies, a thick wedge of each. Or perhaps tonight Gene
would make the mulled rum from his old Colonial recipe,
ceremoniously plunging the antique iron he had heated in the
coals into the small pewter mugs he used only for this drink.

Time now for Winnie to draw our attention to the fireplace
in which burn whole limbs of trees with small branches and
clusters of dead leaves still sticking to them, as though with
such a fireplace they needed neither chain saw nor axe, but
burned whatever a windstorm blew down, or lightning struck
and severed, just as it was.

"I won't soon forget the night we decided there had to be
a fireplace—that fireplace there—behind the Victorian match-
boards that were up there then," she says, a tall showgirl type
who now looks both suburban and matronly, and whose
hair has been turning for years, imperceptibly, from blond
to gray.

"For a while," he—Gene—says, "I just wished I'd gone for
a long walk instead." Since moving to New Hampshire, he has
let his gray hair grow long and shaggy in the back, and has cultivated a goatee. He often wears shirts with string neckties, tight
leather pants he calls his "leatherstockings," and either mocca-
sins or cowboy boots.

Winnie again: "We just stood awhile, afraid for some
reason, I guess, to begin. Then when he did use the bar on the
first board, there was this sound—"

"More like a cry, Winnie, remember?"

"Far more than just a rusty nail leaving a dry board," she
adds. "But it wasn't the house crying out. We hadn't hurt
that."

"It was something *in* the house," he says. "Something we
had to let out."

"And when the first board came out, there was this cold
draft of air, enough to make you shiver. Like no air you would
want to breathe."

From the chimney, of course, we offered.

"Ah, but the flue was closed," he says quickly. "Had been shut tight for years."

"Whatever it was," she says, hugging her elbows, "there had been no way out for it until that night."

"We could be certain of that," he explains, "because the carpenter had written the date in pencil on the back of one of the boards."

"Now it's in here with us," she says, "staying with us. Sometimes it passes right through me—on the stairs." And we would look at those stairs. "Or in the hallway out there." And we would look at the hallway, too. "Or just when I'm walking through a room, any room." And we would shudder.

And shudder equally at the stories Gene would tell. For he was always telling us how he, or someone else, had actually *seen* a ghost—which ghost, and when and where, varied from tale to tale. He was a first-rate storyteller, careful to establish atmosphere and build suspense, with the knack of rendering dialogue without the use of "he said"s, acting out the parts instead. It was his training in the theater, we supposed, perfected from long practice in the classroom lecturing to his students. It would take that blazing fire and a dozen drinks for him to find his tongue, though. Then he would speak as though from the depths of a trance, which had the advantage of allowing him to disregard the interruptions of people like Norman Chase and Gardner Slim, with their jabs of skepticism and attempts at wit. It was always difficult to say what Gene intended from these stories. Were they the embodiment of those facts he supposed supported his belief in ghosts? Or were they merely his notion of diversions that would entertain? Often we would catch a ring of something we had read before. The headless Civil War soldier with the cannonball that had shot off his head tucked beneath one arm and the head itself beneath the other; the masked highwayman accosting the lost traveler at Crazy Corner on a moonlit night; the Revolutionary War lieutenant shot to death in a duel behind the inn, walking

down old logging roads with a dueling pistol in his hand and
a breast you could see through; the mysterious lantern carried
by unseen hands across the pasture on moonless nights, passing from one Hoitt graveyard to the other. Even their dog,
Franklin Pierce, a Schipperke, curled up before the fire, looked
at first apprehensive and then downright frightened by these
stories, and he was pointed out by Gene as evidence that even
a dumb animal knew the awful truth of what his master spoke!

It was during the telling of these stories that we sometimes
wondered if all this talk of ghosts wasn't the Linquists' way of
making fun of us. After all, what must we have seemed to
them but rubes and rustics, ingrown, superstitious, old-fashioned stay-at-homes? They were outsiders, weren't they, from
a different part of the country, accustomed to a different sort
of people from ourselves? In their more sober moments did
they really think we saw ghosts? Talked about ghosts? Lived
with them daily in our houses? It was hard to tell. Because
sometimes we caught the touch of irony, the tone of in-
sincerity. Sometimes the joke was even obvious. But their
laughter never cut deep enough to be malicious. And it was
even possible that the laughter was double-edged, directed at
themselves no less than us. At their preoccupation with "old-
ness" when they were themselves so new. At their passion for a
history that was not theirs, but ours.

They were Midwesterners, you see, not Yankees, and they
were still conspicuous among us in the stores and on the streets
with their shouts of "Howdy!" and their arm-waves that were
so wild and enthusiastic that they seemed they must be intended to warn us off instead of welcome us. Gene would still
speak with his arm draped around your shoulder, for he believed in the power of his touching people, as though he could
pass some therapeutic radiation from his flesh to theirs, a
technique he had consciously practiced on his students; Winnie would still speak to you with her face so close to yours that
at first some of our local men thought her interest in them was
more than neighborly. She was a Midwesterner by birth, he by

an earlier migration, for he had been born somewhere in the East—New York State, we thought—and had gone to Dartmouth, but then had moved on to the Midwest when still a young man. His mother had been a Hoitt, and he had often summered as a boy in this house he had inherited as a man, along with all the worldly goods of Mamie Hoitt, his mother's aunt who had lived in it until she died, aged ninety-five. This inheritance included the estates Mamie had herself inherited from at least half a dozen families and subfamilies of spouseless or childless Hoitts, of which apparently, for a brief time, there had been many, for local gossip had always maintained that the family was a chilly, standoffish, but healthy lot, its members doomed to live long but lonely lives and then die out like tall roadside flowers that had grown rank and woody but, somehow, had never gone to seed. For over three-quarters of a century their estates had arrived first by horse and wagon and later in pickup trucks and even moving vans. These she had stored unopened, caring little for what they were, and not at all for how she might make use of them, only that they came to her and to no one else; stored them in one room after another until she was confined entirely to the kitchen, sleeping fully dressed before the wood stove upon that tattered couch she shared with several dogs. How lucky the Linquists were that antique dealers, or worse, hadn't beaten them to that treasure of silver, pewter, china, glass, and furniture that awaited them inside those shut-up rooms. Because what a difference it had made to them. It had not only let them furnish the rooms with the authentic pieces they could not have otherwise afforded, but to restore the house itself with the money they made from selling the pieces they could not use. For the house today looked nothing like it had since any of us could remember. Long before our time Mamie's father had transformed what was then just another subsistence farm into a Victorian showplace, adding dormers, verandas, and striped awnings to the house, and a wishing-well and gazebo to the newly leveled lawn. During the latter years of Mamie's stewardship, new and old alike had been allowed to run down to something close to ruin. It had taken the Linquists their next six summer vacations to bring the house back to the Colonial it had been in its earliest days. And when they both retired prematurely several years ago and moved up here for good, some said it was to devote themselves to the full-time business of maintaining and living in that house.

To many of us who had grown up in similar old houses set in isolated outposts of this rugged and wooded countryside, it was not easy to share their feeling for such a place. Some of us —like Roscoe's wife and Maurice Dube—could not begin to understand why the Linquists would choose to live as they did when they could have so easily built themselves a snug little ranch house, or bought a house trailer, on the main road.

For the Linquists, however, the experience was new. They had no memories of another and less comfortable time spent in so lonely and old a house. They had been city people, and then suburban people, living in a well-to-do suburb outside Chicago. There she had worked as the office manager of a small travel agency owned by what we came to understand was a group of bored and useless women, and then had sold real estate for another group of women no different from the first. He had been the drama coach and public-speaking teacher, and later the assistant principal, of the local high school. Apparently they had managed a life of what they themselves called insecure and shabby elegance, playing bridge and golf and tennis and even exchanging supper parties with the parents of the children Gene had taught, Winnie driving about in a battered station wagon, Gene in a battered sports car. Somehow they must have learned how to make their leanness look fashionable. Or, at the very least, eccentric. And, in any case, acceptable. They had managed to "put on a show," as Gene had said. Surely they must have made themselves the equals of most people in that town. To begin with, they were tall and handsome, both of them, as was Penelope, their only child, and this alone must have helped their show considerably.

Indeed the measure of their success could be taken in Penelope, who had been both president and valedictorian of her high school class, having made the Linquist household the hot center of the brightest and most popular boys and girls.

Their house had been Tudor-style, in red brick, the size of a small ranch house, and only half the size of the houses of their neighbors. They had neither the time nor the interest to keep up the house and yard, and what was in their neighbors' yards a cultivated wilderness was in their own the real thing. There was often a pane of glass missing in their storm door that Gene would somehow never get around to fixing, a broken window patched with cellophane and cardboard, a plank thrown down across the puddles in the walk in spring. Today the Linquists referred to this house as their "hotel." "Halfway Inn," Gene had called it once, jokingly. "No, 'Wrongway House,' " Winnie had corrected. To hear them tell it, you would think they had lived out of a suitcase for twenty years, waiting to go home. Only back then they had not known that home was here.

For Winnie it had taken only one visit to the East for her to recognize that this was her part of the country, and only one stay at the old Hoitt place for her to determine that this old and unfamiliar house would become her home, her real home. "This is where I belong," she told us once. And then, forestalling the objection none of us would ever think, much less be rude enough to voice, she added, "After all, who are we these days if we're not a free people—free to move around?"

What she said was true enough. We had read the articles in the papers, seen the statistics, watched the specials on television, all of which informed us that our countrymen were moving back and forth across the country, and how out in California they were changing houses the way the rest of us change cars. "No wonder house trailers and a bumper hitch make a lot of sense these days," Gardner Slim had said. And, he might have added, it was no wonder that houses made to look like house trailers, even though they were without wheels and about as a mobile as a barn, were very much in style.

"I mean," Winnie continued, "are there really such people anymore as Easterners, Westerners, Southerners? Isn't it true that none of us sit long enough in one place to become one or the other—except for some of *you*, of course? But the rest of us, the vast majority of us, have our choice of homes, don't we? We become what we want to, where we want to, don't you agree? All we've ever needed is a covered wagon—or a moving van."

After she returned to her Chicago suburb from that first visit to New Hampshire, she became ashamed, she told us, of the few pieces of modern maple Colonial furniture she had, before then, always treasured, having now seen the real thing. Nostalgically, she subscribed to the New Hampshire, Vermont, and Maine magazines, with their color photographs of autumn scenes, lighthouses, covered bridges, snowscapes, sugaring-off. Such magazines, along with the oversized books of photographs of famous New England homes, still graced the cobbler's bench that served them as a coffee table. She still read histories and biographies of the Puritans, the settling of New England, the Revolutionary War. She and Gene had made pilgrimages to the historical sites of Salem, Plymouth Plantation, Sturbridge Village, and they tried to take an annual trip up the Maine coast and down to Cape Cod. To her women friends in the Midwest, she sent gifts of Vermont maple syrup and sage cheese, along with cakes of barberry and blueberry soap, and would have sent them Maine lobsters had she been able to afford them. These women, she maintained, had looked upon Eastern people as aloof, icy, snobbish. She, however, knew we were simply independent, tolerant, and considerate of another person's privacy. In the expectation, of course, that he in turn would be considerate of our own.

Strange to say, the Linquist fondness for New England was often at the expense of their old home in the Midwest, which they had been known to run down as some people do their neighbors. To them the Midwest was overpopulated, overindustrialized, traditionless, flat. If any of us planned to vacation in the Midwest they discouraged us. If we cast aspersions on the Midwest, they agreed with us. If we had good experiences to relate, they doubted them, or tried to convince us they were exceptions to the rule. As was the case when our Major Bill Yarrow, who had once been stationed at an air base outside Detroit, told of the Michigan farmer who had walked across his hayfield to offer to put Bill up for the night after he had seen his car with its hood up beside the road. Or they even questioned our judgment, as when Norman Chase, an avid gardener, proclaimed that Iowa, because of its fertility, was the most beautiful state he had ever seen. And if they themselves had guests from the Midwest, they were downright disappointed in them if they didn't immediately resolve to throw it all up back home and let the Linquists help them look for real estate to buy out here.

"It's all so ephemeral back there," Gene would tell them. Or tell us.

"Don't you know they tear down their best buildings before they have the slightest chance of becoming old?" Winnie would say, and then go on to recite the latest nineteenth-century skyscraper and Frank Lloyd Wright landmark that had been demolished for a new high-rise or a parking lot. "Why, it's a sin to grow old out there—it's impossible to grow old out there. The whole place is like a gigantic gold-rush camp—built right over the gold mines. Someday the gold will all be mined out underneath it, and the whole camp will just cave into this gigantic hole—that is, if the whole darn place doesn't just pick up in the middle of the night and move away first."

"It's the places that are the ghosts back there," Gene said. "Not the people. Ghost towns, you know."

"No, it's not the people," Winnie agreed. "There are no ghosts out there. It's not like here."

Now, wait a minute, we said. Why should our neck of the woods be favored over other places?

"But don't you see it's not old enough out there?" she answered. "The people don't have the history, and they'll never have it. They don't have the—what?—the mystery of the past!"

"Ah, yes, the mystery," Gene would say. "The *murder* mystery. Ferret out the truth behind the coming of every ghost and you're bound to stumble on—a murder!" And he would turn from the coals he had been poking at, and, still hunched over and transforming himself into an evil-looking Capuchin monk, give us his comic demonic face.

"Oh, you can't pin it down to something as exact as that," Winnie objected. "It doesn't have to have anything to do with violence. Or with evil. My guess is that ghosts always have to do with a passion. An old, deathless passion, stronger than life." And her eyes would blaze.

And then, wouldn't you know it, they would be off on their subject of ghosts again. As if, in this instance, even talk of the Midwest would lead naturally into this theme.

Still, it was amazing that for all their talk of ghosts, they had at that time apparently never made so much as a single firm—much less confirmed—sighting of one.

"But can't you *feel* it?" Or him. Or her. It was Winnie's favorite retort to those who doubted the existence of her ghosts. And the implication was that you were not to distinguish between a presence felt and a presence seen.

"Look," she explained, "you know something is behind you. You just know it. And then you whirl around quickly, and just catch a bit of it—a flash of it—disappearing around the corner, or out the door. Something you're not sure you recognize. And sometimes you hear a sound, too, like a swish, just as the thing goes. Maybe it was the hem of a gown—the tails of a frock coat. . . . And haven't you ever whirled around to see yourself in the mirror and caught a flash of something else leaving one side of the mirror just as your own reflection entered on the other side? Maybe somehow you push it out. Maybe it even comes back into the glass as soon as your reflection leaves. How do we know?"

Such flashes were the best that she could do.

"Sometimes," she said, shooting forward in her chair, leaning into the ghostly spatter from the Revere lantern, "I know
they're watching me. Even when I'm asleep. Or just as I'm
dozing off, I hear them whispering. Sometimes they even call
my name."

We tried to tell her that these experiences were common to
us all. Failing to add, however, that they had not become the
obsession with us they had become with her. In any case she
could not believe that our experiences, such as they were, could
be like *hers*.

Ghostly noises, though, they heard aplenty. Car doors
slamming just outside the house. But when they looked out,
nothing in the driveway. Never anything in the driveway. Nor
anywhere along the road. "And you know how isolated we
are out here," Winnie said. "And what a commanding view
we have of the road."

It was Warren T. Fisher, the lawyer—as you might have
guessed—who first pointed out the fallacy of her assumption.
"Then they must be ghosts of very modern men indeed," he
said, "alive at least since the manufacture of the Ford."

He had caught her off guard with that one. It made her
think. "I see what you mean," she said. "They would have
had a horse and carriage, wouldn't they? I suppose it must have
been a carriage door we heard."

"But they don't sound the same at all," countered Warren
T. Fisher, unwilling to surrender his advantage. For, like the
rest of us, he knew how she associated her ghosts with the
olden days as much as with a passion and with a mystery.

"Maybe your ghost has come to spirit you off in a new
Corvette," Major Bill Yarrow said.

"Or maybe it's old Mamie herself," said Gardner Slim.
"Years ago she and that half-wit brother of hers used to drive
a Model T."

We were quick to give her a way out, though. "Sound does
funny things among these hills," Polly Fisher said.

"Who knows, perhaps they were real noises after all,"

Winnie said, retreating even further. "Only we just haven't discovered where they come from yet."

She did not mention the car doors again.

The same could not be said for the ghostly noises inside the house, though. What they maintained were something more than just the creaks and groans of an old house settling on its sills, or the scratching of mice in the walls and squirrels under the eaves. And that same high note they heard plunked over and over again on the piano, and always in the middle of the night. Or the droning of what Gene claimed was an aeolian harp.

Probably just the hot water in the pipes, we offered, none too sure of ourselves, for too much of this kind of talk could leave its dark impression on us, and we could become, like them, oversensitive to sudden sounds, unreasonable drafts, and fantastic flickerings of light.

And just when we were worked up to such a state, the wind might swoop down against the barn, making that drawn-out and almost human moan that would send the blood into the scalp and the heartbeat racing.

The Linquist ghost! we cry, using mockery to mask our fright. Can't you hear it howling?

Then the wind might come down the flue, and clouds of smoke would billow out into the room.

The ghost again! we cry. Can't you see it coming in clouds of smoky ectoplasm into the room?

"Oh, we don't count that sort of thing," Gene said calmly.

"We know very well what that is," said Winnie. "Besides, it's not the Linquist ghost—not *our* ghost. It belongs to—" and she indicated the house and the land beyond its windows —"to this!"

We could try to counter with the authority of Bob Cressman, and of every other old-timer in the town who had pronounced the old Hoitt place without a history of haunting.

"Oh, but it wouldn't, don't you see?" Winnie said. "Not to their knowledge, anyway. It was only when we brought back the house to the way it was . . . a way they had never seen. . . ."

There it was! Out in the open at last. It couldn't be clearer. The ghosts came with the house and land. They lived behind the paint and finish of the paneling, in the patina of the wood, and deeper, in the very grain; were even more integral to the house than this, and were in the oaken timbers of the framing, and in the lime that fixed the bricks of the foundation; were in anything those people from an earlier age had made or touched, leaving some reminder of themselves behind, so that today that essence came off the walls in some vague, transparent human form like the centuries of odors from all the meals the many families had cooked and eaten in these rooms. —And, look here, they were in the outbuildings, too, and outside as well, in the woods and fields. For what the Linquists implied was that to bring back the house to what it once had been—and been in its earliest age, too—was also to bring back all those old human sins and passions that they believed were the irrefutable source of ghosts. As though they believed that by having made a renovation that was exactly right, they had made a home, too, a context—a proper context—for all those ghosts. And believed something more besides: that by their living here and by their *feeling* for the place as they did, that nothing less than ghosts—and our ghosts at that, you might have said—would have been their due.

CHAPTER 2

BUT IF THE LINQUISTS had judged themselves the only possible
companions of two centuries or more of ghosts, how much
more so must they have convinced themselves that they were
the only proper custodians of that haunted house. Because—
well, look here—didn't there have to be a better reason to explain their having worked so hard and with such exactness upon
that house than just this nonsense of bringing back the
ghosts? Sometimes it seemed they must have had a secret and
unspoken suspicion that they had only to remake the house
successfully in "its image" in order to remake themselves.
(Although why these happy people should want to become, at
their age, other than what they nicely were would have been
a mystery to anyone who knew them.) Or maybe not so much
to remake themselves as to carve out for themselves a pair of
roles that would accommodate that house. Roles that might
go a long way to assure them that they belonged to the house
as much as they seemed certain that the house belonged, in
trust, to them.

"Period pieces for the house," Helen—Mrs. Gardner
Slim—had said, with the innocent insight of that jolly good-
at-heart she has always been, "that's what those Linquists

would make of themselves—just you wait—if only they could!"
And, come to think of it, didn't her notion go a long way to
explain those Linquists, though? Not that they were conscious of what they were doing to themselves. Certainly not
as conscious as they had been about their renovation of the
house.

No doubt about the success they had had with the house,
though. Didn't we all agree that it had been the undisputed
highlight of the tour of Colonial houses our historical society
had organized to help celebrate the three-hundredth an-
niversary of the first settlement inside our town? What an
opportunity that day of house-seeing had given the Linquists!
And not just to show off their house, either. But to create the
whole effect. To test their roles. Who in that caravan of cars
coming up that narrow road could forget the first sight of
Gene, waving at us from beneath the ancient creeper vine that
framed the front door? So fantastic a sight that, on second
thought, we wondered if it could possibly be Gene. Because
wasn't it more likely that we had all traveled backward inside
some infernal Linquist-invented time machine? Or, failing
that, the thing before us was an illusion—a mass illusion we
had all seen? Or a ghost—the ghost of one of our own old-
timers? Or, if an old Hoitt, a lookalike for Gene?

He was dressed in leather breeches and buckskin jacket
trimmed with leather fringes. A powder horn dangled from his
belt, an antique muzzle-loader was in his hand. But even with
his beard and long mane-like hair worn almost hippie-fashion,
he resembled more a buffalo hunter of the old West than any
soldier of King Philip's War. "Welcome," he called out to us
as we walked up the driveway, the older folks among us limp-
ing and leaning on each other's arms, the older women
dragging their purses. "Come on in, and see it as it really was!"

In the parlor we saw a Winnie we had never seen before. In
the typical Puritan gown: the skirt and white apron, the
neckerchief and turned-back cuffs, a band of that snow-blond
hair she had parted in the middle and drawn away from her

face, New England-style, showing beneath the muslin cap.
Why, she could have just stepped out of a turn-of-the-century
illustration for a Hawthorne story, or a Longfellow poem. She
greeted even those of us she knew well with what Helen Slim
said later was the formality of those local women who, dressed
up for the olden days, guide sightseers around old taverns and
plantations, delivering a memorized lecture and letting themselves be looked over as though they were themselves one of the
artifacts. As always, she came close to greet you, too close.
Smelling of lavender, too. Not the lavender of a perfume, or a
sachet, so much as the living plant itself. As though in passing,
you had run your hand up the branch of a bush and then
rubbed your palm across your face.

And at her side, a tall beauty we had not seen so much
of lately that we could recognize her straight off through
her disguise. Why, Penelope, we said, recovering from our
double-take, how good to see you home. Home from Wellesley,
we meant, where she had a scholarship, a fact Winnie tended
to forget you knew—and forgot that day, too, several times
within our hearing. She was wearing a simple green full-skirted
dress, which, she explained, was a Quaker dress in the style of
two hundred years ago. What a standout she would have been
in any meeting house! And Gardner Slim, leaning his big
crew-cut head toward hers, winked at her, saying, as he pretended to straighten his bow tie, "Why, don't you make me
want to be a young fellow again, and living back there when
you did!"

As Helen said, hadn't they put the time and effort into the
research and sewing of those clothes. How they shamed the
costumes many of us were wearing. Which were no more
than the standard costumes for the bi- or tri-centennial cele-
brations of the towns in our area. The men in string ties, black
jackets, and derbies, or silk hats, so that they looked like
coachmen or country doctors in the nineties of the last
century, or small-town out-West businessmen in the standard
cowboy film. The women in long dresses of calico or gingham

checks, with matching sunbonnets, so that they looked like the
frontier womenfolk on a covered wagon in that same cowboy
film. A few wore a more eighteenth-century dress: housecoats,
usually, disguised with a ruffled shawl collar and held at the
bosom with a brooch, along with a ruffled Martha Washington
cap. Of the men, only old Bob Cressman, and maybe one or two
of the other selectmen, wore a frock coat, knee socks and
knickers, and a three-cornered hat.

Even Dwight McCracken, Penelope's good friend of the
past year, had been put to work that day and was waiting for
us in the living room, lecturing us on the firedogs even as we
entered. We wondered how Winnie felt about his being here.
She had made no secret of her suspicion that he had run off
with another girl, nor of her opinion that this was a good thing,
too. We suspected he had shown up unexpectedly, for he wore
a makeshift costume not that much different from his usual set
of clothes. Faded denim bell-bottoms and a denim shirt, and a
straw hat with a wide brim and a small round crown. We
guessed the costume had been Penelope's idea. Possibly his
own. (He was full of such brazen innocence.) He was a Cali-
fornian by birth, and shorter than Penelope, with a full beard
he had a habit of stroking, and long hair like General Custer's,
a strand of which he often favored with his fingers. We had always figured he was a far cry from that Ivy Leaguer Winnie had
admitted to imagining her daughter would someday marry. How
he liked to look up the old-timers in the town and find out—
well, not so much how *we* did things as how we did them when
we were young—or how our dads and granddads did them.
Why, he outdid the Linquists in guiding us around their
house, and in telling us what it was we saw. How happy he
was to do it, too. And how perfectly at ease. You would have
thought he really was the specter of some young fellow who
had lived in our town in years past.

You would have thought all the Linquists were the specters
of our past. And wasn't that the very effect they wanted? But
surely there was more to it than just their showing us how they

had redone themselves in keeping with that house. Because weren't they also showing us who *we* were? Or, worse yet for us in their eyes, what we *had been*? As though we had somehow forgotten the existence of our forefathers, or lost touch with whatever it was that was the keystone to ourselves? Although old Mrs. Bob Cressman had not seen the house and the Linquists in quite those terms. She had viewed the Linquist renovations on the house for the first time only that day, stumping about on her cane, her pink face framed by that same sunbonnet that almost hid her blue hair and that she still wore blueberrying, when she also strung a coffee can around her neck. "If only Mamie could see her house now," she had said to Winnie. "It wasn't ever so nice when she had it. Nor quite so *old*, either. You know, don't you, that she always wanted it fixed up—fixed up right, too." Then she whispered as though the two of them—in this small matter, anyway—were in collusion against old Mamie, who might have been understandably misguided, "But she would have wanted it fixed up in the modern way. She had had enough of those *old* ways. . . . But it's *your* house now. To do with like you want to. It isn't hers—not no more it isn't."

As far as all of us were concerned, it was their house, no matter what we called the place. And if they wanted to use it to try to tell us who we were, along with who they thought they had become, that was their business. But you couldn't help asking yourself every now and then just who these people were—really were—who were welcoming *us*, these newcomers who were good people, pleasant people, the best of casual friends and whom we liked despite the lord-and-lady roles they came awfully close to playing. They had studied us, perfected us, showed us up, *brought us back*. They knew about us, all about us, or at least everything they needed to know, or so they claimed. But what did we know about them? Because didn't it—shouldn't it—work both ways? Who were these Linquists, anyway?

Come to think of it, we didn't know so very much about

them after all. We knew that both of them had been married before, both brief, childless marriages. Although we had yet to hear Winnie mention her first husband, there was some speculation that he had been a fighter pilot killed in the Second World War. By contrast, Gene spoke so often of his first wife, and in such friendly and even intimate terms, that we sometimes mistook news of her for news of Winnie. We even knew, and remembered, her name: Sheila. Other than this, very little about their lives before their marriage to each other was known.

We did gather that Gene had been the sort of drama teacher who had tried to make culture as popular as football, taking his classes on frequent outings to the theater and viewing the social pleasure of the trip itself as being equal to the performance upon the stage. In the classroom he championed the social side of education. School was where you learned to get along with other people. It was where youth was to have its fun, if not exactly its fling. "This is the best time of your life—make the most of it—you'll never have it better," he used to tell his students. If he had a favorite piece of philosophy, or advice, to give anyone on life, it was surely: Think young. Or so we learned, not only from what he let drop in conversations with Gladys Chase, who taught school in the neighboring town, but at town school board meetings when he rose as though to have the last word on every matter, that long hair and beard making him—in those days before the tricentennial when we all grew beards—stand out among us as though he were the town character, or poet.

Too often he spoke with a condescension that, in all fairness, was likely innocent, coming as it must have from all those years of trying to treat large children as his equals, and with the deliberate ambiguity of someone accustomed to being the cultural superior of the wealthy men and women who employed him. Sometimes you could actually watch his predicament: he didn't know whether to butter you up or put you down, and so in his confusion he did a bit of both. He gave the strong immediate impression that he was both intelligent and naughty. Actually he was a bit foolish and, despite what he was to do later, eminently decent. He might have been something of a dandy, might have even been fancied as a ladies' man, and young ladies at that, for he was most at home with them, going so far as to treat mature women, including our own wives, as young girls, and must have been a sensation with Penelope's girlfriends at the pajama parties, and later at the beer parties, back in their Midwestern suburban home. He might have been mistaken for a bachelor, too, a spoiled and fussy fellow, even though he was a father and husband of some long standing. Give him his due, though, he was probably a genuinely eccentric man. He was an enthusiast— an "idea man," he once called himself, and that implied youthfulness on his part, didn't it? He had plans for "getting into the art business," and often talked of opening an art gallery in the barn. Given the seclusion of his house and the lack of interest in buying modern art on the part of the year-round or even summer people in our town (the vacationing Boston policemen and retired shop foremen and postal clerks, along with the widows of clergymen), and the lack of money to buy it even if there was the interest, the idea was nothing short of folly. He was much involved in the high school drama club, in the Town Players, a sometime adult group he had himself founded, and in the summer stock company of a neighboring town. He did not seem so much a frustrated actor or even director as he did an impresario who had accepted the world on a small scale. He was—to be unkind, perhaps—a bit of a busybody. He was also an amateur, something he himself must have recognized and accepted some years past. Besides which, he was competitive, and if he did not pretend to be the best of the amateurs, he probably saw himself among their ruling class. Why, then, was he happy here in our small town? Perhaps because he knew very well that here at least he would be the leader in those areas in which he could show more enthusiasm and experience than the rest of us. How strong his feelings for New England were, or how strongly he felt those ties of family and place, was difficult to gauge. Did he feel this was his real home? His spiritual home? We had no reason to suppose he was incompatible with retiring back here. Because he certainly was not the type to have retired to Arizona or Florida, although he might have gone to Mexico. And Warren T. Fisher's daughter said he was the sort you saw retired in Spain. On the Costa del Sol.

Of course on the day of the house tour when he was done up in that frontier, or backwoods, getup, he had to let us know that he was acting, that it was as much good fun for him as it was for us that he should perform so well in so obvious a role. Look how *right* I look, he seemed to say. What a strong splash of theatricality there was about the man!

But Winnie, poor woman, could never quite bring off her part. She always looked so *real*. And it was a reality you couldn't easily change or mask. She was like an actress without a style or method, who wore her clothes like a costume. A former Las Vegas showgirl, you might have said, playing the part of a Navajo princess in a movie—it was as alien and as obvious as that. Oh, that was not what you felt about her necessarily, but it was what you felt *she* felt. It was embarrassing, too. How wooden she looked in comparison to Gene. Small wonder she tried to keep the distance of a room between them, maintaining Penelope at her side instead, her arm firmly around her waist in the pretense it seemed of introducing her to friends, as though acknowledging that she was the star of the occasion, and that her mother wanted nothing more than to reflect her light. In costume or out, she always seemed so out-of-time and place.

But then she had always been a different sort from Gene. Although she had lived all her life in the Midwest, she must have been as much a stranger in that lakeshore suburb as she was with us. For some reason she would have been a stranger anywhere. Of her early life we could only guess that it had taken place in the shadows of the city, in a neighborhood that had changed, or that no longer existed, and that it had not been privileged. It may even have been hard. She had gone to business school as a young woman, and some time after had taken no more than a few college courses in the evening. Even so, she had managed a role as the wife of a cultural leader of their community, had been a mainstay, if not a leader, in the church choir and the P.T.A. If she was not interested in art and public affairs, somewhere along the line she had learned to convince others that this was not so. Take that travel agency she had managed: hadn't she who had never been anywhere advised seasoned world travelers how and where to go and where to stay? That must have taken skill, that must have taken audacity. And what about her work in that real estate office? What had she—had either of them—ever bought or sold in real property? What on earth did she know about selling expensive lots and big expensive houses? Would it be too unfair to suggest that she must have made so thorough a study of saying and doing the right thing that today she could almost do and say it naturally? But if she had aimed to please, her pride had not allowed her to seem inferior to those she had caught up with, or courted.

But even here, in the role of what we, in our ignorance, had to accept as the *real* Winnie, her performance was not entirely convincing. It was not without its rough spots, artificialities, imperfections. Sometimes she was aggressive when it would have seemed more natural to be passive, too timid when she might have been bolder, and surely this betrayed how she was not always at her ease. But there was a recklessness about her that would belie her attempts at self-control, a not-knowing-any-better that showed itself in frank and even intimate revelations that were all the more shocking for being rare, and therefore were always unexpected. They troubled a good many of us, and were often the subject between husband and wife on the drive home. "Doesn't it frighten you," Gladys Chase said once, "that that woman—that any woman—that anyone—should be so—"

"Honest?" Warren T. Fisher helped.

But that wasn't it, although Lord knows she could be that. "Shameless?" Norman Chase further helped.

"So *deep*," said Gladys, putting the name to it at last. And wasn't the implication that to go so deep into oneself was not safe, was not decent? In this how different she seemed from ourselves. . . .

We all had our favorite anecdotes of those sharp moments of embarrassment she had caused us. Once she had said, after a group of us had come from seeing some film or other, "Why is it that the good husbands in books and movies are always bad lovers? And that bad men, evil and selfish and downright mean men, are fantastic lovers? And that the poor heroine is always torn between a good man and bad sex, and a bad man and good sex?" It had come out of the blue, too, as though she had interrupted our conversation on the foot-dragging of the state legislature just as she thought of it. Another time she confessed, "I married Gene because I must have thought—and I'm only just beginning to understand this—that a handsome man would protect me from the iceman." She seemed to have searched for the right word, and to be satisfied with what she found. But just what did she mean by the "iceman"? A lover? A cold husband? Death? We were afraid to ask. But the implication to the women present had been clear: either they already knew this about themselves, or if they did not, now having heard it, they had no choice but to acknowledge that what she said was so. Maybe she was merely being "complicated," deliberately so. Although it seemed more likely that she was without that sort of guile. We remembered how Warren T. Fisher had once almost shouted out in response to whatever it was that Winnie was trying desperately to tell him, his hands up before him as though to hold back an attacker, his voice plaintive to the pitch of anger. "Honestly, Winnie, have you no shame? Are we to have no secrets of the heart anymore? Because if you can tell me that—why, by jeepers, Winnie, you will tell me *anything!*" And once Major

Bill Yarrow, whom Winnie had cornered near the hearth, had had that embarrassed look about his face that meant he was pretending not to understand whatever it was she had said that he understood only too well.

We often wondered how her suburban friends had regarded these sudden outbursts of depth and candor. Had they recommended on the sly, to Winnie's befuddlement, the services of their own psychiatrists? Because she must have been troubled, although she herself could not have known it. Passionate, too, someone suggested. Possibly on the brink of a nervous breakdown. More likely she revealed herself because she could not imagine that she was different from the rest of us—or from anyone, for that matter—and so expected you to acknowledge in your own heart whatever she confessed to finding in her own. She did not understand how—or even *that* —she was unique.

The interest of these Linquists in the house we understood. Or thought we did. But the interest in the ghosts was something else, a fascination far more complicated than it seemed. It was probably no more than the theatricality of the subject that attracted Gene. But what was there about the character of Winnie that would explain her interest in the things?

You might have known the subject would come up during the tricentennial tour of the house. We could hear Gene proclaiming to the stragglers, the Massachusetts and Connecticut summer people who had mixed among us, the women in their cowl-shaped sunglasses and swollen lumpy slacks, and the men in their plaid trousers and white high-heeled shoes, who were looking at the ceiling and listening to Dwight lecture them on anything from wainscoting to the making of mortar from seashells, "You know, of course, that this is the town's only acknowledged haunted house." Emphasizing "acknowledged" as though the rest of us were much too frightened or ashamed to own up to the haunting of our own.

Acknowledged, yes, but authenticated? we asked.

"Feeling is believing," Winnie said, the Puritan mistress of the house, finger in the air like a teacher.

Which sent them both onto the subject of their ghosts again, and the retelling of any of several shopworn anecdotes. The usual drafts and noises and how the coats kept falling off the hallway hooks and they would hang them up again only to have them fall off again.

And they could be counted on to tell us something of the Frenches, too. For the Linquists did not always have to sense the presence of ghosts in anything as ethereal as the pranks of poltergeists or the air shut up for a century inside their flue. They could summon up spirits that had bodies, histories, names. And the first and foremost of these were John and Amy French. God, in those evenings spent at the Linquists, didn't we hear about those Frenches, though! A bachelor brother and spinster sister, the children of a mother who had been a Hoitt, they had been master and mistress of this house back in the eighteen-forties. Winnie had discovered Amy's diary in the attic among the dusty litter of acorn shells and snake-skins, and Gene would sometimes give us a dramatic reading from it that would bring tears to Winnie's eyes and the eventual outburst for him to stop, that it was too pathetic a document to read. Amy had been a keen observer of field and garden, preferring the melancholic times of late autumn and deep winter, which inspired in her the gift for small poetry. On her pages you saw the small birds she had seen pecking the seeds from the spikes of mugwort and dock that poked above the frozen snow; the tunnels through the snow she had discovered in a thaw, made by the mice in a path from their nests to her southernwood, the bark of which they ate; the upturned clay of the mole runs she had discovered in the lawn in early spring. She had also set down her fears concerning her brother's failing health, along with her prayers for his recovery, for she had daydreamed for years that he would one day enter the ministry and eventually run for a seat in the general court. Alas, a green winter, which, as the old saying goes, fills the churchyard, an outbreak of influenza, and John, the more delicate of the two, took shivering to his bed. Broths, bedside vigils, the tender nursing of the faithful Amy—all for nothing in the end. "Cut down by a bitter wind, like vetch beneath the scythe," as her diary had so cruelly put it. Another month and she, too, was gone. Winnie said it was as though his death had robbed her of the will to live. Nothing more had been entered in her diary after the day of her brother's death until the day of her own, when she had managed to write in her feeble hand what Winnie deciphered as "Got up to walk with John." They had only been in their early thirties. Today they were buried side by side in one of the two Hoitt cemeteries, both tombstones bearing the inscription "We hope to meet again."

"And they do meet again," she—Winnie—had told us once. "Here in this house they loved so much. They're holding hands, just as he did when he was lying in that bed—in there—and she was at his bedside. Only now they hold hands as they walk from room to room. They're still with us, you see. There was a feeling between them too beautiful, too powerful, to die. Sometimes I think I hear a sigh—her sigh." And heard it always on a drizzly, foggy day, she might have added, for she associated the Frenches with those early-winter evenings when, after you have rearranged the bouquet of dried roadside weeds for the third time, you throw yourself upon the window seat and, with a scratchy throat, sigh yourself, looking out.

But the unfortunate Frenches were not the Linquists' only ghosts. "Now, Belle Hoitt," Winnie would say. "She's another *presence* entirely. I'm sure she is."

What sticks-in-the-mud and scarecrows the Frenches were compared to Belle Hoitt, who had lived as a young girl in this house a century ago. Hourglass girdles, obscene bustles, the cleavage of creamy breasts, a black silk stocking rolled halfway down a plump milk-white thigh—these were the pictures the Linquists painted from what little they knew or could guess about her. We never knew for certain how much they actually knew, only that their suspicions about her life and character seemed awfully close to what we ourselves suspected was about right. And our own ignorance, or reticence, concerning her only increased these wild erotic Linquist speculations.

"There's some secret there," Gene was fond of saying. "Some shameful secret—a mystery—a crime—or worse. Something indescribably—"

"Indiscreet!" suggested Winnie.

"Indecent," countered Gene. Then, turning to us: "And a conspiracy on *your* part to keep the secret to yourselves. God almighty but she must have been a wicked thing for *you* to protect her after all these years. Why, none of you even knew her."

"But don't you see," said Winnie, teasing us, "it's not her they think they're protecting—it's *themselves.*"

They had even tried to get information about her from Bob Cressman on the tour day, asking if he had seen her when he was young. But old Bob in his three-cornered hat had said no, he hadn't seen her, and didn't know of anyone alive who had, and said also, within the hearing of a good many of us, that he didn't know a thing about her either.

Well, he knew more than we did, which was either a little bit (what might have been for the Linquists another piece of the puzzle) or nothing at all. Still, those of us who did know something could never figure out why we could not bring ourselves to tell the Linquists what we knew. Which was no more than what we had managed to hear—or overhear—and remember, going back a good many years.

Belle Hoitt was also buried on the land in a Hoitt graveyard —not in the old orchard with the Frenches, but in the newer graveyard, on the upper slopes of the pasture behind the house. An immense Baldwin apple tree grew out of her grave, the only tree of any kind within the graveyard. Whether this was the living memorial she had herself requested, or the consequence of her kin's unwillingness to tend her grave because of some unknown scandal, the Linquists did not know. Neither did we.

The Linquist interest in the Frenches we thought we could

explain. As Polly Fisher said one night in all innocence, "You know, I believe the Linquists are *like* the Frenches." And she might have gone further, too, had she been able, and said that perhaps the Linquists wanted us to think they were like the Frenches, that perhaps they wanted to believe this of themselves. Because weren't they always considerate of each other, and affectionate, if only in the smallest ways? They pecked each other on the cheek, they held hands—once we even saw Winnie reach out to take his hand while he was reading from Amy French's diary. We went so far as to wonder if they didn't see in the Frenches some antecedent to themselves, or even believe that the Frenches had been reincarnated in themselves.

The fascination with Belle Hoitt, though, was not so easily explained.

Oh, with Gene it was simple enough. For him it was good manly fun to imagine the company of so fleshy and feminine a ghost. Belle Hoitt, far more than the Frenches, was the subject of his ghostly tales. How he liked to speculate about her shady history before that roaring fire of his, with us, his friends and neighbors, well-fed and half-drunk, around him at a late hour. Although ghostly terror more than ghostly licentiousness was the mood he favored most and captured best, summoning his ghastly cast of characters from the flames and eggplant walls. How he could transfix us with his gesticulations, crouches, tip-toeings, sudden turnabouts and springings forward to the dramatic demands of his far-fetched and terrifying tale.

Behold the ghosts! (He might begin with such an unexpected and unnerving cry.) Returned to replay in spirit that same bloody scene they once played in the flesh, and to the death, as living men.

See it over there, materializing before your very eyes? There! That stuff! That thing! It takes a bit of firelight, a piece of plaster, a puff of smoke, a touch of glass and—presto!—behold the man!

Now he feels—that man there—through the moonless darkness for the walls, passing like a blind man from room to room

until he finds—of course!—the stairs, up which he starts to
creep. . . . Quickly, all of you, after him!

And so you follow him up, stair by stair. Follow the back of
that beaver hat and muffler, the long waistcoat and the dry,
scuffed-up wellingtons, the creases of which are filled with
dust. . . .

Hear it? . . . The wind, you say, making the old house creak?
Be satisfied with nothing less than the dreadful, unhappy truth!
Look for yourself! Look at him steal down the pitch-black
corridor, then, with his forearm, push in the heavy door to the
first bedroom—the one on the left. In he goes, disappearing for
a moment into the fog or smoke or dust that seems to fill that
room, while you hang back and watch him from the door. Now
he pulls apart the embroidered curtains of the fourposter. Eases
in his arm . . .

Sounds like someone fluffing up a pillow, doesn't it? Now
like someone pounding down a pillow. Now like the rustle of a
straw mattress and the squeak of the ropes that serve as springs.
Suddenly you feel the unseen body hurtle past you in the darkness of the hall. Edges of empty sleeves and pants legs brush
against your clothes—and you smell, just for a second, an odor
like toadstools rotting in a muddy shade. Then you turn and
begin to follow the slamming of shoulders against the narrow
walls along the staircase. The boots kick and stumble on the
treads, they blunder beneath you across the parlor—this room
here! Now the door—that door!—it's thrown open—wide
open—is left open!—an awful wind howls into the room! Then
horse hooves on the hardpan of the road. . . . They're heading
east—at a gallop—up that ridge.

Then, for the first time, you hear the screams behind you.
The bloodcurdling cry of waking from the nothingness of sleep
into a world of pain racing pell-mell toward the nothingness
of death. "Murder!" the voice is crying. "Oh—somebody—
come and see!"

You look in between the curtains and see the victim thrash-
ing in his sheets. . . . Go ahead, look in!

But just as you do, *his* hands emerge from the gloom and seize the curtains from you. Out comes his head, so close to you that you could take it in your hands. Eiderdown tumbles out of the gash in the tucking of the goose-feather bed that covers him. It floats in the darkness of the room; it blows against your face, goes up your nose, you begin to sneeze. . . .

Then the man, struggling to rise up from his bed, pulls the curtains down upon himself, and—God help you—on you, too! And tangled up in curtains, feather bed, and bloody nightshirt, he crashes to the floor, taking you with him. There you listen to the death rattle in his throat while his blood pools—makes a great pool—seeps through the cracks between the floorboards, drips down into the parlor—drip! drip!—this parlor!—on the floor right here! . . .

These stories Winnie usually ignored, favoring instead the unraveling of some silent story of her own. She would sit, glass of sherry warming in her hands, and stare into the fire as though her husband were not bombasting upon his stage and no guests were in her house. What was she seeing in those flames? we wondered. Surely nothing as frivolous and transparent as highwaymen and headless horsemen. Maybe the spirits of Amy and John French, their chalk-white faces cheek to cheek, their melancholy eyes shut tight as the coughings spilled out of their blue lips. Maybe the buxom, rosy-cheeked Belle Hoitt throwing back her head and laughing. Whatever it was she saw, it was she, we always said, who had the power to have a vision that would be more than just a made-up story. Because the stories were Gene's way of looking at the matter. But what was hers? What has *she* seen? we wondered.

CHAPTER 3

EVENTUALLY SHE SAW the real thing—if "real" can be applied to anything as insubstantial as an apparition. How remote it must have seemed from those playful perceptions of her intuition that she had shared with us. Because—well, first of all —she saw it not in the dead of night but in the daytime; and not inside that antique house of hers, either, as it sat in Colonial costume in a Pilgrim chair, but out-of-doors, in modern clothes. Nor was it feminine as, obviously, it would have been were it the specter of Amy French or Belle Hoitt. Even the weather, which came from the outer reaches of a hurricane and was far more Floridian in feeling than Yankee, must have gone against what she would have thought appropriate for such a sight. Clouds that looked like rivers dredging up their bottoms, heavy winds, a balmy temperature, a rainbow whenever the sky cleared in the east, and that soaking rain that fills our wells before the frost seals off the ground for winter. In such weather she had found herself outdoors. Walking in the rough pasture behind the house in a kind of vale overlooked by slopes of evergreen intermixed with those almost purple patches of barren hardwoods. Outdoors for no other reason, she supposed, than the exercise in a romantic tramp through the drenched and blown-down grass while she watched the trees trimmed of their dead and weakest branches and the last stubborn leaves tossed high into the blow. Just above her stood a ridge of pasture and a sprawling orchard of about a hundred trees. Leafless trees that day, and so severely pruned by Gene and Dwight that fall that they looked blasted by a war, almost artificial, as if faggots had been wired haphazardly to all the trunks. And above this ridge and orchard, only sky, blowing as though above some remote Atlantic island. And then against the sky, suddenly that man.

She would have thought he would show surprise that in such a deserted landscape a woman could suddenly appear before him. And, as if awaiting him, staring, out of all places, at the very spot where he suddenly appeared. But he didn't speak to her, didn't wave at her, didn't so much as startle at the sight of her. Only turned and walked through the orchard along the ridge, away from her and toward the woods.

There was nothing extraordinary about his presence. Wasn't it deer season, with the reports of rifles sounding throughout the morning from the woods? She assumed he was a hunter who was also a stranger, a presumptuous fellow who had ignored the signs that proclaimed this was posted land and then ignored the woman on whose property he trespassed. Lord knows, it had happened before.

But once the man had worked free of those apple trees that had in part obscured him, she saw that he was without a gun. Nor was he wearing the brilliant orange or red check of a hunter, but a lightweight jacket almost the color of the sky, and baggy bell-bottoms almost the color of the grass, and oxfords instead of boots—black with pointed toes, like a dancer's shoes—and a rain-soaked fedora with the wide brim pulled down all around the crown. Although a trespasser and stranger, he was no hunter, the only role that accounted automatically for the other two. Who was he, then? And what was he doing here? The nearest inhabited house this time of year was nearly two miles away, and even if her neighbors were having guests, this was no weather to tramp a great distance in, and no season to be out in the woods in so dangerous a set of clothes.

Oddly, it was just then that she heard a rifle shot, and instinctively turned in the direction of the woods from which she thought it came. Equally as odd, it was precisely then that the man turned to stare down at her, as though he thought the shot originated not from the woods but somehow from her. Certainly if he had pretended not to see her earlier, he could make no such pretense now, and she anticipated not only his greeting but some offhand comment on the shot.

But although the man stared at her, he did not stop to stare; did not so much as alter his stride. Nor did he turn to her anything but his face, which he showed by cocking his head at an improbable angle, as though the distant shot had been a signal not unlike a sergeant barking at his platoon, "Eyes right!" Even the swing of his arms became military. So did his stride, which, with its exaggerated lifting of his knees only to set a pace more like marking-time than marching, resembled that of an old veteran in a legionnaires' parade. And his wave, when at last he gave it, could have passed for a half-hearted military salute.

It was strange, too, that having refused to look at her before, he now could not look anywhere else. Which meant he had yet to see the fieldstone wall separating woods from pasture that he was fast approaching, and she was on the verge of calling out to him to look sharp. But just when he seemed about to blunder against that wall, he snapped his head forward, saw what lay ahead, and lifted his leg to step across the stones. Then, as he stepped over at a place where the stones were more scree than wall—or even as he began to step over—as he lifted that long lean leg not to stride forward with as before but to swing above that heap of stones and take himself into the juniper that grew beyond them, he stopped and held that pose of stepping over, with neither foot in contact with the ground on either side, airborne and yet suspended where he stood.

That is not to say he failed to move, for move he did—with a dreamlike determination, too—but without the knack of getting both legs together on a given side, so that instead of climbing over or stepping back, he only went back and forth like a hobby-horse a pants leg had brushed against and set to rocking. All as though some mysterious power—or invisible hand—had descended on him, and was unable to decide on which side of the wall it wanted him, and so was content in the meantime to hold him up by the back of the belt while his legs made the motions of walking through the air. And if this was itself not enough to leave her open-mouthed, the man grew luminous, with a halo effect around his flesh and clothes. This light wavered, waned, grew bright again, grew blinding, went on and off and then grew dull, fading until the man became a patch of fog that the wind, which at that moment actually howled, blew through but not away. And then as the light faded, the fog faded, and the man vanished into the background of the woods beyond the wall. And in that moment just before he vanished, she had seen *through* him and glimpsed the gray fieldstones with their crusts of green moss and blue lichens that he had straddled, and the juniper and birch that awaited him beyond the wall, and she had heard him—or what was by then only the remnants of him—say what sounded like "Hello, again."

In reply she said nothing, did nothing. Her mind lagged behind her senses—might well, in this instance, have never caught up with her senses. She knew only that her body had become inadequate, that sixth senses had become appropriate: that they were in the air. Knew also, as soon as the man was no more than seconds gone, that it was too late to scramble after him with any hope of catching him; too late even to shout after him with any hope of being heard. Not because the man had managed in so brief a time to take himself so far away, but because, unaccountably, he no longer was. Not only where he was last seen before he left, but anywhere. But beyond this immediate faith in the miraculous, her under-

standing of the mystery was confused and weak. Her mind
fluctuated between doubting the performance of her senses and
the reality of what she had heard and seen. For no midsummer
noonday sun had been out to scramble her brains, no glaring
snow to blind her, no fog, no nor'easter of driving snow or
rain, nor was it nighttime, when with a minimum of imagination any tree trunk can be made to move. Nor was the man at
any time so distant that he could have been anything but
clearly seen.

Besides, hadn't he given from the outset every indication
he was what he seemed—a man of certain form and matter,
three-dimensional, solid, opaque, who lived and breathed? In
the orchard he had blocked out those portions of the trees
he had walked before, while the trees had blocked out those
portions of him that had passed behind the trees, and when
he had stepped into the open pasture, he had hidden those
portions of the clouds that blew behind him, and his feet had
hidden the grass they trod upon. . . . But now she saw that
precisely in her perception of his feet had been a forewarning
of something strange about the man and scene. She had seen
the grass depress beneath his footsteps, stick out about the
edges of his soles, and, after his feet were lifted, had seen the
grass quiver—individual blades of grass—and slowly begin to
rise; had seen the rotten apples beneath the trees those feet
had walked among, seen the heel of the left foot dig into the
sod for surer footing, may have even seen the ground water
flood the sodden heel-mark his shoes had left behind. And she
had seen all this even though—given the distance between
them, not to mention his position over her—she could not
have seen it. . . . And she had seen more, too. For although she
had not seen *through* him, she had somehow seen *behind* him.
Had seen that cloud, that patch of sky, that leafless apple
bough, even though the density of the man's head or legs had
hidden them from sight. If the man himself was unnatural,
what must she say about the eyesight that had seen him in the
fields?

And what about sound, too? "Hello, again," the two words spoken just before he disappeared. Only he could have spoken them, since no one else was around to speak them. And he could have only addressed them to her, since no one else was around to hear them. But now she recalled that his voice had been no louder than a whisper, which meant that he had been too far away to have been heard. But she *had* heard him, heard him clearly, too, as if he were not seesawing upon that field-stone wall but standing next to her, whispering in her ear.

Not only that, but she now remembered how she had looked away from him, not only when she heard the rifle shot, but several times. Once she had as good as put her back to him. (It was when she saw him appear upon the ridge, and he had embarrassed her by failing to acknowledge that she was there.) But as she gazed down upon her house and barn, she still saw the man before her. Oh, not anywhere around the house and barn, as if he could move magically about the landscape, popping up and materializing in any hunk of space he wanted to, but saw him walking on the summit of the ridge behind her, making for that wall. She had seen the house and barn, you see, and that ledgy, grass-grown, and washed-out trail—puddled in the low spots—they called their road, which wound up the wooded hill to where their tin mailbox stood on its upright, the red flag up; and had also seen, and at the same time, too, the man upon the ridge, alone and dark against the moving backdrop of that sky, making his pathetic march across the ridge, his face turned toward her in that formal and inappropriate salute. Had seen him literally with eyes in the back of her head. Had seen him without benefit of eyes. And not in her mind either, but even so somehow *in space*.

She guessed—or better yet, divined—that what she had witnessed was not the involuntary activity of her mind and senses, but the expressed will of something other than herself, some spirit that had manifested itself in the body of that man. And she had seen him not only outside the limits of her senses, but against her will—against her will!

How could she bring herself to go up the slope and search the woods and wall when she was afraid even to look there— or at that path along the ridge, the orchard, those portions of space the man had made the stage setting for his drama of passing by? She feared she would see him reappear among the apple trees. Or worse, that she would catch sight of those storklike and airborne legs still stretched interminably across the wall.

Her house might have sent her running home if any light was shining in the small-paned windows. A light would mean that Gene was there, and that she would be able to share the man with him and, by sharing him, weaken the hold he had on her. Or better yet, rid herself of him entirely. She would only have to let Gene persuade her that he was real. Or that she had seen him come and go, not in the dimensions of space but in the backfire of her own senses. But no light—not so much as a glimmer—shone through those panes. And wasn't this in itself a mystery? For the grayness of the hour and overcast should have meant a light turned on somewhere. That is, if there was anyone inside the house who wished to see—or to be seen.

Desolate, that was how the house looked. All the more so in the bleak November landscape. The car was gone from the grassy driveway beside the house, which meant that Gene must have gone off, taking Pierce with him. Nothing near the house except those few shrubs and the same grass that was in the pasture, differing only in a near-circle around the house where it had been lately mown and was a different, darker green. The starkness of the house repelled her. No shadows angled from the eaves to dull the colors of the walls and cornices; no shadows fell from the roof and walls to dull the yard. The same sunless greenish-yellow light that was in the orchard was down there, too, consistent in every stretch of yard and wall. She did not like the way the house was overemphasized within this light, the lines unrelieved by any awkward angle, that leather-red paint undiluted by the contrast of any other color in the monotonous run of clapboards along the walls from house to ell to barn. Such a tenuous and nervous light it was, too, as though it could not last, as though it would end in thunder.

She had a feeling close to loneliness, close to desperation. The place was so austere. So unfamiliar. She could not believe she had lived or summered in that house for the past ten years, that she could have made its taste and history her own.

As much as the man upon the wall, the house beguiled and taxed her senses. She wanted to shake her head, blink her eyes, palm her ears, jolt all her senses as she might a radio or clock that would not function, or function properly. She seemed menaced on either side. For a reason she could not explain (could not believe existed) she felt closer to the man than she did the house. As though the man, for all his disappearing, was more real to her than was the house; as if he had beckoned her to follow him, whereas the house would drive her off. And yet she did not feel she would be safer with the man. But since when was safety her foremost consideration? What did she care about safety, given the thrilling desperation she was feeling? As though she could become, all in one sensation, lonely, homesick, and aroused. As though a man—a real man had brushed against her in the dark. And wasn't this the reason why instinctively she turned and once again encountered what only moments earlier she had not been able to bring herself to face—the orchard and the path along the summit of the ridge that ended at the wall—fearful that she would see the man a second time, and this time scramble after him, calling out for him to stay? But the man was not upon the wall, nor was he in the woods beyond. Nor had he backtracked along the pasture to the orchard. What choice did she have now but to walk down the slope and home?

She had no wish, however, to reach her destination. There was no promise that the house would steady her, would give her sanctuary. It was still so much the prisoner of that uncertain light. To take herself into it would be like walking on the moon, or underwater. She had the sensation that time was at odds with her understanding of it. Why, the man's passing on the ridge had taken no time—no time at all! Perhaps she had never even left the house, had never gone out that door. She was in there now before the fireplace, picking up a log, poking at the coals. Or at one of those small dark panes, peering out.

She grew impatient. If only some new perception, or just a darkening or brightening of that light, would change the scene. Or some sound, any sound, so long as it was natural. But nothing happened to relieve the peak of her anticipation. Even the back door, which had been left open, did not blow to and fro, but hung motionless out over the granite stoop at a right angle to the wall. And this door did not invite her. It repelled her—terrified her! It should have been closed, closed tight! Who knew what besides bad weather might have blown indoors?

Later, with the door shut tight and chained behind her, she went from room to room, calling for Gene at the closed doors and up the steep and narrow stairs. Fool, she told herself, you know he isn't home. But the silence of those empty made-up beds and all those empty chairs could not convince her she was in the house alone.

Then it occurred to her that to make herself responsible for the open door only multiplied the mystery, only intensified her mood. When she had knelt before the fireplace and lit the kindling beneath the logs, something had come over her, replacing her will, wiping out her consciousness. What an overwhelming urgency she must have felt! She had dropped the poker, the box of matches, had run to the door, must have thought it madness to spend the time to close it. And look there: the plastic raincoat she had worn just now was torn in the back below the collar; in her hurry she must have torn it off its hook. And she had walked out into the high wet grass wearing sneakers and no socks, and her feet were cold and soaking wet. All as though she had been commanded by an unheard voice to go into the pasture and wait there until the man appeared. And all of this had taken time, too—no little time! It must have taken time!

But the maple logs in the fireplace were burning on the irons as if only the last draft across the threshold had set them blazing. The flames seemed to burn only on the bark. She put her palms before the bricks, but felt no warmth. Again she began to doubt that she had left the house. Why, she could have done little more than run up the slope and down again, sprinting at a pace beyond her years. Either those moments had been outside of time—time as she knew it—or else had happened with the compression and intensity of actions in a dream.

But she was wet! Her hair was wet, water dripped from the hem of the plastic raincoat, the soles of her sneakers left damp impressions on the floor. The wetness proved she had been outdoors.

She dried herself in a large towel, which she wrapped, turban-fashion, around her hair, and then brewed herself a cup of tea. The smell, taste, and heat all persuaded her that she was awake, and real. If only her mind could concentrate on things as homely as tea leaves and rising steam!

If only Pierce had not gone with Gene but had walked with her in the pasture instead, he might have barked at the man, or chased him, proving that he, too, could see what she had seen. Because what was important, she had begun to realize, was that the man's miraculousness had been revealed to her eyes alone. Would he have been there, she wondered, as any other man—any *real* man—would have been there if she had stayed indoors? Was it possible that he was there only because she was there, and, taking it a step further, that she was there only because he was about to come there? If so, didn't this mean there had to be some bond between them that could, at the very least, join them—the man-ghost and the woman—in the enigma of his appearance and passing by?

But if they were as close as all of this, why hadn't she recognized the man? Come to think of it, what was it about his face that troubled her? Why, she could not remember it—she hadn't even looked at it—that was what troubled her about his face!

By the time her tea was cold, she had begun to wrestle with the naturalness of the man's coming, with the unnaturalness of his going. To her surprise, she judged the coming more suspicious than the going. Because wasn't it likely that he had not walked up the slope of the other side at all, but had emerged from the very ridge itself, bursting through the ledge and sod like a dead man rising from the grave? Or that his body had never been born on earth, never walked the earth, nor returned to earth, and when she saw the head poke above the ridge, no body stood beneath it, and when she saw the torso, no legs supported it, only blowing rain and wind below the waist?

Now she wondered not only at the miracle of the man's going, but—having seen the elementary logic in any man's going, that it presumed beforehand his coming—wondered also and, what was worse, shuddered at the miracle of his coming. For the real wonder was not that he had gone, revealing at his departure how he could dissolve himself into nothing more than air, but because of that revelation, that he had come—had come at all.

CHAPTER 4

"THERE, YOU SEE, what did we tell you? 'Hello, again,' it said to Winnie. *Again*, mind you, that's the key word." It was Gene, confronting us at a late hour before his roaring fire. He was excited, full of argument and vindication. He actually seemed to screw a long filtered cigarette into the long white cigarette holder he often favored. As he leaned over the piece of kindling he had poked into the fire, his white, winglike hair glowed red, as did his goatee, and his eyes dilated, crossed, and glared ferociously as he sucked through the long holder, the long filter, the long cigarette, until finally the tobacco burned. "Which not only proves that he was here before, but that Winnie—or one of us—saw him here."

"Well, if that's the case," said Norman Chase, our county forester, leaning against the chimney in his flannel shirt and tweed jacket like a country gentleman, "I can't imagine why we haven't heard of him before. I can't imagine how you or Winnie could have kept that first visit such a secret."

"But don't you see?" Gene said. "We didn't know ourselves. The first time around we didn't see him disappear, and so we must have assumed that—whoever he was and wherever we saw him—that he was as real as you or me. I mean Winnie would still be thinking the man in the orchard was a real man if he hadn't disappeared. . . . Or maybe we didn't actually *see* him. We didn't have to see him for him to have been there, you know. We could have just heard him moving about the house. Or out there in the woods. . . . Or felt his draft. Just goose pimples on the back of the neck. . . . But you'll admit now, won't you, all of you, that he's borne out what we've been trying to tell you all along? The place is haunted. It's alive with its own history. You can't refute that."

It was apparent that up to now we had failed to take the ghosts as seriously as the Linquists would have liked. Now, they believed, we would have no choice but to change our attitude, if not our minds. We had yet to be convinced, however, that our sense of humor was out of place and our skepticism unjustified. "You have to keep your eye on Gene," Warren T. Fisher said, clapping Gene on the back and winking at the rest of us from his hard-drinking lawyer's face. "He ties tire chains to his ankles, throws a logging chain over his shoulder, and then tramps about his attic in the middle of the night— moaning with indigestion!"

"While Winnie," Gardner Slim said (we wouldn't leave Winnie out of it), "tiptoes through the downstairs, slamming doors—if she doesn't rap on them first!"

"And opening windows, too," Norman Chase offered, "in high winds, and thunderstorms."

"Or—and listen to this," Warren T. Fisher said, "when Gene sneaks a few drinks downstairs (after the more than enough he already had when the rest of the house was up! ha-ha!), he goes bump against things in the night!"

No one laughed more than the Linquists at all of this. They could afford to be amused now, they could afford to indulge our humor. After all, they knew the truth now. Or the first stage of it, anyway. They had had the "experience."

However, the experience—as they chose to call it—was not one that Winnie cared that much to talk about. And what an about-face this was from what we all expected! We knew the experience had not amused her, and suspected it had disturbed her. It had become one of the few subjects—like personal sex of the most explicit sort—that she was usually careful to avoid. Left to herself, she would not say much about the man she saw. "It's not that I can say definitely what he looked like," she had explained to Gladys Chase, "so much as I can say what he didn't look like." But even though the face was no more focused than a blank slab in her recollection, she was certain it had been a familiar face, one that she would recognize in the end.

It was Gene who retold most often the story of her sighting, and explored its implications. As though in the eyes of both of them she had earned, through her vision, the status of a high priestess whose rare pronouncements were best proclaimed and interpreted by Gene. And it was Gene who broadcast the news outside our small circle of friends and into the town at large. So that at Tolman's Garage, where Gene would have his car serviced and inspected—and where a good many of our locals (including Bob Cressman, who speculated in cut-over mountain land in partnership with Tolman) hung around, peering up beneath the oil lifts in search of rust on the undercarriages of other people's cars or watching the oil drain out of the crankcase of those same cars—you could have heard not only Gene telling the story of Winnie's ghost but, in his absence, the locals refuting whatever it was that he had said. And not so much because his assertion of a ghost as fact had cast a dark shadow upon the good name of our town as because it infringed upon the privilege of Cressman and his friends to be the sole guardians of the history and knowledge of the town, indicting them for what was in their eyes their own ignorance of themselves.

"I can tell you this much, boys," Bob Cressman said. "In my lifetime of almost eighty years, nobody's seen a ghost inside the boundaries of this town. Not that's come to my ears—and nobody's ever accused me of not listening to what's been said!"

"He's the drinker, ain't he?" Tolman said. He was bent over

beneath a car, looking up at the tie rod he was feeling with his hand. "I could understand if *he'd* seen it—seen two of them fellows, walking along—and holding hands!"

"Of course," Cressman said, "there was old Hi Hall. Forgot about him. . . . You must remember him, don't you, Ben? Or was he before your time? . . . Now, there was your fellow that saw things you could see through. Said he could, anyway. But then he was blind in both his eyes by then, and didn't he like his liquor, too! Rough-and-tumble old bird. Always fighting with his brothers and his father's cousins. Used to say the only Hall that could lick Hi Hall was alco-*hol*."

"Had to put a lock on your radiator in winter!" Tommy Lehoux said as we all laughed. "He come to your house to visit, and you'd be all froze up in the morning!" Lehoux was a skinny old fellow, with taped-together eyeglasses with milky lenses on the tip of his pointy nose, and a mysteriously chewed-up ear. He had worked for Cressman, or the town, which was usually one and the same, hauling timber, gravel, sawing down trees.

"Now, when I was a boy," Cressman said, "I used to talk to old men in their nineties. They'd tell me all sorts of stories that went back to when they were boys themselves. And I never once heard them say anything about a ghost. You figure it up, between those men and me—why, we must stretch back pret' near to the end of the eighteenth century. Pret' near two centuries. And I never read anything about any ghost either." And didn't we all know that Cressman had read everything written about our town and just about everything of a historical nature written about our state? "And I don't believe there's been but a half a dozen suicides and two— maybe three—murders in the history of the town, and that's not so bad for three hundred years. . . . But, mind you, never a crime of violence at the Hoitt place. No, sir, never—not on your life."

Whereupon Tommy Lehoux recalled that hunting accident when that Massachusetts fellow was found shot to death in the woods, and his companion, who was also his business partner, was drunk. Or pretended to be, Ben Tolman said. Which led Bob Cressman to the subject of those skeletons and pieces of bones discovered in the woods even into this century. . . . And hadn't he and his brother, Tommy Lehoux said, when they were small boys, come across the skeleton of a hand poking up through some leaves way back there in the woods, and weren't they some scared, screaming their heads off and running all the way back to tell their father, who had just laughed at them and told them they were seeing things, and sure enough, you guessed it, they walked all over those woods and never found the spot again. They were the bones of Indians, Bob Cressman said, who, during those early smallpox epidemics, had gone off alone into the woods to die—at least that was what he always figured. And Tommy Lehoux recalled that old Swedish fellow they had found frozen to death in his unheated cottage a month after he died, sitting upright, stiff as a board, in his easy chair, and who could say there wasn't the possibility of foul play? While Tolman recalled the woman they had found head-first down the old well out in her barn, and how he had to go down and bring her up, and Cressman speculated on the probability that a certain family, infamous for its suspected incest and certain arson, had poisoned a great-uncle, who was well up into his nineties, on their isolated, mud-surrounded farm.

And they might take up the subject of the Linquist ghost again, or be reintroduced to it by Gene, a mile down the road in the Village Green Restaurant, a one-story box that looked as though it were built from packing cases, which was on or near no green but in the middle of a paved parking lot. Nor was it in the village (there being no village as such in our town, only widespread houses, the oldest of which were at one time working farms), but on the main highway that ran through the town. Here teams of carpenters and well-drillers and the road agent and his gang and any number of retired Massachusetts men had their morning breakfast—a plate of hamburgers or home fries and eggs—bunched up together in the steamy, smoke-filled booths, their loud talk full of greetings and laughter. Of course Cressman and his cronies gathered in a battered, tape-patched booth up front which they jokingly called "Town Hall," loitering over cigars and mugs of that coffee that stayed a mud color no matter how much cream you poured into it. And it was here that Cressman, after Gene had stopped to speak to him in passing on his way out, remembered that something violent—of a sort—had happened out at the old Hoitt place after all. Way back in the eighteen-eighties a boy had slipped while reshingling the roof, fallen off, and broken his neck. "Used to be a stone there, too—craziest thing you ever saw—marking the exact spot where he was killed. It was on the east wall, right between a pair of windows, right up against the foundation stone."

"They know it's there, do they?" Harvey Deming asked. He was both owner and cook, and in his slack moments he would squeeze in beside them in his white, floor-length apron and smoke a cigarette.

"I can tell you this much," Cressman said. "If they had known it was there, boys, don't you think we would have heard about the thing by now?"

"You sure it's still there, Bob?" Ben Tolman said. "Somebody might have hauled it off."

"Well, it must be forty years since I saw it," Cressman said, "and it was just about covered over with earth and leaves back then. I'd guess it was still there, though buried under about a half a foot of grass."

"Don't know who he was, do they?" Lehoux said.

"Well, the stone would tell us, wouldn't it? Looked just like a tombstone, had the fellow's name and dates of birth and death, and a line or two about his having fallen from those eaves and landing exactly there. He must have been new to town. Probably come down from Canada, looking for work as he was traveling through. A lot of them came down around then."

"Say," Harvey Deming said, the thought having come to him just about as it was coming to all of us, "he isn't buried out there, is he, and that's his tombstone?"

"I wouldn't think he was," Cressman said. "They wouldn't put a body right up against the foundation of a house, would they, especially when the fellow was a stranger? But then again, I don't know where he *is* buried. Not around here, anyways."

"Well, maybe that explains it," Dicky Beers said. He was Cressman's grandson, and the town's only full-time police-man. "Maybe he's the Linquist ghost."

"Only," Tommy Lehoux put in, lowering his voice in the smoky collusion of that booth, "they don't know it—don't know nothing about it."

"Now, I don't believe there's any ghost out there," Cressman said. "But if there is—" And he leaned forward, squinting, tapping his finger on the table.

"You can bet it's him!" Dicky Beers said.

"You mean," Cressman corrected, "you can bet that if the Linquists knew about him, they would say it's him."

And they smiled with the satisfaction of conspirators who, to be successful, had only to keep to themselves the secret knowledge of the stone and the dead youth it commemorated. Because how could the Linquists interpret the town history, *their* history, if they were ignorant of what *they* knew? There was no ghost, they said, but if by chance there was, it was they and not the Linquists who would know who, historically, the fellow was. And even though Bob Cressman never asked us not to, none of us ever told the Linquists about that stone.

Gene learned only that Cressman doubted, for historical reasons, Winnie's sighting of the ghost. His reply had been smug in triumph: "Cressman doesn't know everything."

And it appeared that maybe Cressman didn't know as much about the history of the Hoitt place as the Linquists did. For the Linquists had been busy sorting through the past. And how much less romantic and how much more scientific their inquiries had become. Of course they were helped by our tri-centennial celebration, with all the work being done by the old families on their old houses and their old families, and by the new families on their old houses, in preparation for the publication of a new history of the town. Maybe it was Winnie's determination—over some objections—to write an article on the town ghosts (but only *if she could discover any written references to them,* she had finally conceded at a historical society meeting to a group led by Bob Cressman) that had inflamed the Linquists' interest in research. Because there was no denying it had become compulsive with them. They were at it all the time, all day and half the night, work-ing as a team. They began to keep to themselves more, to be satisfied with each other's company, and nothing more. They entertained less, and turned down most invitations to our houses. Sometimes one would show up without the other for a single drink, looking distracted and impatient to get back to the other and to work. They were living on the knife's edge, and loving it, working with that timeless fanaticism of poets and scholars. For a while they looked disheveled, a bit dis-solute. They were so careless about their appearance and their clothes that you would have thought they were a pair of secret drinkers—or tireless lovers—or both. And didn't Winnie con-fess how much it had aroused her (as she gritted her teeth and shook her fist in mock intensity), this looking into old books, records, diaries, letters? Wouldn't you call it the thrill of the forbidden, she herself suggested, this compulsive trying to discover how best to open a locked door behind which were other people's things—secrets you were not meant to know? It was, she informed us breathlessly, almost the excitement of stealing.

Gene shared in this passion, of course, but not, we thought, to her extent. When they passed on their information to us, he would suddenly reach out and rub her shoulder; she would often seize and squeeze his hand. And once when we had called on them unannounced, and they had both gone into the kitchen to fetch us drinks, we caught them standing against the counter with the refrigerator door wide open, he with his unshaven cheeks and she in her housecoat, kissing.

But they were not so fond of their seclusion that they failed to seek you out when they had new suspects and theories to relate. They had gotten hold of an old map someone had discovered down in the county courthouse at Exeter, which, if they interpreted it correctly, showed that in the seventeenth century a log cabin had stood on the Hoitt land, approximately on the same site as the present house. "We've always assumed," Gene explained, "that the ghosts came from *this* house. But why couldn't they have come from an earlier house, one that's no longer here?" He cited the instance of the ghost of Irish monks heard chanting in a pasture where once a monastery had stood—and that English ghost that walked down the upstairs hall of a great manor house, through an outside wall where there once had been a door, and into a wing of the house that had burned down in the seventeenth century and was now only fresh air above the kitchen garden. To support his case, he got out a portfolio-sized book with grainy photographs of English and Irish ruins. The log cabin, built apparently by a first settler in the wilderness, allowed their imaginations to range back to the earliest days of settlement in the state. No one knew for certain how early, although the date of 1630 was mentioned. The ghosts of Puritans, witches, the victims of Indian raids—all were possible presences and explanations now.

Not only this, but they deduced from something in the history of the town published a hundred years earlier, at the bicentennial, that the large Hoitt house had for a brief period after the War of Independence seen service as an inn. This was more than plausible, since the Old Crown Road had been the main stagecoach route between the state capital and the coast until what was now the main highway had been built around 1800, and many of the larger old houses along it—less than half of which had survived—had served at one time or

another as inns. "Even Lafayette may have stayed here," Gene
said. "We know he traveled down this road on his way to the
capital to make a speech. . . . You don't think your man was
General Lafayette, do you, Winnie? After all, your fellow
acted like a soldier."

"Not like a general, though," she said, laughing. "Not like a
Lafayette."

"Just think of all the people who could have spent a night
beneath this roof," Gene said. "Think of all that could have
happened in these very rooms."

And he might lapse into one of his stories again, which we,
his guests, would inevitably turn into the parlor game we
called Guess the Ghost.

"Look at the buxom barmaid upstairs in bed with the
English captain, her big tits flopping out of her unlaced bodice
as the pair of them—the captain and barmaid, I mean—roll
about the feather bed. Don't be afraid to come closer and
squint a bit. Don't be shy. Don't be afraid to let yourself become excited. Of course, you have only candlelight to see
them by. Look at his red coat on that ladderback chair. Listen
to the wench laughing, the captain panting. She isn't certain
she's been in *that position* before. . . .

"But what's that? Did you catch it, too? Footsteps on the
stairs. A clodhopper's feet. A plowboy—the girl's local swain
from over the mountain—lumbers into the swim of your
candle. He stands in the open doorway, mouth open, eyes
bulging, watching them root about in a tangle of unmade bed.
Now he comes into the room and—"

"Beats the limey officer to death with a cowbell!" shouts
Norman Chase.

"Better yet," says Gardner Slim, "strangles the girl with his
dirty hands."

"Does up the both of them," Warren T. Fisher suggests,
"and quite right, too."

"Wrong, the lot of you," says Gene. "He comes only to beg
the barmaid to leave the English captain's bed and return

with him to her father's farm over the mountain. But while he pleads with her, the girl orders him out—the idea, tramping in here with his muddy boots—while the officer makes fun of his simple clothes. He won't go, though, not without the girl. Won't even go when the captain, in his nightshirt, draws his sword. Look at him try to take the barmaid in his arms. Oh, the captain warns him all right. But in the end he has to run him through. . . .

"They buried him out there, you know, buried the plowboy." He turned to the window that faced the pasture in the back, a mysterious sentimentality in his voice. "The two of them buried him, the barmaid and the officer. He carried him on his back while she carried the spade and lantern. You can see the lantern out there some nights. A teardrop of yellow fire bobbing in the dark."

Then he said to Winnie, "It was the plowboy you saw. He probably wanted to show you where they buried him. It must be somewhere in that piece of woods you saw him heading towards. Or even right there where he disappeared, beneath the wall. . . . Of course! That's it! Beneath the wall! What a perfect spot to bury a man! What dolts we are! Why didn't we think of it before? It all fits, doesn't it?"

You can't say we didn't try to lighten their single-mindedness, which was only in keeping with the good humor of Gene's stories. One evening Norman Chase presented them with the gift of a ouija board, saying, "Now I'll find out once and for all who the fellow is. I won't have to listen to any more of these *speculations*." It bore the name of The Talking Board, was a child's board, really, with a smiling sun in one upper corner and a smiling man in the half moon in the other. The Chases insisted that we gather around the big table in the dining room, turn out all the lights except the candles and the lantern, and prepare to receive a message from Winnie's ghost.

It was determined that the fingertips of three hands at most could touch the plastic pointer at the same time. And the

Fishers and Norman Chase were the first to volunteer.

"Say, aren't there any directions to this thing?" Warren T. Fisher said.

"You don't need to know anything except to sit still," Gene said.

And sit still they did. They even managed to keep quiet. Their hands grew warm, grew sweaty, fell asleep, but still the pointer failed to move.

"But you can't just sit there, sillies," Bonny Yarrow said, having come in from the parlor. "You have to ask it questions. Nothing happens unless you do. Something like"—and she turned her face to the ceiling—"is there a *presence* here?"

"Anybody home?" Norman Chase called out, cupping his mouth with his free hand.

He had no sooner spoken than the pointer began to move as if of its own accord, taking arms and fingertips with it as it indicated the word YES at the top of the board.

"My God, it's working!" Bonny Yarrow said.

"Don't be foolish, Bonny," Major Bill Yarrow said, looking on. "It was Norman doing it."

"Doing what?" Norman said, incredulously.

"You know very well it's you," Bill said. "Pushing it."

" 'Tisn't."

" 'Tis."

"Nonsense, 'tisn't."

" 'Tis, too."

Polly Fisher ignored them. "Who are you, O spirit?" she said.

The pointer slid about the board, spelling out from the arc of alphabet: W-I-N-N-I-E-S F-R-I-E-N-D.

"Can you be more explicit, O spirit?" Polly said.

H-E-R-M-A-N, the pointer spelled.

"Herman who?" Warren T. Fisher asked, more of Norman Chase than of any spirit in the air around our heads.

"Not Herman—at least I don't think so," his wife said. "Her *man*. Winnie's."

"You mean," Warren said, "that you have to interpret the thing?" And, turning to Gene, "I could have told you myself that her man, so-called, was already in the room."

"But he's only here in the flesh," Gladys Chase said.

"Are you the man she saw outdoors, O spirit?" Polly asked. "The man who disappeared?"

I A-M, the pointer spelled.

"Who are you?" Polly said.

But before the pointer could begin to move, Winnie said impulsively, "Where are you now?" And then, "Why have you returned?"

The pointer ignored this and began to spell, M-Y N-A-M-E I-S A-D-M-I—

"Oh," Polly said, lifting her fingers from the pointer, "you're doing that."

"It's Warren doing it!" Norman Chase said to the rest of us. "I can feel him moving it—by God, I can, too!"

"You were about to spell Admiral Nimitz, weren't you?" Major Bill Yarrow said.

"That's right, we were talking about him before dinner, weren't we?" Norman said.

"I guess I know when to throw myself on the mercy of my friends," Warren T. Fisher said.

"Admit it," Polly said, "you were doing the other answers, too."

"No, I wasn't, either," he said, surprised. "One of you two did *those*."

"Either that," Bonny Yarrow said, "or there was a real spirit here after all, really speaking to us."

"Oh, Warren," his wife said, "if only you hadn't interfered."

Later Gene said to him, "I don't know how you could expect us to believe that Admiral Nimitz would be our ghost. Why on earth would he come *here*?"

Because neither of them—but most of all Winnie—took kindly to any suggestion that the ghost was not, in some way, family—Gene's family. Winnie preferred the skeleton in the closet, the proverbial horse thief at the end of the rope, to any passing stranger. Besides, as she was quick to point out, her ghost had appeared almost midway between the two Hoitt graveyards, in one of which Belle Hoitt was buried, while John and Amy French rested in the other. She could not see how her mystery man could have been John French, insisting he would only be encountered in the company of Amy, although she would not rule this explanation out. But it was Belle Hoitt who had become her fascination, her fixation, her favorite explanation for the ghost.

The uncovering of the true story of Belle Hoitt had been the biggest prize of their research. Winnie had, in the course of contacting all of Gene's Yankee relations, written to the daughter of a cousin of old Mamie's who was living up in Maine. She had been more than willing to pass on what she had heard about the mysterious Belle Hoitt from her own mother's lips, corroborating, in good measure, what some of us had already known, or guessed. She had run away from the Hoitt farm at the age of fifteen, and gone to New York—to do what, no one knew exactly, and apparently most people were afraid to guess. This was around the time of the Civil War. She had turned up next in Paris, where she had been celebrated as an international beauty, becoming almost overnight a wealthy courtesan. How Winnie liked to speculate on the identities of those famous men she had been the mistress of. "And not just a mistress, either, but confidante," she would be sure to add, implying the hypnotic power of the charm and intellect she had exercised upon—whom? The Prince of Wales. The French chief of staff. Le Duc de Something-or-Other. Claude Monet. Who knew? If Winnie was right, she had turned such men into pawns, puppets, playthings. But at the height of her powers she had been afflicted with a fatal disease, and if those people who knew her back then had known what ailed her, they had never said, including Mamie herself, who must have actually seen and spoken to her second cousin when she was herself a small girl. Because Belle came home.

But without a word beforehand that she was coming, without so much as a word having passed between her and the family in those more than twenty years, and probably without a proper welcome, too. She had died within a few weeks of coming back. She was only thirty-eight. We had always heard that she had died in this very house, but the daughter of Mamie's cousin said no, not in the house; her family would not have her in the house. She had died instead in the inn at Crazy Corner. Her money, if she had any, she must have left to friends or charity, for there was no record of it coming down to any Hoitt.

"What a personality she must have been," Winnie said. "What independence, what courage for a woman of her time —of any time, for that matter! What a liver-of-life! She's still with us, you can be sure of that. Even the roots of that apple tree she's buried under can't pin her down. Her kind of spirit survived—you know it did!" She even claimed you could always tell when she came into the room, for she gave off a smell like perfume, like that plant—valerian—on a humid summer afternoon. One night she surprised us by adding, "And she smells like something else, too—I know, like sex!" It was as though the notion had only just occurred to her, and she had surprised herself as much as us by saying it. Another time she said, "She walks because she has to, because she is driven to look"—and here she gave Gardner Slim, who just happened to stand beside her, a mock embrace—"for men!"

Gene could go along with this. Once he even claimed that Winnie's talking of her could "get him hot." He liked to joke that Belle's ghost—even though she had been his relative, albeit distant—was always trying to push him into bed. "What a lusty slut," he would say about her. And: "Every family should show a high-class whore on some branch of its tree." So much for Gene's interest in Belle Hoitt. However, Winnie seemed not merely to believe in her, but to identify with her. But she also identified with Amy French. How was it possible for her to reconcile them both within herself? Besides, wasn't she far more like Amy than she was the infamous, mysterious Belle?

Her intuition told her that the man she had seen had something to do with Belle. "If only we knew more about her," she complained. "There must have been a local lover in her life. It would explain so much if only there was."

But why go back so far? we countered. Why couldn't he be the former lover or suitor of old Mamie Hoitt?

"What lover?" Gene asked, surprised.

Well, we didn't know of any, we said. But then again we wouldn't know, would we? And we recollected for them the ghostly noises they used to hear, suggesting it was Mamie's ghostly lover come to call in his ghostly car.

Gene was repelled by the idea of his great-aunt having a lover. To him she had always been old, very old. "But she was young once," Winnie said.

Winnie, however, was not about to trade a Mamie for a Belle Hoitt. She was certain Belle had been the sort of girl who matures early physically. What we would call "over-sexed" today. Before girls like her could run off as she had, they would have to have an experience first, perhaps several of them, she argued. How else could she know that she was attractive to men? Or that she could use that attraction to her advantage? Or that the local men did not measure up to her needs and taste? For Belle, Winnie favored only one affair, with an older, married man. That would explain why she hadn't married him, why she had had to run off. Or just maybe—and this was possibly her favorite speculation—the reverse was true, and he, the lover, had been willing to sacrifice everything —family, reputation, business—for what he had come to understand would be his last romance, whereas she, the child-woman, had viewed it from the beginning as nothing more than the first of numerous affairs. . . . And couldn't she have returned home to see that lover once more before she died, having made the sentimental discovery in her final days that her first love was her one and only? If so, she had found the tables turned. Because he had not forgiven her, had not come to see her and utter a last hello, a last goodbye. "It was *his* ghost I saw," Winnie offered. "It was coming from some graveyard in the town to visit Belle's grave. To make up for his not having come to see her before she died!"

This, then, was the difference between herself and Gene. He insisted, facetiously, on sin as the primary force behind the manifestation of her ghost, a vestigial guilt from the gloomy Puritan past. She argued, sincerely, for simple passion. He mock-thundered revenge. She whispered regret, and a meeting of the twain in a last beyond-the-grave attempt to put an old wrong right.

CHAPTER 5

EVEN PENELOPE, who had been known to join her mother in the fun of resurrecting the Frenches and sending them on their business about the house, was drawn into the new mystery. Winnie had written her a long letter setting down the whole episode of the man in the pasture, and Penelope the next time she telephoned home had asked, "Your ghost— he wasn't poor John French?"

In her next letter Winnie wrote, "I don't know why you keep calling it *my* ghost. More than likely he's a Hoitt ghost of some sort. An ancestor in your family, not mine. I only married into the family, into all these old characters in their interesting old past in their lovely old houses. I don't think we'll find any Schmitz ghost back in Illinois or Wisconsin, do you?" Winnie's maiden name had been Schmitz.

What troubled Winnie more was Penelope's reply that Dwight had become interested in her "experience," that he had read her first letter like a detective in search of clues. Had they found any footprints? he wondered. Any squashed apples? Anything the man might have dropped? Because, Penelope explained, although they might not be able to prove he was an apparition, they just might be able to prove that he was real. Such questions Winnie ignored. No, they hadn't found any footprints, or anything else. They hadn't even looked. How amused those two would be to learn that she had ignored what was so obviously the first scientific step.

For it turned out that Dwight had become interested in ghosts—or apparitions, as he preferred to call them. And if Penelope was right, he was not unusual in this. Today subjects like telepathy, ghosts, ESP, spiritualism, witchcraft were all the rage. The shelves of college bookstores were crammed with books on all those subjects (she was sending her mother several, including one on the Salem witch trials), and she and Dwight had recently attended a symposium on the super-natural at a college in the Boston area that had featured a Romanian doctor and his Scottish wife who billed themselves as "The Ghost-Detectors." They had pronounced the college field house haunted, a possibility no one, until that moment, had so much as suspected. She and Dwight had laughed their heads off—they were such amateurs, such pathetic frauds. But—seriously—you could even take college courses in such subjects, they had become that respectable, that scientific. Dwight had taken a course in parapsychology, and had his own theory of apparitions, too. A theory that might go far to ex-plain Mother's experience. He would tell all about it when he came up with her during the next vacation period.

Winnie didn't doubt but that he would tell them that, and a lot more besides, far more than they might care to know. She might have known that sooner or later the supernatural was bound to become another of his fads. Because that was what his interests were—fads. He drifted from fad to fad, and his record in school, as far as Winnie could tell, had al-ways varied from brilliant to indifferent. Still, give him his due, if he was capricious, he was hardly shallow, or lacking in enthusiasm. Perhaps he exhausted an interest from the sheer intensity of his study of it. Naturally, just as he became the master of it, he went on to something else. Hadn't he taught himself to play both classical and flamenco guitar, and learned in one month more about photography than Gene, a camera enthusiast, had learned in twenty years? He knew all about opera, ballet, hypnotism, throwing pots, pipe tobacco, home brewing of beers, automobile mechanics, the cultivation of a vegetable garden, and the gathering of edible mushrooms and weeds. He was both a mechanic and a naturalist, and could often seem simultaneously to be an optimistic technologist, who believed that science was best left unbridled, and an unyielding conservationist, who predicted planetary doom. Maybe this confusion was the legacy of a father who taught high school metal shop and mathematics and of a rural upbringing on the northern California coast.

When he was taken with a subject, he talked on it endlessly, dominating any conversation. But he never argued, was never arrogant, was always the patient explicator of his special knowledge. If he knew nothing about a subject, but had an interest in it, he would only listen, asking an occasional question. Expert or beginner, teacher or student, he had no other roles.

Like the Linquists, he had a preference for New England, which had become one of his few lasting enthusiasms, and in this much, anyway, he convinced them of the soundness of his taste. He had come all the way East to college, remained here, and was now teaching part-time a course called Outdoor Survival at a small college in Maine. Recently he had picked up their interest in old New England furniture and architecture, which had gone far to please them. However, by the next time they saw him he had become so complete and outspoken an expert that they didn't know whether to be grateful to him for supplying them with insights they had not had before, or indignant that he would presume so much upon their special area.

He was such a different sort of student from Penelope. She had always been so single-minded and consistent, with a strong interest in her studies, and in doing well in college, which she had prepared for since grammar school. Hadn't she been an honor student in every subject she had studied? Archaeology had been her great love and sole ambition since as early as Winnie could remember. She had even gone as a high school student on "digs" at Indian sites in downstate Illinois and once as far away as Alaska.

To Winnie the difference between Dwight and Penelope was just too much for her to give their friendship any chance of lasting. And a good thing, too, she thought, because he was so wrong for her. She had thought that they were seeing less of each other these days, and were on the verge of breaking up, although perhaps the wish had been father to the thought. She was certain the trouble between them stemmed from his having another girlfriend. The name of the girl was no secret. Lisa. Penelope herself had casually dropped it several times in conversation (Lisa had done this . . . done that . . .), and once in a letter (Dwight had gone somewhere to see his friend Lisa). All Winnie knew was that if she were in Penelope's place she could not have brought herself to so much as mention the girl. At least not without a sharp lash of irony.

But then Penelope had shown up on the day of the house tour in the company of Dwight, dashing her hopes that they were about to separate. Now he was coming here for the holidays—to help out with the ghost, Penelope said. But even granting him his fascination with the supernatural, wasn't that just a ruse to justify his invitation?

She sat at her favorite desk—an inlaid William and Mary piece—her reading glasses on the tip of her nose, and wrote to Penelope by the weak light of the small lamp, using dashes for punctuation. How much she wanted to tell her of her own disappointment with Dwight, of her dissatisfaction—no, her outrage—at his treatment of her. She wanted to say right out: I do not want him up here. She was afraid that Penelope meant his coming here to be a signal of a change in their friendship. Or worse, that it would reveal exactly what that change would be. Why, she had only to bring him here to speak half of what she wanted to say, and to prepare Winnie for the rest.

But Winnie could not bring herself to set down her true feelings. Instead she continued their dialogue about "her" ghost, working in, with a wealth of detail, the information she had discovered about Belle Hoitt, and her suspicions as to how she related to the man who had disappeared. When Penelope came home, Winnie would find some way to tell her how she really felt. She would do so, first thing.

But when Penelope came home with Dwight, they all talked about the ghost instead. Winnie herself had been the first to bring it up—had been quick to do so, too. On the first night, no more than an hour after they had driven up, as the four of them sat before the fire drinking wine and snacking on cheese. They had all jumped eagerly upon the ghost. The ghost would be fun, it wouldn't be any problem. Except intellectually, of course. No, the problem was Penelope, she who Winnie had always predicted to her friends would be no problem in "those difficult years."

After she had recited without much interest her experience in the orchard, Dwight said, "It sounds like he was a soldier you've seen before." He spoke in that flat, nasal drawl that to Winnie made a Midwestern voice sound lyrical, and in a tone of voice she considered vaguely feminine.

"Ah, yes," Gene began, "the headless Civil War soldier. Or our old friend the Revolutionary War captain—"

"My guess," said Dwight, interrupting, "is that he's never been here before, either as a ghost or as a man."

"You don't think he came from our graveyards?" Winnie said, disappointed. "Or from the house somehow?"

"How did you say he was dressed?"

Gene was ahead of her. He caught on immediately. He said, "I see what you mean, Dwight. The style of clothes."

Winnie said, "Not in today's style, but reasonably modern. Say, the style of thirty years ago."

"There you are, then," Dwight said.

"I beg your pardon," Winnie said. "I am where?"

"Well, if the man was one of Gene's ancestors, or anybody else who lived here a long time ago, and died or was killed here, you'd think that no matter where he was buried, in your graveyards or someplace in the next county, that he would have shown himself dressed up in old-fashioned clothes."

"If it was a spirit I saw," Winnie argued, "what does it matter what he was wearing?" She didn't like the way what should have been a simple give-and-take conversation was being turned into a vehicle for Dwight's instructing them. "If a spirit has the power to make itself appear before us in the flesh, why shouldn't it have the power to wear whatever it likes?"

She thought her argument was first-rate, and was disappointed that neither Penelope nor Gene was quick to second it.

"But what you saw," Dwight said softly, almost apologetically, "why does it have to be unnatural?"

"You see," Winnie said, turning to Gene and smiling bitterly, "he *doesn't* believe us after all." She laid her hand on Gene's forearm. You're on my side, aren't you? the hand was meant to say.

"But isn't everything that happens in the world natural?" Dwight asked. "Isn't there some logic behind everything? It's only that in some cases we can't explain yet what that logic is. Apparitions are a natural phenomenon—they have to be— and they obey certain laws. For example, we know you don't have to worry about an apparition pushing you off a balcony, or dragging you off to the crypt. And despite what you read in Gothic romances or see in the films, there's never been a single case of a ghost strangling anybody. Or even leaving so much as a damp footprint. They're nothing but air."

"One wouldn't give you the key to a lost treasure box?" Gene said.

"I wouldn't say that," Dwight said. "Because he might—

but it wouldn't be a real key. And it would disappear when he disappeared. . . . But one of the laws an apparition obeys probably has to do with the clothes you see him wearing."

"Ghosts must wear the clothes they would have worn when they were alive," Penelope said.

"But they don't necessarily have to be the spirits of dead men, do they?" Dwight asked.

The question startled Winnie. Until now she had taken for granted that a spirit was the special province of the underworld, or of some spirit world divorced from the real world of flesh and blood, of the here and now.

Penelope picked up the argument. "If a man's spirit survives him after life, surely it's not unreasonable to assume that he has that same spirit in him while he's still alive—if, by spirit, we mean his immortal soul. But I don't see how the spirit can leave the body before death lets go of it. And I don't understand how it takes on as an apparition the very human form it managed to leave."

"Neither do I," Winnie said quickly, hoping that even so small a difference between them as this might be an indicator of a deeper breach.

"Now, wait a minute, Penny," Gene said. "You're going too deep for your old dad. You're too theological for your old dad's agnostic blood."

Winnie turned upon him such a look of disappointment. Why did he have to make himself into such a fool? He should take Dwight on, head-on, and put him down. Should show Penelope that he was not the man her father was. At least Winnie had some vague notion that this should be so.

"Ah, but what if it isn't the soul, Penny, but the mind?" Dwight said, his tone that of the patient teacher with his brightest pupil. "Or the spirit of the mind, if you want to call it that. But the only question that really interests me is this: Was it Winnie's mind at work here, or someone else's?" He looked over at Winnie. "You see, you hallucinated the man—

there's no other explanation. My guess would be that your hallucination didn't originate with you, but with someone else. It was a case of his mind, and your mind, and your eyes."

"The mind of the man I saw?"

"Telepathy." Dwight tapped his temple with a fingertip. "He sends you the message, you receive it in your brain and pop it out through your eyes like a movie projector. You visualize the message, in space, three-dimensionally, in technicolor."

"Good heavens, is this your theory of the thing?" Gene asked.

"It's a well enough known theory. It's a case of mind—and another man's mind at that—over your mind, and your eyesight. You receive his signal on some unknown wave-length and it activates that part of your brain that controls your eyes—it must be something like that. Then your brain decodes that message into a visual image, like the electrical signals they send that, put together, make up a photograph. When it's decoded, your eyesight goes haywire and actually sees the man, or whatever it is, before you there in space. It's like the power of suggestion—his suggestion."

"Must be a hell of a powerful suggestion," Gene said.

"More like a command," said Winnie, letting the conversation drop for the evening. She studied Dwight, though, before she cleared the cheese and wine. His face was in the firelight, and she was reminded of the remark she had made once to Gene that, with his beard and long hair, his gapped and slightly buck teeth, and his small dark downcast eyes, he resembled a melancholic but simple-minded woodchuck. He was looking at her, too—or, rather, acknowledging her study of him. There was a look about his sleepy-eyed face that both mocked and challenged her, and at the same time wished her no malice, only the most open-hearted friendship. He knew that she disapproved of him, and of his visit here, and that she was powerless in the face of him. She had only to look at his face to know this. He would be patient with her, he would be kind, but he would be superior, his firelit face said. In patience, friendliness, knowledge.

She was furious for half the night, tossing and turning in her bed, thinking up a barrage of answers to his arguments—and why hadn't Penelope seen through his logic instead of supporting him? And what help, in God's name, was Gene? She would have to drop this ghost business; she should not have brought it up in the first place. She had let herself become sidetracked into what was no better than a game. And yet, she had to admit, she wanted to learn all she could about the meaning of her ghost.

After breakfast Dwight asked if she would take them out into the pasture and show them where she had seen the man. They all went, turning the expedition into a walk through the new snow. Gene and Winnie in the tight-fitting and expensive ski clothes—down to the edelweiss headbands—they often wore, even though Gene had not skied since his Dartmouth days, and Winnie had never skied at all. Penelope, in her maxi-coat and high Cossack cap, towered over Dwight, who, bell-shaped in his olive-green soldier's greatcoat from the Second World War that still bore the red diamond shoulder patch, and with his beard and wild hair, looked—or so Gene claimed—like a crazy Bolshevik revolutionary just commissioned a general in the Red Army.

They had just begun to pick up their discussion of last night when Gene said, as though he had given the matter a good deal of thought, "But he disappears in the end, Dwight, old boy. He gives up playing as a man. He becomes—what?—ghostly. You can see through him. According to Winnie, he obeys the laws, has you thinking he's a man when—poof!—off he goes."

How grateful Winnie was to him! Had he been as angry last night as she had been, his mind churning in the bed beside her own?

"But that must be because the power of the message fades," Dwight said. "Or else the message is all done. It's the end of the sentence. Either that or the power of the person receiving it to translate it visually runs down. Like a weak battery. Like a motor running out of gas."

"But while you can translate it," Winnie said, "you see what he wants you to see?"

"If you're properly plugged in, so to speak—of course. And in your case it looks as though the man was himself the message. He wanted you to see *him*."

"And if you heard him," she went on, "you would hear what he wanted you to hear him say?"

"Why not?" he said. "Can't sounds be hallucinated as well as sights? The message merely affects the ears, not the eyes."

Now Winnie was thinking aloud. "And this message—it is sent to me, to me alone, and you say I receive it without knowing it?" She thought she had come close to refuting him, that his theory was becoming just too complicated to be believable.

"That would be the theory."

"But why," Winnie said, "does anyone send a message?"

"I don't know—you mean the particular message you received?"

"I mean," she said, "that people don't receive messages of this kind every day. This is the first apparition I've ever seen, really *seen*. And I've always felt I was one of those people who have a special antenna for receiving them—in this house, anyway."

"All I know," Dwight said, "is that these messages seem to come to a person at a time of great stress—not his stress necessarily, although it could be, but certainly that of the sender. If the receiver was under stress of any kind, there would be good reason to suspect a subjective hallucination. In other words, that you made up the apparition yourself, Winnie. But you weren't under any special stress when you saw your man. . . ."

"I wasn't?" Winnie said.

"You said you felt blank and passive that afternoon," Penelope reminded her, supporting Dwight.

"Which makes it sound to me as though someone else's stress was responsible for your hallucination," Dwight said. "That and the fact you didn't recognize the man. I mean if it was your hallucination, and yours alone, surely you'd hallucinate someone you knew."

"But who could the sender be?" Penelope said. "Someone close to Mother who had just died—or was dying?"

"Someone just bashed up in a bad car crash?" Gene suggested. "And at the very moment Winnie saw him?"

"You didn't get a telephone call or a telegram later that night?" Dwight said.

Winnie shook her head.

"Oh, well, maybe he'll get in touch with you again," Gene said. "In his own way, *again*. And maybe this time he'll clear up the mystery, once and for all."

"Usually," Dwight said, "the two parties involved in this sort of experience are extremely close to each other. Lovers, neighbors, relatives, good friends. They would have to be, to communicate in that way. That's why a sister tends to see her brother when he is in trouble of some sort, or just at the moment of his dying. Of course she doesn't know he's in trouble or dying until later. She just sees him in the setting of her living room, walking past and saying hello, or goodbye, or 'Tell Dad I did my best.' "

They had come to the stone wall, which they walked along, Winnie having pointed out the spot where the man had disappeared. What an incongruous sight they made, tramping through the woods of hemlock, their shiny faces dusted with the powdered snow the wind sent up in sudden gusts, Gene and Winnie in their glossy bright blue-and-red futuristic-looking ski clothes, Penelope looking like a giant Russian countess of pre-Revolutionary days, Dwight—in Winnie's eyes, anyway —like an American G.I. of thirty years ago.

It seemed to Winnie that because she was without any new objection to his theory, she would have to go full circle and repeat an old one. "What you say," she said, "it's all very interesting, Dwight. I'm sure it is. But this house—this property—has a history, a unique history. There's plenty of food for ghosts here. I just can't believe that what I saw didn't have something to do with the people who used to live here, who are buried out in those graveyards. There are such things as haunted houses, you know."

"Sure there are," said Dwight. "But I would think the more talk of a haunted house, the more suggestion in people's minds to hallucinate the ghost they've already been told is there. And especially if the word gets around where exactly the ghost is supposed to walk—you know, a certain staircase or balcony —and what he is supposed to wear, or say. Unlike your experience, Winnie, those are simple cases of subjective hallucinations. Besides, as far as we know, you were the first to ever see this ghost. That would seem to rule out his having been a haunt. And aren't you also forgetting the matter of his modern clothes?"

"Reasonably modern," Winnie corrected. Adding, in further argument, "Still, we have had certain signs of their presence here before."

"Belle Hoitt and John and Amy French," Penelope explained.

"And who knows who else?" Winnie added, pleased with what she interpreted was Penelope's support.

"Well, what about that?" Penelope said to Dwight. "Can telepathy come from dead people? You don't really believe in this survival of the spirit after death, do you?" Winnie couldn't decide whether she was picking a weak spot in his argument or setting him up so he could show himself off.

"I have my doubts about it being possible" was all that Dwight said.

"But we've not only had certain signs before he came here," Gene said suddenly, "but certain signs after. Just recently, too.

Winnie saw him again—she didn't tell you?—this time in the *barn*."

"I only thought I might have seen him there," Winnie said. It was not information she wanted known.

"I tell you, he is getting closer to the house," said Gene. And then, winking, "I think I even caught a glimpse of him myself."

It did not appear that Gene expected to be believed. Certainly Dwight, who smiled and looked at him dubiously, did not take him at his word. In any case Gene's statement put an end to that portion of the conversation, and they went indoors.

But once again it was a reflective and bewildered Gene who reintroduced the subject, this time as they sat at supper. "You say that because of the modern clothes he was wearing," he said, "and this problem of survival, that this fellow Winnie saw has nothing to do with the house or land. But then why was he here? I mean, what *has* he to do with?"

Dwight seemed almost amused by the question. "He was here," he said, "because Winnie was here. Because if he has nothing to do with the place, why then he must have everything to do with Winnie."

It was the explanation that Winnie, to her surprise, discovered she had been dreading all along. "He was here because I was here?" she said, hoping she made a good show of looking disbelieving.

"I can assure you, Winnie," Dwight said, "it's either you or the place. And we seem to have ruled out the place."

"But you seem not to have heard me very well, Dwight," she said, making no attempt to control the edge to her voice. "Or else I haven't made myself perfectly clear. Because I thought I told you I didn't recognize the man."

"Well," Dwight said, "isn't that the mystery?"

"Winnie, think carefully," Gene said. "Are you sure you never saw the man before?"

For a moment they made her doubt herself. "I don't think so. . . . No, I'm sure I haven't."

In the long silence that followed, Dwight and Penelope smiled at each other, and Gene stared, with his long legs crossed, at the smoking cigarette in its holder, which he held upright, spinning it in his fingertips. It was final now. Penelope had sided with Dwight, and Gene had sided with *them*. Winnie felt as though they were in some youthful league against her. Felt also as though they had accused her of some shameful but unspecified crime, and that they were embarrassed for her because she could give them no answer to defend herself, not even a lie, so powerful was their truth. Still, it was out in the open at last, what they had all been thinking.

"But if your theory about this business is right," she blurted out at last, in a voice that all but pleaded with them to accept this interpretation, "then that means that these telepathic signals got crossed up in space. There was a mix-up, don't you see?"

And when it appeared from their puzzled looks that they did not see, she added, "That would explain it, wouldn't it? No wonder I didn't recognize the man, or see how he was relevant to me. I intercepted someone else's message!"

"Good heavens, you didn't!" said Gene with that theatricality she suddenly realized she despised.

"The ghost was meant for someone else—it wasn't meant for me!"

CHAPTER 6

THAT NIGHT, Winnie, fresh from the shower and with a towel worn like a turban on her head, sat up in her bedroom close to the fire Gene had built in the small Count Rumford fireplace and read the term paper that Dwight had taken out of his backpack after supper and given her to read, explaining almost bashfully that she might find something in it that would give her some further insight into the nature of her experience with her apparition. He had written it for a parapsychology course at the university, presenting in it what he seemed fairly certain was an original theory. Most of the documented and reliable sightings of apparitions, he asserted, had occurred in the nineteenth century, in the British Isles. This, he reasoned, was because so many Englishmen, Scotsmen, and Irishmen at that time were emigrating to places like America and Australia, and settling as colonialists in India, Africa, traveling to the four corners of the British Empire. Such a worldwide scattering of people had been unprecedented in the history of the world. People today could not begin to imagine how many families, lovers, and good friends had been separated by this wanderlust. The man who was untouched by it would have been difficult to find. And yet although these people had the means of transportation to travel anywhere they wished upon the globe, they had no easy or instant means of communication by which to get in touch with one another if the need arose. They had no radio, telephone, telegraph, or even a swift and efficient mail service, so that they were often months and even years apart. In their desperation to reach each other in a hurry in matters of life and death, or deepest love, what means of communication did they have except their instinctive power of telepathy? Not that they were conscious of this power or, when they used it, that they had done so. He reckoned that the people back then must have been more attuned to sending and receiving telepathic messages than they were today. Possibly because inventions like the telephone and telegraph, which were mechanical extensions of man's telepathic communications, had pretty much replaced telepathy, thereby dulling the faculty in people. After all, what need was there for telepathic communication today? He predicted that if a study was made it would be discovered that the incidence of people sighting apparitions in the twentieth century had decreased since the nineteenth century. And if someone did try to get in touch with someone else by means of telepathy in these times, he suggested it was because that person did not know how to get in touch with the person he wished to reach, or where that person was.

The paper, which had been typed faintly on onionskin, had received, without comment, the grade of A.

"If you want to find out why Dwight thinks they saw ghosts in the old days, and not so much these days," Winnie said to Gene, "you can try reading this."

Gene was in bed, his head propped up on a pillow, reading the century-old town history. "I'd think we would want to find out why we see ghosts these days," he said.

"Oh, he says something about that, too," she said, finding the pertinent lines and rereading them to herself.

"Remind me in the morning," he said. "I want to continue with this now. Maybe I'm onto something—something fresh."

He was searching the town history for the historical background and personae he figured he needed to write the drama the town planned to stage next summer as part of the tricentennial celebration. The town historical society had already asked him to write the play, but there was still some debate as to who would stage it, Gene or Lester Marcotte, the English teacher and drama coach at the town high school, the man who had had the amateur drama world of the town all to himself before Gene moved in. The society wanted to be fair to both men.

Winnie threw a piece of split birch on the small fire, then hunched over it, rubbing her hands. "You were very good to believe me about my seeing the ghost," she said. "Some people, I know, didn't. Anyway, I wanted to thank you." She suspected she had told him this to learn if, after their talks with Dwight and Penelope, he still believed her.

"You don't have to thank me," he said, putting the book down. "I had to believe you."

"Even now?"

"Even more so now. After all, I've seen one of them myself."

"Oh, you haven't either," she said, laughing. "Not really, not like I have."

"But I have, too. Oh, not here, not now. It was a long time ago. It's funny, though, how it came back to me today—or was it yesterday?"

"It's odd that you never mentioned it before," she said.

"Well, that's because I didn't think of it before. It didn't even dawn on me that I'd seen an apparition until Dwight explained that theory of his. Then, of course, I knew. But the experience wasn't that extraordinary. Nothing very mysterious about it, either."

"You can feel that blasé about what you saw?"

"Well, it happened such a long time ago. Long before I even met you. Besides, it wasn't as if she frightened me."

Winnie unwound the towel and let her hair fall toward the

flames. "She?" she said, her voice not much louder than the sound of her breath. "What do you mean, *she?*"

He looked surprised. "Why, the ghost—the apparition. Who do you think I mean?"

"Your apparition was a woman?" she said, with her back to him, shaking out her hair.

"But didn't you see a man?" he said. "What's wrong with my seeing *her?* Maybe, old girl, we can't pick and choose our apparitions. Believe me, my experience with her doesn't come close to yours for the mystery. Her appearance was explainable, was explainable all along. Besides," he added, shaking his finger at her, "I *recognized* her. All I saw was Sheila, good old Sheila."

Sheila—his first wife—she might have known. Sheila, who was very much alive, and still in the blush of the best health. A less likely apparition she could not imagine. And if so now, how much more so when she had been young.

Gene had always felt free to talk about Sheila in front of her, treating her as though she were not his former wife but a friend whose long and fond acquaintance they both had shared. Winnie, for her part, never spoke about her former husband in return. Nor had Gene asked about him. He wasn't jealous, she knew; he simply didn't care. Not about him, nor about her early life, which her first husband had, in some small portion, shared. More than likely he would have to remind himself that she had once had a husband other than himself. Which suited her. She just did not care to remember the man, even in the secret safety of her thoughts, much less out loud to Gene. Her life with him had almost become the blank it was to Gene. She had not had to deliberately forget him, either. It had just happened. As she had forgotten all but a smattering of incidents and images out of the things that had happened to her before the age of five.

But Gene still corresponded with Sheila, if infrequently. Hadn't they exchanged Christmas cards as recently as last year? One always telephoned the other every year or so, usually at Christmas time, and invariably just as the other claimed to have been thinking of calling first. "The old telepathy at work again!" Winnie would hear Gene joke with her on the phone, first thing.

Over the years, Winnie had met Sheila several times, always whenever she had been passing through Chicago on one of her many transcontinental treks. Then the three of them would meet downtown and have supper at a nightclub in the Loop, where the camera girl would snap their picture—Gene, who had worn a pencil-stripe mustache back then, with his arms around both behatted women. Winnie liked Sheila well enough, although she judged her flighty and flirtatious, and questioned both her depth and her taste. Sheila's forte, however, was physical. She was a good-looking, big-boned blonde, with a year-round freckled tan and sun-bleached hair, and the broad back and shoulders of an athlete. Unlike Winnie, whose small interest in sports was confined to golf and tennis, she was not only first-rate in those sports but an expert horsewoman and swimmer as well. Several years ago she had served as the coordinator of girls' water ballet for the state of Nevada, whatever that job entailed. Gene often told the story of how, as a teen-ager, she had run away from her well-to-do Boston family and joined up with a water-ballet troupe performing at a natural-springs resort in Florida, and later worked in Hollywood in the chorus of those ballet bathers seen in the swimming-pool sequences of those epic, glamour-ridden song, dance, and swim films. Since her marriage to Gene, she had been married to an aging nightclub crooner Winnie had never heard of before, not even back when he was supposed to have been popular. She had seen him once, long after Sheila had divorced him, on a late-hour television variety show, an older man in a tight, doublebreasted tuxedo and an enormous bow tie, who wore his snow-white hair at shoulder length. Next Sheila had married the owner of a large automobile agency, in Colorado, called Lincoln City. Then a horse rancher (although Winnie couldn't be certain that the owner of the auto

agency and the horse rancher weren't one and the same man),
at which time Sheila had sent them colored snapshots of herself in cowboy hats and tight blue jeans. Her most recent boy-
friend (or had she married him?) had been the baseball
manager for some team in the minor league Western League,
Lefty Something-or-Other. She had never felt the least com-
punction about telephoning Gene from places like Las Vegas,
Phoenix, and Los Angeles to ask his advice on present boyfriends and future husbands, and—because she was oblivious
to the difference in time from west to east—in the middle of
the night, too. She had two families of children (after having
none with Gene), and now lived somewhere in Arizona. A
wealthy Eastern girl, she had made a comfortable home for
herself among the sunny Western middle class. To Winnie
she had always seemed like an Eastern girl in Western dress,
a Mayflower growing in a southern California rock garden.
She liked the West, the desert, dude ranches, sun. And Winnie could imagine her best in a setting of palm trees, sunglasses, outlandish straw hats, greasy sunburns, and tall fruit-
decorated drinks sipped through long straws at the side of
kidney-shaped swimming pools. Her marriage to Gene, Winnie
could only explain as having been somehow a marriage of con-
venience, as though the one had married to give the other
citizenship, or to satisfy the requirements of some eccentric
will. She suspected that Sheila, having returned home to the
East that first time after running off, had tried unsuccessfully
by marrying Gene to throw herself back into her old world
and ways.

"When did you see her?" Winnie said.

"When we were going together, before we were married."

"We? You mean you and I?"

"Before I married either one of you. This was back when I
was living in Boston. I had a furnished room to myself in the
Back Bay, close to the Charles. How terribly overworked I was
in those days, what with attending the theater school, and
taking dramatic lessons, and working towards my master's de-

gree, and acting in one amateur production and trying my best to direct another; it seemed like I was always either reading a book or learning off a part. A thought didn't run through my head but that it wasn't the line from some piece I'd memorized. I don't even think I knew who I was from one minute to the next. I never knew, I guess, what part I was supposed to play. Spin me around fifty times and then throw me into a gallery of fun-house mirrors and you'll get some idea of how I felt back then. Of course, I was young then, awfully young. And there is nothing you won't do then, nothing you think you can't do. I don't think my mind has ever been so active since. No wonder I was dreaming all night long, the strangest dreams—night after night, too. . . ."

As he spoke, she saw the big, airy room in the Back Bay, with its high ceiling and many windows. The walls and ceiling all painted that antiseptic white that was so popular in the thirties. No pictures on the walls, either—he wasn't allowed to put up any—only several of those large frameless mirrors, silver rectangles that gave the impression they reflected only white. And the Victorian-looking, Nile-green couch that made up into his bed at night. Saw him sleeping—no, tossing and turning—on that couch, because it was summer, and quite warm out. Then saw him suddenly with his eyes open. Something had startled him awake. It wasn't a sound. Wasn't a light. Just his sixth sense that someone else was in his room. Oh, he knew immediately it was nothing hostile. On the contrary, knew that it was safe enough, and pleasant. So he sat up. He looked around. One of the windows was up, and the chintz curtains were sucked out the opening. (How clearly he could remember it once he set his mind to it.) There was a hotel across the street, with a neon sign that partially lit the room all night. And he remembered, suddenly, that there were two narrow, rippling bars of light across the floor. She was sitting on the floor. . . .

"Sheila was?"

"Yes, Sheila, sitting on the worn Oriental beside the couch, facing me," he said. Now Winnie noticed how less theatrical than usual he had become, and how oblivious he seemed of her, as though he had returned to his memory solely to satisfy himself, listening to the soft-spoken ramble of his own nostalgia.

Noticed this but also saw from what he said Sheila sitting on the floor beside the couch and smiling—Winnie knew that smile—smiling as though she had enjoyed watching him sleep. Her knees were drawn up and skirt-covered, and her arms were wrapped around her knees. Wasn't it a favorite position of hers that he had often seen her in before, and precisely there, too, in that room? He admitted he was half-asleep. Even so, he knew she was there. At first she was not quite in the pathway of the light shining through the window, but then she must have moved, because light was falling halfway up her knees. He could see her stocking feet. (Where were her shoes?) The light shining through still another window must have struck a mirror on the opposite wall—yes, that was it—and reflected back across the room, for only the top of her hair was lit up: he could see individual hairs sticking up and blowing, slow-motion, in the breeze. At the same time, he could hear the noises of traffic in the street below, such as they were at that hour. Then he spoke to her, actually said something, something ordinary—he didn't know what.

"Good to see you." Or, "What are you doing up?" But didn't the very insignificance of what he said prove beyond a doubt that he believed that she was real? Granted, he was never fully awake, but he wasn't sleeping, either. Nor was he dreaming.

Later, when he looked back on it, he knew he could not have dreamed it. Because how often do you dream you are in the very room you are sleeping in, the same room exactly, looking exactly as it would in the light of that particular hour if you were awake? He never had, not to his knowledge.

Sheila didn't answer him, though. Never spoke a word. Too busy smiling, he guessed. All she did was sit there smiling. He

must have believed she had somehow managed to slip into his
room. She was living nearby on Beacon Hill then, with an
aunt, an alcoholic and socially prominent matriarch, and he
knew she often went out walking late at night. (This was
when the family was trying to keep her in the East and make
her give up that water-ballet business and her work as a
chorus girl in those Hollywood swimming-pool films.) He
simply figured he had left the door unlocked. Or that he had
left his key at her place, and that this was her way of returning
it. Satisfied with this foggy explanation, he fell back on the
couch and went to sleep.

"You turned away from her?" Winnie said.

"Goes to show how tired I was, doesn't it? Say, I wonder
what would have happened if I had tried to kiss her? The
bubble would have burst, eh?"

But he woke up again, right away, certain that only a few
seconds had passed. Only a deadly quiet now. The breeze was
still cool, the curtains still sucked out the open window. He sat
up and looked around. She was gone. She wasn't anywhere in
the room. Even so, he was still convinced he had seen her in
the flesh. Why, if she had let herself in, why couldn't she have
let herself out? She had only wanted to check up on him—that
was it. And having satisfied herself that he was well, and rest-
ting, she had left. How thoughtful of her, he said to himself,
how unspeakably nice. Then he fell asleep again, and didn't
wake up until dawn. The room had become light, although not
yet with sunlight. Sea gulls were screaming in flight between
the buildings just outside the window. From the couch he
could see the door—the only door. It was chained and bolted
from the inside.

For the first time Winnie looked away from the fire, looked
at him. She said, "What did you think had happened, then?"

"That I had just seen an apparition."

"Well, if you believed that then, it's odd that you would
forget it."

"But I knew very well there were such things as hallucinations. Good Lord, Winnie, I'd been drunk before. And I'd heard about dope addicts, mystics, the d.t.'s. And I knew how my mind was overworked and hyperactive at the time, and that I had been given to dreaming. I assumed I had hallucinated *her*, and didn't think another thing of it. It never entered my head until Dwight told us that theory of his that *she* might have had something—or, indeed, *everything*—to do with her apparition being in my room."

Winnie put the screen up before the fire and climbed into her bed. Gene put out the light, and she turned immediately to face the window and the starlit sky above the darkened, snow-blue pasture. "If that's true," she said at last, "she must have felt very close to you. She had to, to have been able to come to you like that. You would have had to feel very strongly—powerfully—about each other."

"I don't doubt that," he said. "The truth is, Winnie, I was like a schoolboy bitten by the love bug. We were great pals—and still are, in a different way, of course. But when you think about it, hasn't there always been that telepathy business between us? It wasn't just the physical chemistry; there must have been something mystical between us. And then, you have to remember, she was accustomed to being in my room at night—oh, not every night, and never all night. And maybe, on that particular night I saw her apparition, she was in her own bed in her aunt's house on Beacon Hill, wanting very much to be near me. But whether it was her telepathy or my hallucination, or some combination of the two, I don't think it's so extraordinary. It's explainable, at least."

"And Sheila," Winnie said, "she wasn't ill, or in some kind of trouble when her apparition came to you?"

"In perfect health! Happy as a little girl on a teeter-totter. She was so gentle to look at, sitting there that night, and she made me feel so looked-after and peaceful, that I never once considered when I saw the locked door in the morning that she might have come to see me because she had a nasty accident."

"And she knew nothing of what you saw?"

"Aha! I only wish I could tell you that on that very night she dreamed she came into my room and saw me sleeping on the couch, then heard me speak to her. You know, I'd like very much to have known what it was I said. And, who knows, she may have dreamt just such a dream, for the truth is I never mentioned it to her. I forgot all about it. . . . Say, it isn't much of a story, is it?"

"It isn't just another story, is it?" she said, seizing on that possibility but knowing very well it was not that.

"It's my one and only ghost story," he said. "Just as it happened. Or just as I remember it happening."

She rose up on her elbow and looked at him for a while through the rise and fall of the firelight within the dark. "So that's your *real* ghost story," she said. Then, lying on her back, she said, only to herself perhaps, because for all she knew he was already fast asleep, "I only wish I knew what was mine."

Wished she knew it the long night too, during all those wakeful spells of restlessness that passed, unhappily, for sleep. All night long she woke into a cave of phantoms, the light of that dying fire turning the darkness into what resembled shadows that leaped across the ceiling or trudged, quivering, along the walls. A dog barked across the snowy fields, sounding wolf-like. Barked again—and again—until Pierce answered with a growl downstairs. Suddenly, "Winnie!" someone—she almost recognized the voice—whispered in her ear. She thought she smelled smoke, sweet smoke, lavender. She was sure she smelled smoke. Then she was in the hallway, with the flickering light she had left in her bedroom breaking out of the door she had left open into the house at large. In an instant she was past the open door of the guest bedroom in which she had quartered Dwight. That most medieval and least used of all the bedrooms, so much a museum of the best upstairs pieces that their friends had often said they should fix a thick rope across the threshold so that visitors could look in but not enter, the same room that Dwight admired more than any other, and the favorite setting for Gene's ghost stories of murder, adultery, and orgy, and, as often as not, of all three, though in the same story, in which the fourposter was made to serve a violent or lustful purpose, and the crewelwork bed curtains were sure to be brought down on someone's head. In that moment of passing the open door she saw in the flicker of the small candle that lit the room the spiral of sweet smoke uncoiling from a cone of incense burning in a saucer set, of all places, on the floor, and saw through that coil of smoke Dwight sitting on the pine blanket chest at the foot of the bed, barefoot, shirtless, his body surprisingly slim and hard and tan and strangely vulnerable, and Penelope, in her flowered, quilted bathrobe, leaning back against the dresser, both of them drinking from big china mugs what must have been the warmed-over hot chocolate she had watched Penelope preparing earlier in the kitchen. And immediately she saw the turnabout: that Penelope had come to *his* room. And saw the incongruity, too: the half-naked boy, the girl in her nightwear, the romantic candlelight, the exotic incense in contradiction to those childish mugs of hot chocolate and the chasteness of that wide-open door. They had been speaking, too, although she had been too soon beyond the door to know exactly what. She was certain only that she had heard Penelope say, "Lisa," but in a voice so unlike her own—so serious, so flat, so soft a voice, so utterly without a trace of feeling—that she could have believed some third person was in the room. And heard Dwight's answer, too, given unintelligibly in a whisper that sounded like what she would have called a coo. She seized her bathrobe at the knees and hurried past the door again. She could have heard her daughter and an older woman speaking in the counterfeit baritones of men for all the sudden ugly apprehension that she felt.

In bed again, she watched the failing firelight on the walls, then lost it to a superwoman with a moon face, naked except for a sequin-coated bathing cap, swimming a lazy backstroke across a marble swimming pool. How healthy she looked, how muscular and brown, how happy, too! Slowly she raised one leg until it stood perpendicular to the glittering surface of the water, while wave after wave of girls in bathing suits dived in to join her from all sides of the pool, their splashes like small neat fountains of exploding diamonds, looking all together like petals closing on a flower as they swam toward the swimmer in the center of the pool. Then more light and shadows dancing on the walls, and the muted breakup and final flaring of a burnt-out log. Just before the faceless man in his baggy clothes walked in front of her across the pasture, waving at her and calling out "Hello, again!" as he blew up in smoke upon the wall, and she was left to face the lonely, unlit house below and, beside it in the road, the mailbox with its red flag up. Then she was awake, rigid and awake, remembering the girl she had just seen sitting silently on the floor beside the bed, hugging her skirt around her knees and smiling at her as she watched her sleep. Sheila! Come back to haunt her. His first wife.

What bitterness she felt! What disappointment! Where was the mystery, the tragedy, the passion, the history, in a woman the likes of Sheila? How could she create, if only for the briefest moment, a world outside her flesh?

Oh, she had had it with these ghosts! No longer did they have the power to terrify or entertain her but, like her problems with Penelope, only to depress her and to make her wish that they did not exist.

Because how many people in their lifetime get to see an apparition? One in a hundred? a thousand? ten thousand? Surely it was a rare enough phenomenon. But both she and Gene had seen an apparition, and she could not help but contrast his experience with her own. He had seen a woman he knew and loved, who loved him, too. She could see the purpose and the beauty in the apparition he had seen, for the force behind it had been her love, or need, of Gene. She could understand how such a mystical and sympathetic bond could culminate, under the right circumstances, in a vision of a loved one that surmounted the natural obstacles of time and space. But what had she seen? A cosmic miscalculation, the misfire of telepathic signals, a dead man's prank. It might have been slapstick, a pie in the face, for all its significance and passion. What, was farce or simple error to have the same power to upset the universal laws as love? Where was the meaning, the justice, in the revelation she had seen?

CHAPTER 7

AND—COULD ANYONE please tell her—where was the sense in Penelope taking back the likes of Dwight? And why should she, Winnie, be the one to confront her with suggestions of what the wasteful consequences of this mistake would be? After all, Penelope was a lot closer to Gene.

To Winnie, who in no way resented that her only child was made in her husband's image, this was only as it should be. Hadn't she always prided herself that she was not a mother who used her daughter as an imitation, or extension, of herself? And a good thing, too. Because it was apparent to one and all that Penelope, who was handsome in a rawboned Nordic way, with a long jaw and a mouthful of strong teeth, bore a striking resemblance to Gene. She also shared many of his mannerisms, including the first stages of what Winnie called his "scholarly stoop." Although Penelope had been known to play golf and tennis, she was not the athlete he was, and her form was more comparable to her mother's than to his. Nor was she the dancer he was, which had been only too painfully apparent whenever they had danced together at the parties Penelope had given for her school friends in the basement of their suburban home—although, thank goodness, she was lighter on her feet than Winnie. Winnie had often tortured herself with the possibility that her school friends had called her a "horse of a girl." Strangely, Penelope had made no attempt to improve herself, nor given any indication that she suffered with her fate. And it was this innocent and honest awkwardness about her, which often embarrassed Winnie for both their sakes, that Winnie suspected was her legacy. It could not help but remind her of herself, not as she was now, but what in the misty and best-forgotten past she used to be. As though Penelope had been born with those same wayward ears that Winnie had had pinned back on her own head before she ever met Gene, and she had only to look at her daughter to suffer with the secret knowledge of why this was so.

And didn't Penelope remind Winnie somehow of herself as she stood now in the doorway of the kitchen as though afraid to enter, drinking a cup of camomile tea while Winnie scrubbed the sink—looking, in her self-conscious costume of overalls and railroad man's bandanna and wire-rim glasses, like a lady riveter or welder in a defense plant during World War II. But if her presence made Winnie uncomfortable, it also presented her with an opportunity she was afraid to lose. She said, "If Dwight wants to eat a New England boiled dinner while he's here, maybe you had better give me a hand."

Penelope seemed surprised, seemed pleased. "You're a mind reader," she said. "I wanted to help, but I was afraid to ask."

She did not explain why this was so, and Winnie did not need to ask. It made Winnie nervous to have Penelope about the kitchen, she was so careless with a knife. And so messy, too, unable to keep the waste pieces on the cutting board, or to clean up after herself, afterward. Since Penelope had been a child, Winnie's contention had been that she made more work in the kitchen than she performed, and rather than put up with her carelessness, she preferred to do the chores herself. She had never been able to bring herself to instruct Penelope in what were such self-evident and simple-minded skills. To have to do so would be an insult, and an admission, on her own part, that her daughter lacked, in some small way, instinct and common sense. Nor had she been able to tell her what chores to do. Besides, with so little work to do herself, wasn't it wasteful to have help? And didn't it waste Penelope, who had so many other and better things to do?

Reluctantly she assigned Penelope the job of cutting turnips and cabbages into wedges while she herself scrubbed and scraped potatoes in the sink.

"Did I tell you I'm learning how to cook?" Penelope said, looking up.

"Careful," Winnie warned, watching the blade of her knife bend as she appeared to stab instead of slice a turnip. "I'll tell you what, I'll do the turnips, you peel the potatoes. You're just not used to that dull knife."

"You can give me a good knife someday, if you want," Penelope said. "I can't wait to get my own kitchen."

"Oh, yes, you can," said Winnie. "Because, believe me, that day will come sooner than you know." And will not come at all, she would have liked to add, if you're lucky.

"Cooking, I should imagine, can be just as much a creative adventure as anything else," Penelope said. "Oh, I know there must have been plenty of times when you hated feeding us, although you never let on. But you must have liked doing a lot of it; you must have found something in it that expressed yourself. I mean you were *making* something."

"Maybe," Winnie said. "Now and then." But she wondered how it was possible that Penelope could know so little about her mother. Or was it because she, Winnie, during all these years had refused to let her learn even this much? Oh, she had always been able to prepare the German dishes she had picked up from her parents, and she had picked up some French and Swedish dishes along the way; she could do that much with competence and a sense of show. But she had al-

ways hated cooking, hated kitchen chores. At best she had
submitted to them with a good, if mindless, grace. She had
never viewed the kitchen—this kitchen or any other—as her
special room. She had taken no special interest in doing over
this kitchen, either. All she wanted was a place that was
practical and did not embarrass the rest of the house, which
explained the presence of all the modern appliances in cop-
pertone disguised in settings of red brick and unpainted
panels made of old weathered boards. To have returned this
room literally to the old days would have meant returning it
to the old ways, and Winnie was having none of that. Even
now, as she and Penelope worked at the vegetables while
Dwight read philosophy in the parlor before the fire and
Gene the morning newspaper over coffee at the Village
Green, she felt they were no better than domestics working
for little more than room and board.

"Say, I know," Penelope said. "Let's put in some beets.
You know how Dad likes red-flannel hash made out of the
leftovers."

"If you like," Winnie said. "If you'll wash them, I'll peel
them after they're cooked." The kitchen would resemble the
site of a bloodbath if Penelope was allowed to take her knife
to them.

Penelope said, "It's odd that you never put up any food.
You never canned or froze anything. I don't even recall you
making jam or jelly. But I suppose that's because we never
had a garden. Not even flowers. I know if I'd lived in the
country as long as you have, I'd have a garden. A big garden.
Vegetables and flowers and clumps of herbs, all mixed up in
one big garden. In neat rows, though. I'd live off the land if
I could. Sometimes I think of all those apples in the Yarrows' orchard that rot because they can't give them away—
they'd give you bushels if you'd take them. And all the things
like elderberries that Dwight's pointed out going to waste
along the road."

Winnie said something in her own defense to the effect

that one could just not do everything. But what Penelope had said was true enough. Bill Yarrow, with that orchard he had dreamed of keeping when he retired from the Air Force, and Norman Chase, with his interest in conservation and agriculture, among others, had made the same observation before, although Penelope made it sound less like an observation than an indictment. Winnie and Gene had no stake or interest in the land itself, had not much more feeling for it than city people spending weekends in the country, except, of course, as it was the bare stage on which the set, in the form of this house, had been built, and where the cast of characters had appeared. For herself, she knew nothing about growing things, and cared even less; besides, it was too late to learn. And Gene's only connection with the land was to make sure that he hired a man once each summer to mow the fields, and to cut brush himself an hour a day, every day, weather permitting, working with an axe or hook and hauling what he could not use for kindling to the town dump where it was burned. Cleared land, he liked to call the product of his labor. But it was not for the land's sake that he did it, or for the sake of acquiring firewood, but for his own sake. It was his daily exercise, which, he claimed, kept him in shape.

"Do you realize I don't know how to do anything with my hands?" Penelope said. "I've never had to use my hands. Except to type pages—"

"Oh, come now," Winnie objected, "that's not true. You've worked with a spade, and with a small pickaxe, too." Which was a reference to Penelope's work on her digs.

"Oh, digging for arrowheads and pieces of old pots," Penelope said. "But I'm too far advanced, too valuable to be doing that anymore. Now I'd just work with a dusting brush or a small scraper. Or maybe I'd work with a paintbrush and label shards. Besides, I've had enough of other people's damaged artifacts. Don't you think it's time I made my own? I'd like to try my hand at so many things. Weaving, dyeing, potting. You know, it's just occurred to me that my brain got developed before my hand, and that that's backwards from the way it happened to the human race. We only got our brain because we learned how to use our hands. All I want to be able to do is what other people have already done, and do it the way they did it. Doesn't it bother you that I can't even begin to do what you do?"

The question did not demand an answer of Winnie, and so she gave none. It seemed to her that their talk had taken them to a point where it was now possible for her to steer it in the direction of Dwight. Not that she had ever been afraid to broach any subject with Penelope, but only rarely, and then in her own fashion, did she care to speak her piece. She preferred instead a course of indirection, of asking questions she hoped would subtly declare the way she felt without committing herself to so firm a stand that she was cut off from qualification or, if need be, retreat. After all, who was she to tell her daughter—and a daughter like this no less—what she should do? Much better to give her the right to deliberately misinterpret her, or to pretend that she had not understood the implication behind her indirection. This gave her the satisfaction of making her feelings known without appearing to treat a precocious daughter as her inferior. "I suppose you want to see so much of Dwight now during this vacation," she began, refusing to look up from her paring, "because you know you won't see much of him next summer." Last summer Penelope had gone on a university archaeological dig at a Stone Age site in New Mexico, and as far as Winnie knew, she planned to return there this summer.

"But I'm not going anywhere this summer," Penelope said. "Neither is he."

"It can't be because you can't tear yourself away from him, can it?" She managed to make this sound like a joke.

"I've been on so many digs," Penelope said, "and I was on this one last year. Besides, I don't feel right anymore about doing my work on American Indians."

"Maybe you can do work in Colonial archaeology instead," Winnie said. "You're interested in Colonial things. I just saw an article in one of the magazines about a site they're excavating down in Massachusetts—down in Newburyport."

"I want," Penelope said, "to do something else for a change."

"Then you're interested in something else?" Until this moment she had been afraid that Dwight would throw up what little he had to keep him in one place and on one track and would follow Penelope out West. Instead she was staying behind to be with him.

"Only in what I told you," Penelope said. "But what else in the long run, if that's what you mean, I don't know exactly. I'll just feel my way around this summer. I'll probably take a job."

"What kind of job could you possibly take?" Any sort of job would be a terrible waste of time and talent. She didn't need the money, and she could use the time to advance her studies.

"Oh, working part-time as a secretary for this professor in the philosophy department. A friend of Dwight's."

"In an office?"

The disappointment must have registered in her voice, because Penelope said, "If I remember, Mother, you worked in an office—and not so long ago, either."

"But I had to," she said, angered by this analogy. "You're different."

"How am I different? I'd be interested to know. . . . But if it will make you any happier, I'll also be taking care of the professor's children. They have a summer place in New Hampshire. It's not that far from here."

"I suppose," Winnie said, "it doesn't pay much more than room and board."

"No, not much more," Penelope agreed.

Winnie said, "Oh, dear, don't tell me you're going to be one of those girls who gives up studying for her R. N., gets married, and works as a practical nurse putting her husband through medical school?"

"Dwight isn't really interested in continuing with school," she said.

There it was again, that directness she had noticed in Penelope's responses to her ever since she returned home. It cut through Winnie's tact and answered her as though her question had been explicit and not implied. And she did it with such a coolness and cocksureness, too, along with— what?—such an even temper that with so little effort made her seem so superior. Oh, she couldn't say what exactly. Only that it was new to her, and was definitely something Penelope had picked up from Dwight.

Then Penelope said, "Dwight and a few of our friends have a house they're going to fix up and live in this summer—"

"Whereabouts?"

"Here."

"In town?"

"Jessie Farnum's place near the mountains."

"How did he get that?"

"He just drove by and saw this empty house he liked. He found out who owned it, wrote to her, went and saw her. I guess she liked the way he felt about the house. She's an old Yankee, you know. He can live in it rent-free if he does some fixing up."

"And you want to help him?" The job, the sudden need of money, the staying around here, the interest in things domestic were becoming clearer now.

"I just want to try a simpler, more honest life," she said. "I just want to return to the best of the way it was. Because this modern world, Mother, is taking us quicker than we know to Armageddon."

"But you can't throw yourself away like that," Winnie objected. "You can't really return to the past. Not your own, not anyone else's."

"Look who's talking," Penelope said. "What have you and Dad been doing in restoring this house if you haven't been trying to bring back the past?" Then, as though she had just thought of it, "Aren't you literally trying to make the past come alive again with all your old ghosts? And isn't that because you really want to know the people who lived here back then? I just want to go you one better." Then she added, "For a while, anyway."

But even this final touch of sanity did not satisfy Winnie. Was it possible that Penelope was deliberately using her as a model? Did she want, in obedience to some fashion of the moment, to relive her mother's life? It made no sense if this was so. Surely it was the clothes that Penelope had taken to wearing lately that had started her thinking along these lines. Not only the worker's costume she was wearing now, but the used clothing from the thirties and forties she picked up in the secondhand shops down in Cambridge, so that at worst she looked like the denim-shirted daughter of a sharecropper or an urban blue-collar victim of the Depression, and at best like a threadbare and wrinkled fashion model who had just stepped out of a nineteen-thirties issue of *Vogue*. In such disguises how much she could remind Winnie of herself. Not that Penelope was aware of this effect. Because her model was not a Winnie she had known. But it troubled Winnie to see her dress herself so. And not only because the costumes demeaned and ridiculed her, but because they were proof that so unique a girl could surrender to the passing fad.

"Look at yourself," Penelope said. "You didn't have to go to college. And you're bright enough without it. It isn't necessary to be successful, or happy."

"Times were different then," Winnie said. "And I was a far cry from you." And then she surprised herself. She said, "All I know is that I wish I were young again and had all your opportunities—how I wish I were that young again!"

Penelope was interested. "You sound like Father," she began.

But Winnie, who did not want the focus of their talk to switch to her, broke in, choosing her words carefully, "You don't think you're wasting yourself, that you might be turning around too quickly? You don't think you'll regret it later, do you?"

Penelope thought a long time about this. "I don't see how I have a choice in all of this," she said with difficulty, as though she knew she was entering an area where it would be difficult to make her mother understand. "I can't say when I came to the end of one thing and started on the next. So how can you regret what you didn't know you were about to do?"

Winnie, as always, admired her honesty, but was appalled by her confusion. Was this the girl who used to be so clear-headed, level, dead-certain?

"And I wouldn't worry about Dwight," Penelope said, looking directly at her. "Whatever we do together, we'll do as equals. Although I'd be surprised if we could ever be as close as you and Dad. I don't know that we have *that* kind of understanding."

Such an observation unsettled Winnie more than she let on. She had not known that Penelope could stand back and examine her parents' marriage, especially where it concerned the quality of their affection. But far worse was her surprise that the observation should strike her as being so completely wrong.

"But then again," Penelope added, giving her mother a look Winnie would have expected from a woman in her thirties, "we'll see if we stay together long enough to find out."

Here it was at last, the opening Winnie had been looking for. She said, "At least you recognize it's a fickle world."

"Or that I'm a fickle girl."

How she would have liked to say, Good for you if you are! Instead she said, "I don't think you are. You're much too faithful, to anything you latch on to. You move too slowly, and you don't give up easily." Only at the last moment did she manage to keep from adding, And that is the sad thing. For a moment she was overcome with pity for her daughter. It came upon her like a sudden sickness. Then, seeing she was about to miss her opening, she said, "But so what if you are fickle? Isn't *he* fickle? With women, I mean."

"Mother, do you know something I don't?"

"Only what you know well enough already. Lisa, this German girl?"

"Oh, the other woman."

"Aren't you sophisticated to put it like that?" she said, unaware that she had turned around to face her and placed her hands on her hips. "And aren't you the odd one to put up with it? I know I wouldn't." She did not like holding herself up as an example to her daughter, and regretted immediately speaking as she had. Far better if it were the other way around, the roles reversed. But only as recently as yesterday Dwight had called Penelope Lisa, and she had been about to ask him just who he thought her daughter was when Penelope caught her eye and winked, as though acknowledging they shared the amusing secret of his embarrassing and very *male* mistake.

"Maybe I don't have your strength?" she countered.

"Strength?" Winnie said instinctively, wondering what she could be getting at. For the first time she questioned Penelope's sincerity. However, she was not about to let herself be sidetracked along this line. "Does he still see her?" she asked.

"She's gone home to Germany."

Winnie received this news with mixed emotions. If Penelope was rid of a rival, she was also rid of the likeliest means of getting rid of Dwight.

But then Penelope added, as though she had no choice but to be ruthlessly honest, "She left him."

As Winnie trimmed some of the fat off the slab of grayish corned beef, she tried to get a picture of this Lisa. She would be blond, athletic, speaking English with a soft lisp. She probably squinted, too. Intellectually she was tough, and stubborn, and when it came to Dwight, at least, she was a lot shrewder and more selfish than Penelope. "Was she a college student, an exchange student of some sort?"

"No, just an office worker. Dwight met her when he went to school in Munich. He made the arrangements for her to come over here. She worked as an *au pair* for some friend of his family's out in California at first."

"Well, she didn't amount to much, did she?" Winnie said. In her eyes, Penelope had humiliated herself in competing with such a girl. And for the affection of what? A Dwight.

"I don't think she ever pretended to be what she wasn't," Penelope said.

"Does he still care about her?"

It was a painful question for Penelope. "I want to understand the situation. . . . I'm willing to go out of my way to be sympathetic. . . ."

"Do you think she will come back?"

"To haunt us?"

"No, to spirit Dwight away . . . to make you unhappy. . . ."

"That," she admitted, "is a possibility I just might have to learn to live with."

"How do you know," Winnie said, "that she hasn't given in to some whim and that she isn't on a Lufthansa flight at this moment, headed your way?"

"I don't."

"Then why get hurt?"

"Oh, I don't think she can hurt me."

"Oh, can't she?" Winnie said, thinking, Then the more fool you. Because really, it was too much. It was one thing to tie yourself up with a man when you had every reason to believe he would be faithful and then have to put up with the presence of another woman for the sake of the children and the marriage, but another thing entirely to tie yourself up with a man when you knew very well there was another woman he had no intention of giving up.

She returned to this subject later when they had finished with their chores, and faced each other across the kitchen table, drinking tea. "You remember what your father always told his students. Have your fun first, all the fun you want, move around, date a lot. Find out who other people are, who *you* are. Don't tie yourself down too soon. Because the important thing is to stay young as long as you can, stretch out your youth while you can. Then when you're ready to make your move, just be certain that it's solid." Then, perhaps again inspired by Penelope's candor, she asked, "Or does he give different advice to his daughter?" Because the truth was she didn't know what he might have told her.

Penelope appeared to be recalling past conversations with her father. "No," she said, "I'm sure he's said as much to me. But then it's always hard, isn't it, to remember *what* he's said?"

This observation Winnie ignored. "Would he be disappointed if you did otherwise?" she said.

"If he was disappointed, Mother, how would we know it?"

Surprised by these back-to-back criticisms of Gene, she restrained herself from adding, We wouldn't know it because he wouldn't show it, and he wouldn't show it because, quite likely, he wouldn't feel it. And even if he did show it, how could we be certain that he meant it? Surely Penelope was not suggesting that although she might have a closer friendship with her father, she and her mother were more clear-sighted and sincere, possessing deeper souls? But Gene was a subject that was irrelevant at the moment, and one she would have been reluctant to pursue at any time. Instead she seized on something Penelope had introduced earlier, only she disguised it a bit. "You don't ever want to be able to look back and have to say it was just here that I made my mistake even if, as you say, you had no choice but to make it."

"And have it come back to haunt me, you mean?"

"In a manner of speaking."

Suddenly Penelope said, "Then what do you think I should do, Mother?"

This so disconcerted Winnie, who had gotten up to cover

with cold water the bowl of already bruised-looking sliced potatoes Penelope had not known would discolor if left exposed
to the air, that for a while she could only stare in silence at
the tap water spilling over the rim of the bowl and swirling
around the stainless steel above the drain. Had Penelope
ever asked her opinion on so personal and important a matter? She could not remember.

When she saw her mother's hesitation, Penelope added,
"Not that I'll do what you say . . ."

At a complete loss, Winnie said, "I think you should be
. . . realistic."

Penelope smiled, and immediately Winnie knew she had
said exactly what Penelope had predicted she would say. And
worse, what she had wanted her to say.

"When you say be realistic to someone, aren't you really
saying that they should do something they don't want to do?"

"I suppose that's true," Winnie admitted. But she didn't
care to discover that she could be predictable, or that her
daughter was capable of setting traps.

"To be realistic," Penelope said, "is to do what you want
to do, what you have to do, because that's who you are, the
real you."

"Oh, is that it?" Winnie said, trying not to show her
anger, which was due less to her daughter's presuming to
lecture her than to her suspicion that she had picked up this
idea from Dwight. "Suppose you tell me what it is *you* want?"
she asked, turning the tables.

"I suppose I want to be—"

"Better?" Winnie helped, surprising herself so much that
she caught herself bringing her hand up to cover her mouth,
as though, unknowingly, she had just betrayed a secret.

Penelope was no less surprised. "Better?" she said. "Better
than what?"

Winnie said, "Don't you want to be happy?"

"But you said better."

"Well, you know I meant to say happy. Better, happy . . ."

"Happy isn't better."

"I know that," Winnie said, not knowing anything of the sort. "I said I meant to say happy."

"I hope I am happy. But I want to be real."

"Aren't we all that already?" Winnie said. "The question, it seems to me, is a real *what*?" Oh, what a little fool she was! How could she make a mistake even her mother would not have made? How could she fail to see what even her mother could see? One thing sure, her mother would not have settled for a Dwight. She would have demanded something else from life, something more, something better. Even if she had yet to meet up with it, she would have known it was out there in the world waiting for her. Her disappointment with Penelope was keen. She felt so helpless, too. And it was not only because she wanted Penelope to do better in life than she had done, although, Lord knows, she wanted that desperately enough. The truth was she looked up to her daughter, judged her a far different and better sort than herself, as though she had been born and bred not in her mother's house but in the château of a glittering neighbor. And she was now as disillusioned with her as she would have been with any idealized model she had chosen for herself who had just revealed her feet of clay.

The girl was weak.—What other conclusion could she reach? Penelope was too willing to view life not as a valley surrounded by mountains you had to climb if you wanted to leave where you had been put—where you had to start out from—but as an endurable and easygoing plateau, an Eden of lotus-eaters who could stand still or backslide as the fancy took them. And wasn't that the legacy of Gene? Maybe her honors and rewards had come much too easy to be the making of her; maybe that was the problem. Because she had not had to reach for her high place, and she had grabbed at nothing. She had neither earned nor seized so much as she had received, as a princess might her legal tribute. She had as much as been given the class presidency in high school. She had not had to campaign for it, probably had not even wanted it. And wasn't it possible that she had been popular because her father had been popular, and she had been a decent, good-looking, and bright girl among classmates whose families were, for the most part, too established and well-off to be snobbish? If anything, wouldn't they have gone out of their way to reward the underdog? Her ambition, her toughness, her ruthlessness had yet to be tested: that was it. And what better proof that she was to be found lacking than the ruin she risked making of herself by hanging on so shamelessly to Dwight?

Good God, weren't young women supposed to be so much more independent and "liberated" these days? The irony, of course—and she saw this clearly—was that Penelope was using her freedom and independence only to subjugate herself to Dwight. She had certainly believed that Penelope would do better in this world than her mother did. Because wasn't there always this gradual trend forward, and hadn't she, Winnie, taken a good-sized step that it was Penelope's business—no, calling—to advance upon?

How she wanted to take hold of her, shake her, say to her, Be yourself, make yourself, but whatever you do, don't be Dwight—don't be— Oh, she didn't know what, only that it was something more than Dwight. Oh, Penelope, she wanted to shout at her, just don't be *him*!

CHAPTER 8

SEVERAL NIGHTS LATER, when Penelope and Dwight had gone
to visit a friend of theirs—a former grade school teacher who
was now trying to make his living in these parts as a carpenter, and who was said to have some ideas on how Dwight
might best improve the Farnum Cape Cod he had been
made the rent-free tenant of—Winnie joined Gene beside
the fire where he sat making notes from the town history for
that historical pageant he had been commissioned to write
for the tricentennial celebration of the town. After a while
he looked up and removed his glasses, saying, "It's so damned
difficult to be enthusiastic about putting this thing together
when you don't know what's going to happen to it once it's
done. Maybe you can tell me how in hell's name they think
they can have me write it and then give it to that cornball
Marcotte to direct? Because you know as well as I do, all that
farmer is good for is a pantomime of the forest." Here he
gave an imitation of how Marcotte's actors clomped woodenly
on and off the stage, or stood stiffly delivering their lines.
"Perfect if you're doing 'The March of the Wooden Soldiers.'
Dreadful for Ibsen, though."

If anything, this was an understatement of Marcotte's incompetence. Marcotte preferred to stage the plays of Sophocles, Chekhov, Lorca—his ignorance of which was surpassed only by his inexperience with the art of stagecraft—or any other works that were automatically impossible for his pickup company of well-drillers, grocery clerks, retired postmen, and high school sophomores to perform. Often his actors had to read their lines from mimeographed crib sheets while on the stage, and even then they stumbled over the longer words, or had to be prompted by Marcotte from where he sat perspiring in his front-row aisle seat, his legs crossed and revealing his white wool socks and the black oxfords that Gene had once described as looking as though he had to cross a hen yard to get to school. For Marcotte's audiences, attendance at the town hall or high school auditorium was grim business, a parental or communal duty equal to that of listening to a long-winded and mumbled funeral sermon. Gene's audiences, on the other hand, were almost always entertained. He was at his best in his selection of simple plays that the actors could creditably perform, and the audience could honestly enjoy. For this reason he preferred contemporary Broadway shows; or mysteries with British settings and crimes that were not unraveled until the final act. If he could not have them dancing in the aisles, he was fond of saying, then by Jesus he would have them sitting on the edge of their seats.

To Winnie, Marcotte looked like one of those rumpled salesmen who sold cardboard stands of trinkets to truck stops, or a poker player who had held bad cards into the small hours of the morning. He was just a country teacher, self-effacing, insecure, and frightened of any criticism, and she thought Gene demeaned himself by forcing such a man to be his rival.

Gene said, "Of course if Marcotte gets to do the play he'll use his same old cast of incompetents all over again. He has to. He has too many friends in this town that he needs to keep him in his job. That's why he can't be professional about his casting. Whereas I'd like to use as many young people in the line-up as I can."

Gene had never liked to work with older amateur actors, claiming that there was little chance of improving them and no chance at all that they would ever amount to anything. He preferred youth and raw talent, he said. It gave him energy, fresh ideas, new approaches. Best of all, young people were fun. Winnie had sometimes thought that so many years of teaching youngsters would make him weary of them. On the contrary, if he could be believed, it had made him one of them.

"Dionne's very good at getting young people involved in theater," Gene said. "And she's been good for me, too. I've actually changed some scenes because of her critiques. She's got the knowledge, I've got the experience, and we're both full of ideas. We could make a hell of a team—if we could only do the play."

By Dionne he meant Dionne DeMarco, and Winnie was surprised that he had come to speak so well of her. Whenever he had mentioned her before, it was with a deep distrust that bordered on dislike. She was nothing but a know-it-all academic, he had said, pushy and high-strung.

Winnie had meant to ask him about her for some time now. She had learned from her friends that Dionne had barely moved to town, about two years ago, when she divorced her husband (or vice versa), who, to her apparent if unexplained disgrace, retained custody of their two small children. A former high school teacher, she was finishing up her work on a doctor's degree in drama at the state university nearby. She must have been around twenty-seven. Winnie wasn't certain she knew exactly who she was. She suspected she might be the short and fragile-looking young woman with the white skin and dark hair she had seen at the post office once or twice. She had looked intense, conceited, furtive, and something else besides—what it was Winnie could only give a name to now: she had looked guilty.

"Doesn't she have a wild reputation?" she said.

"On stage or off?" He seemed surprised.

"Off."

"May I ask where you heard that?"

"Gladys Chase. Polly Fisher . . . You want me to go on?"

"I don't know anything about it," he said, frowning. Obviously it was unimportant to him, having nothing to do with her professional life. Although he did add, "In any case, she's young," as if that explained, or excused, whatever he thought Winnie meant by being wild. "All I know is she's a great help in dealing with the committee and standing up to Cressman and his pals. The latest news I have is that it's no one else but old Cressman who's behind getting the committee to wonder if it wouldn't be fair play to divide the pageant up between Marcotte and myself. And of course they knew from the start *he* couldn't write the play."

The quarrel between Gene and Bob Cressman went back to the days when Cressman had been a selectman trying to get the Old Crown Road paved. Since the townspeople did not care to spend any money they did not have to, Gene's orations at town meetings on how he preferred his road to remain dirt and just as it was in the old days could always be counted on to carry the vote against the town warrant to have it paved. Which infuriated Cressman, who, quite apart from the fact that his nephew was the road agent and would be paid by the town to do the paving, honestly believed every road should be paved if the time and money could be found to do it with, and that anyone who was against paving in principle had to be told what was good for him, he was that big a fool. Gene was convinced Cressman had become the champion of Marcotte in revenge.

"And just look at this, will you?" he said, opening the bicentennial history written a hundred years ago, which was almost the size of the average dictionary. "Most of the pieces in here were written by members of the old families in the town, and you can't believe how far these families have degenerated in just a hundred years. Here's a piece on the illustrious Perkins family by Nathaniel Perkins, old Mrs. Cressman's great-grandfather, and he was an ordained Congregational minister, a Harvard man, and a poet, too. Here's his 'Ode to the Granite State,' a wonderful piece of doggerel. And what is his great-granddaughter today but just another country lady who could never put two hands together well enough to play a decent church piano. And there's no chapter at all by a Cressman, which shows you the sort of stock he sprung from. But there is one by an Overhill—can you believe it?—on the first settlers of the town, and another by a Beecher on the town's contribution to the Civil War. And obviously these were literate men, with a high regard for education. Unfortunately, as you can see, they wrote in that flowery prose people write when they don't read any prose, only the worst sort of flowery poetry. . . ."

The contemporary William Overhill was the one-eyed keeper of the town dump, where he could be found shooting rats with a .22, or fishing with a long pole about the smoldering trash for small treasures. The contemporary George Beecher owned the town's smallest garage, and was against spending public money on public education, appearing at every meeting of the school board, in the same blue shirt and pants he wore in his garage, to tell it so.

"It's odd, isn't it," Winnie agreed, "how we take for granted that a family keeps rising in the world, that it keeps improving. . . ." She came close to introducing the subject of Penelope with something like: And speaking of families going downhill . . . Instead she appeared to speak out of the blue, saying, "I don't care much for the seriousness of Penelope lately. She used to have such a wonderful sense of fun. You could see it when she got together with her father."

"Well," Gene said, obviously wondering what she was

getting at, "perhaps that was because her father has a sense of fun."

"You mean that Dwight hasn't a sense of fun? And that he has taken your place?" Although she was well aware that this might sound distasteful, she had laid a plan to play up his special relationship with his daughter, believing such a tack had the best chance to provoke him into accepting her feeling that Penelope's change of direction was a great mistake.

"You can't very well act like a daughter with your boy-friend" was all he said.

"It's that word 'act' I don't much like," she said, aware that she was "getting back" at him, for what exactly she could not have said. "I don't know why she can't be herself."

"Easier said than done," he said. "Don't you remember what it was like to be young?" And when she didn't answer he said, "I know I do. You were always acting then. And I've always believed young people learned who they were by becoming bits and pieces of other people they happen to admire, or like, and take a turn at imitating. You can't deny them outside influences. They play roles, change roles, go from one role to the next, only they never give up the old role entirely. Maybe Penelope's far closer to being herself now than she's ever been. In fact, no maybe about it; I'm sure she is."

Winnie said, "That's just what she would say, too. I just think it's a shame, though. I don't like her becoming like *him*."

He seemed surprised. "Is there something wrong with him?"

"Only that he's not *her*. Oh, I'll admit he's not the type I imagined she would see eye-to-eye with someday. It's not that I pictured anyone very definite. I just always assumed that Penelope would do very well in life, that she would certainly have a lot more of everything—" She hesitated, then, deciding she could not bring him down with her, said "—Than *I* had. You didn't expect a bit more of her?"

"Well, I wanted her to be stable and happy." Then he

added as a joke, "Of course I didn't want her to make out so badly that I'd have to support her in my old age."

"It's his influence on her that I don't like," she said. "She's not interested in archaeology anymore, can you believe it? Ever since she was a little girl, she made me feel so proud of her—of all of us—when she would tell people she wanted to be an Egyptologist when she grew up. I mean other girls her age hadn't even heard of Egypt. From the beginning she was so different from the others, so much her own self."

"I don't know," he said, with that long cigarette holder between his teeth. "Maybe I never told you this before, but her precociousness could make me feel uncomfortable sometimes. I didn't like her being so far above the heads of the other kids that she wasn't one of them." But then again, he had never made a secret of his belief that education should be a great democratic leveler of talent—in the social years anyway.

"I suppose you know," she went on, "that she doesn't intend to go back to New Mexico next summer." And she picked up the photograph album from the cobbler's bench and looked through the plastic-coated pages until she found the snapshots Penelope had sent from the sites of her archaeological digs. There she was suntanned and sweaty, in khaki shorts, bikini halter, and sun helmet or bandanna, a small hammer or beer can in hand, squatting above the fragments of a clay pot, or posed with her arms around her fellow suntanned students, or beside some professor with pipe and full beard. For Winnie, what an exotic and head-turning world there was within those photos! In them, Penelope had become so much more than her mother had, or could have, been.

"Still, this business with Dwight," Gene was saying, "it's all part of the educational process, isn't it? I've never believed that the classroom was the only place where we learned about the world we live in. And what's the learning process if it doesn't provide us the opportunity to change— ourselves, our minds, our jobs, whatever? We all have to change. We have to, Winnie, especially at Penelope's age."

"But don't you see," she said, "that she should be the making of *him*? That is, if it has to be this way."

"Which way do you mean?"

"Why, the two of them together, what do you think I mean?" How could she make him understand that although she was fairly certain she still believed Penelope would not merely be better off with the right man but that such a man might be necessary for her to complete herself, she preferred her by herself to the company of any man less than the best.

He fell silent, fingering the pages of the town history and blocking with his hands the pile of pages on which he had written notes.

"You'll agree, won't you," she continued, "that she shouldn't lose what she has to him? Because she has so much more than he has. At the very least there should be some interchange between them. This is all so one-sided, and so unfair."

"Winnie," he said, fingering his beard and fluttering that cigarette holder between his fingers in a manner some men might have considered effeminate, "do you really think your concern—or anyone else's, for that matter—can really help her? If she's to be herself, as you say you want her to be, wouldn't it be better if you simply relaxed, stayed out of her affairs, and let her follow her own head of steam?"

She read the implication in this. It was meant to say that if she was concerned, he was not. But shouldn't he have shown more anxiety over Penelope's well-being than merely this? After all, she was his only daughter, and between them hadn't there always been this special friendship and affection? She knew his worldly-wise philosophy of sympathetic understanding ("Leave them alone, and they'll come home, wagging their tails behind them." That was how he put into a joke his very serious approach to counseling and teaching), but was he so patient and tolerant a man that he could apply this rigid "hands-off" policy to his daughter? It was true that he had never been jealous of her boyfriends, or worried much about her when she was out late, or off by herself at the other end of the continent, and apparently he had not given her any advice at home that ran contrary to what he gave his students in school. But now she began to suspect that his feeling for Penelope was not so deep as it had seemed, or as she had imagined, nor even so deep as it should have been. Was it possible that his so-called philosophy only masked his loss of interest and lack of feeling, a posture he had learned he could put over on his students, who would of course applaud his permissiveness and understanding, seeing it as the consequence of his deep feeling? By God, after all these years she didn't really know if there was a philosophy behind his point of view! All she knew for certain was that his weak spot, that special affection he had for his daughter, which she had hoped to wound in order to make an ally of him against the likes of Dwight, was iron-plated, or else did not exist at all.

"And besides," she said, starting it up again, "he's so *new!*" She seemed to have no other argument left.

"Odd," he said. "I would have thought you would say young. Because of his enthusiasm, I guess. Or, come to think of it, you might have said old. Because he *is* like a little old man, with all his fussy little eccentricities and scraps of information. But I do see what you mean, though."

"I don't mean *nouveau riche,*" she said, "because he's not that. Not anywhere near as bad as that."

"No, he's not like that," Gene agreed. Adding, "He's not a man you can see through."

She was quick to defend herself. "I'm not snobbish—what do I have to be snobbish about? Precious little. And I do like him, I like him a lot. It's just his newness. His Westness, somehow." These were judgments she had never articulated as clearly before. "Maybe that's it, he's so far from the West, and that's why he wants to run off into the woods and play Pilgrim father and frontier settler, living in a run-down house, living off the land with nothing but his know-how and his two hands. . . ."

"You don't think it's just a case of getting away from it all?"

"Oh, sure, if you want to look at the surface."

"How do you know he will stick with it—or with anything else, for that matter—long enough for him to actually do it?" he said in consolation. "It's the idea and the gathering of information that he likes, not the doing of it."

"Well, so many of them are doing just that these days," she countered. "Besides he's not all theory. And he does get his hands dirty. I don't have any trouble imagining him becoming what he says he wants to become, nor with Penelope becoming exactly like him."

Then Gene said, "Look here, if you really feel the way you do, why don't I arrange to have a chat with her before she leaves for school?" He only said this, Winnie knew, to bring an end to the conversation. Even so, she was glad to have made him concede at least this much.

It was Winnie, though, who made the arrangement for their "chat," and as soon as the next day, too. She sent him on a shopping errand to the supermarket and liquor store, and then suggested to Penelope that she go along. To Winnie, it was a reminder of their "buddy" days, which she had viewed humorously as their father-and-daughter romance.

Only when they were gone, however, did she realize the consequence of her little plot. She was left alone with Dwight. And needlessly, too. Because what had made her think Gene could possibly do Penelope any good? He wouldn't keep his promise to talk to her even if he hadn't already forgotten all about it. Now she was stuck with Dwight. That it was her duty to keep him company and make conversation if she could, she accepted. But she felt too uncertain of what she might say or do to anticipate his putting her at ease. Besides, she judged him too humorless, too quietly intense, for easy company.

But as she prepared the supper dishes and then performed her clean-up chores in the sanctuary of the kitchen, he remained in the parlor where he was so quiet she could almost persuade herself he had fallen asleep. How quiet the house seemed beyond the bright factory of this kitchen! She scrubbed the cutting board and sink with trembling arms. Why, she was trembling like a schoolgirl. And feeling that same awkwardness she had known as a girl awaiting—what?—the arrival of a first date. She wondered if he was as aware of her in here as she rattled and banged about as she was of him out there in all his scholarly silence. She busied herself until she found she was going over old ground needlessly, and feared that by now he must suspect she was avoiding him and be close to guessing why.

There he was. She could just about see him now. Reading by the firelight with his shoes off, warming his feet in their heavy wool socks before the flames. In only a week the room had taken on his smells of feet and musk and smoldering elm and something that reminded her of cider just beginning to turn in the jug. If only he were watching television, it would be easy then. She could join him without thinking it was her duty to engage him in small talk. She had intended to ask him if he would like a cup of coffee, but asked instead if he would like a can of beer. She had a beer, too, and seated herself across the room.

She poured her beer into a glass and stared at the sinking foam. He continued to face the fire and his book, and she wondered if he was only pretending to read. He had said nothing since accepting the beer. Oh, he would look up now and then—almost with a start, too—but not at her, only at the fire, sipping his beer. What was in the air between them that embarrassed them and made them shy? Or was he innocent of such a sensitivity, and she was attributing to him a guilty self-consciousness that belonged only to herself? In times past she had suspected that one or two of Penelope's boyfriends had found her—well, *interesting* (because she had always been unable to think about this, she had yet to find a truer word), and she had gone out of her way not to be left alone with them for the sake of the awkwardness she was certain they both would feel. Just now she had barely kept herself from blurting out to break the silence, "Well, here we are alone. . . ." Instead she said, "What's the interest these days, Dwight?"

He had to peer over the back of his chair to see her. "Oh, mysticism," he said, holding up the book, "the East . . ."

"Aha!" she said, seeing this as an echo of her worst fear. "That explains the interest in apparitions."

"In a left-handed way I suppose you're right," he conceded, yawning. "But I tried to look at that as scientifically as I could. After all, I've always been a good son of the Enlightenment and the Age of Reason. Lately I've begun to wonder, though. Maybe I've spent so much time studying the so-called natural world with the so-called scientific methods that I've missed something. I know I've just ignored the possibility of there being another world within us. And all around us, too. Another plane of existence, another dimension of the life force entirely. Another world superimposed upon this world."

"The spirit world?"

"Half the world seems to believe in something like it. It's just a different way of looking at the same old world. I mean why should the wisdom of the West necessarily negate the wisdom of the East? Why should the scientific method be the only way of looking at the world? Why should its laws be the only laws?"

He didn't have to tell her any more. She could predict where this new passion would take him. Braided hair or a shaved head, the mindless chanting of incomprehensible prayers and Yoga positions performed in a saffron robe on the wide pine-board floor of the run-down Farnum's Cape, or in the stand of white pines behind the house. Hadn't she seen the type already around these parts, college kids who mixed a blue-collar or artsy-craftsy life of old New England with the spirit of Buddha, or with something Hindu? As far as she knew, Dwight had yet to immerse himself any less than all the way in any subject he took a fancy to. Only there would be a difference here: once he gave up the sane limitations of the scientific perspective, there was no telling where he would go, and where he would remain. Off the deep end, more than likely. Even if there was not another world around us, that would not prevent him from stepping through the looking glass in an attempt to discover it, and without troubling himself about how he was to find his way back. "What would your father say about your new interest?" she asked.

Unaccustomed to Winnie's oblique lines of interrogation, he was momentarily puzzled. Then he said, "Oh, I see, because he's a math teacher. Yes, but to tell the truth, he's had an exotic interest in the occult all his life. It used to embarrass me."

"I suppose," she said, "that's the California influence on him."

This time he was ready for her, and he laughed, catching her meaning.

This led them into a subject on which they exercised similar tastes: the geography of the country from east to west. He had driven across the breadth of the Midwest, from Kansas to Ohio, five times now, and he agreed with her that it was flat, monotonous, and inhabited by a race of people not unlike the landscape. For him it was just too far from the oceans. Only the East coast for Winnie, and either coast for Dwight. Maybe after the experience at the Farnum place he would settle in Oregon or Washington, or on the northern coast of Maine. There he would buy a sizable tract of timber, build a log cabin, clear some land, grow some food.

"That," she said, "could be a hard life, a lonely life."

"I wouldn't want to be a hermit. I never thought of doing it except with other people."

"How many . . . would you need?"

"Oh, from one to a hundred. I might teach grammar school besides. I'd like to start a school of my own, an experimental school, with an open classroom and no fixed courses. I'd want to become involved in the community, I'd want to be a part of it."

"I can't understand this wanting to go back," she said.

"Not even to find your roots?" he asked, obviously aware that this was bound to strike a chord in her.

"Oh, that—like the interest in folk songs. I can understand that. But to simply shut yourself up during the most important years of your life, wasting the years that count the most when it comes to making something of yourself—I admit I don't understand that. It's just not being . . . realistic?"

Predictably, he was ready with his answer. "But it's realistic to do what you want to do," he said. "It's unrealistic to do anything else." Then he went so far as to scold her. "Like a lot of people, you seem to have it all mixed up."

"Got it completely backwards, haven't I?" she said, aware that he would miss the edge of irony. Anyway, there it was: the proof of the power he wielded over Penelope. It had come to her parroting his platitudes!

Thank God he had pushed her to the point where she could now feel that she had to let him know she disapproved of him. If only because Penelope, as she saw it, should have aimed higher. Because—well, no because about it—she could not understand the girl. Penelope had met boys here in the East whose parents were well-known or well-to-do, and most often both, some of whom she had confessed had shown an interest in her. And Winnie admitted that she had always assumed Penelope would someday marry a man not only wealthier and more intellectual than her parents, but better than the best of them back in their old suburb on the lake. That wasn't unreasonable, was it? After all, hadn't she demonstrated she was the intellectual superior and the social equal to the best of them back there? And wasn't it something like her right to have the best of men, and society's duty to give him to her? That is, if she wanted him—wanted anyone. Instead she had fallen for Dwight, a man who had not made it, who would not make it, who would be satisfied with so much less than he should become. And she knew the reason why, too. He was weak. . . . Oh, he and his friends would, of course, turn it inside out and maintain that he was strong, too strong to be one of those weaklings who are driven to compete for the prizes life offered. He would not want the money, status, security, power, fame that most people wanted. Self-satisfaction and happiness, along with what he would call honesty and peace of mind—that was all the allotment he would want from life. He was without envy, he was untouched by ambition. He wasn't driven to reach, to get up on his toes. He wouldn't catch up, wouldn't keep up, wouldn't even try. God, didn't she know the artistic type he favored? The house painters with half a dozen kids and a litter of muddy dogs living in the shell of an old house in a small snowbound town in Maine, with bare laths on the walls, or sheetrock that had yellowed and had yet to be taped, diapers soaking in the toilet bowl and sinks, the friends of *real* people: lobstermen, lumbermen, unemployed mill hands, illiterates on relief. The fool—he had it all wrong! You always went forward. You never went backward, not if you could help it. That was the way this country worked; it had always worked that way. It was the way the world worked, too.

If he meant to use her own retirement to an old house in the New England countryside as an argument that she was one with him, he had never been so wrong in his young life. This house was for her a step forward, the last step, and the best step, too. She could never think of it as "dropping out," the term he would use to describe his planned retreat into the woods. She supposed if she had called her coming here anything, she would have said it was her "settling in." She would show him how far she had risen—not too far, to be sure, but when you reckoned the distance she had traveled from start to finish, you had to give her credit. She would prove to him just how determined she had been to endure and make her way through social worlds she had had no previous knowledge of, and in the process, just how astute and tough she had become. And she ought to let him sample the slights and insults of those suburban women she had never been thick-skinned enough not to recognize, or numb enough not to feel, those many ways they could make her out to be so much less than themselves, less than their children, and even her own child (although she never minded that), and so much less than Gene. These indignities she had at first ignored, and later parried, and finally silenced, having learned to strike first and reverse the roles. She had never been above the battle. But she had not been beneath it, either. She would make him understand what a wonderful reward it was to have left that life behind and moved on and "up" to this. "You know, I was born back there," she began. "Just outside Milwaukee. My father owned a bakery, a neighborhood hole-in-the-wall. He was a baker—born in Germany, too. When I was a girl, I had to work behind the counter selling sweet rolls and bread every day after school and all day Saturdays and Sunday mornings. The whole family had to work—"

"Have you ever wanted to go to Germany?" he asked.

Surprised by this interruption, she said, "Oh, yes—maybe. When I worked for a travel agency, I had a chance to go there once. To a convention of travel agents, and inspect some new hotels. But it fell through, for some reason." But then, seeing what he meant, she added, "But not because *he* came from there. Not because I would have wanted to go *back* there."

He waited a moment, then said, "What a good thing to be able to make your own bread like that, and to be able to sell it, too. . . ."

"Oh, not such a good thing as you might think," she said. "We lost the bakery—of course we lost it. (You don't know why I say that but, believe me, I do.) Then my father got a job as a CTA motorman in Chicago, on the el. Times were tough then—you kids don't know how tough. You know, when I went to college—" And then, realizing she was giving him the wrong impression, she said, "Oh, it wasn't a real college, just a business school. A secretarial school. I had to work to put myself through it—as a servant in some doctor's house. I had to cook all the meals, make all the beds, wear a pinafore. I had to eat in the kitchen, too, while the family—and there were four girls my age or younger—ate in the big dining room. The doctor was too good to talk to me, and his wife—what a bitch! How she liked to make me wait hand and foot on those girls. And all I got was my room and board. Not so much as a cent extra. And I had to pay the school back out of the money I got on my first job. But that's the way it was then."

Then she was telling him about her early life in Milwaukee and Chicago, her family and friends, while he listened as though he could become as much a student of her life as he had been of those many interests he had mastered and discarded, asking now and then a relevant and sympathetic question that led her on. But gradually his presence grew unimportant, and she found herself reminiscing solely for the bittersweet pleasure of her nostalgia. She was bringing back a world she had set out to forget, and it amazed her that it had been so much sunnier a time and place than she had previously remembered, or imagined. It didn't hurt her, it didn't shame her. It was all right to bring it back. She stopped only when she reached the period of her history that began with her first marriage. There was no way she could get around that block of time. She had no thoughts to think about it, and there was nothing she could say.

In the silence he began to tell her in turn something of his boyhood back in California. A virgin forest of redwoods behind his house in which he played all day, a small fishing fleet chugging into the harbor—she could not say what else, for if she was no longer speaking about her past, that did not mean she had given up trying to listen to its voice inside her head.

Then he was silent, tugging at his beard, while the room grew dark. Neither had remembered to turn on a light, and the fire, which had not been fed, was burning low. At some time she fetched them both another beer, and this time she was drinking hers directly from the can. She tried to make him out, sprawled in that easy chair, and she could picture him wearing that little smile within the foxy beard that came to sharp triangles high up on his cheeks beneath the tiny, puffy eyes. She had to sense him more than see him now, and she was not so conscious of their difference in age. She wondered what the sexual attraction could be between Penelope and him, and decided it could not be much. She could not remember having seen them kiss. She had always assumed they were more good friends than lovers, and suspected now that their friendship depended on something else, a perverse interdependency that fed their separate weaknesses, and made them weaker yet. Ah, but he was sensual, though. She thought: Almost as a young woman must seem to a man. As though, like a cat, he would arch up beneath a stroking hand. Or as though he would remove his clothes before a woman with the studied provocation of a woman before a man, and entreat her—that woman—not that she let him make love to her, but she to him. She knew where it came from, too, that sensuality of his. It was in his flatness, blandness, his soft-spoken supple passivity; that being all of a piece, with no ups and downs. Out of curiosity she tried to imagine herself in her daughter's place, as she had been at her daughter's age, wondering if she would have been attracted to him. She might have, in the blinding, unbreakable grip of an unusual turn of lust.

Then she remembered Penelope and Gene. Shouldn't they be back by now? They couldn't really be parked somewhere talking, could they? And shouldn't she be in the kitchen, setting the supper dishes on the stove?

"Do you know whereabouts in Germany your father came from?" It was Dwight, sounding soft-headed and half-asleep.

"Bavaria," she answered. "A village somewhere—near the Czech border, I believe."

"Oh, yes," he said. "I've been around there. Little towns with onion steeples on their churches. I went to summer school in Munich." For a while he seemed to await her invitation to go on, but this soon gave way to a heavy mood. She thought she knew the subject and the meaning of that mood.

She was seized by an impulse. "And did you have a girl friend there?" she asked, taking, in her own eyes, a great risk.

He came forward in his chair, not toward her but away from her, into the redness of that dying fire. "Yes," he admitted. "Haven't you heard the old saying that if you want to know another country you should have a love affair with one of its women?" And he turned around to look at her.

She was scandalized, not only because his tone with her had been flirtatious, but because he had proclaimed so different and base a feeling for this Lisa from what she had expected, or imagined. Surely it was not a feeling he would have, much less reveal, about Penelope. "And you know Germany?" she asked, hearing her teeth chatter.

"Intimately!" he admitted.

Before she knew it—and she could never have explained it —she was laughing. Laughing like a fool. So was he. They tried to sip their beers, only to laugh anew, choking on their mouthfuls, letting the beer splash against their chins.

She reached out and rapped her knuckles on the windowpane, as though warning a child she had seen outdoors away from mischief. She was looking out the darkened window now. She said, "I wonder where they can be? It's already late." She studied the beer can almost with tenderness. "I've had too much to drink. . . . I have to get supper. . . ." And she slapped her thighs like a man telling himself to get a move on.

He said, "You're so real when you've had a drink."

"Am I?"

"Yes, the opposite from Gene."

"You mean he is—what would you call it?—artificial?" He was perilously close to presumption, to impertinence.

"I'd call it a role."

"You mean when he drinks?"

"Well, even when he doesn't," he said. "Isn't there a sober *and* a drunken role?"

"Is there?" And her voice had arched against her will.

"Certain roles he steps into?"

"Superficial ones, I suppose?" she helped, leading him on. She was squeezing her forearm with her fingers, she was so tense. They were threading such a fine line between an icy argument and the warm give-and-take of a young boy and girl. Surely he was pressing an intimacy between them she could not allow.

"Pure façade," he agreed. "But isn't that the nature of playing roles?"

"Maybe," she offered, "it's the actor in him, always living out his role . . . ?"

"Yes, but he's never really been an actor, has he?"

"Not professionally, if that's what you mean."

Instead of picking this up, he said, "The two of you, are you for *real*?"

She was shocked. She couldn't speak. He had not only acknowledged the seductive atmosphere that had come between them in the dark and smoke and slow smolder of the fire within the room, he had mocked it. Oh, he was not without his special gifts and powers, she saw that now, not without a dangerous insight into herself and Gene.

Then he made it worse. He said, "Oh, I like Gene, but I don't understand for the life of me how you could have married him." He must have interpreted her ensuing silence as a signal of her confusion, because he said, "You don't think that in comparison with you he comes off as something of a fool?"

"Well, he's *Gene*, isn't he?" she managed to say at last, aware that it had sounded as though she agreed with him.

"But didn't you ever think it could have been different somehow?" he said. "That you might have married the wrong man? Because, you know, I seem to see so many bright women your age married to such foolish men." Then, unbelievably, he said, leaning toward her, his body twisted around over the arm of the chair, "Does anything really go on between you two? How can you relate to each other, in any possible way?"

He could have stung her with a poison, she felt that paralyzed, that doomed. She could not make herself bring him up short, put him in his place, tell him he had crossed the line. Her own candor, she knew, had inspired him to say such things, but how dare he voice to her face such a cruel assumption? How differently he saw her from the way she saw herself!

Meanwhile he studied her, his face in firelight, with that mask of simplicity and innocence, unaware of the harm that he had done. Oh, so smug and so superior, so absolutely certain of himself. Of his youth. Of his sex. Of the gentle power he exercised over Penelope. For she did not doubt but that he was a sensualist of a certain low but delicate refinement, and that he had managed to make Penelope discover her own body as much as his. Suddenly she imagined him aroused, easily and habitually aroused.

Ah, what might she have done or said if Gene and Penelope had not driven up just then?

CHAPTER 9

In town they came to talk about the Linquists more than ever. Talked about that Linquist ghost, which Gene now claimed Winnie was almost seeing daily and hearing nightly in their barn, and about Dwight and Penelope and some of their hippie friends planning to move out to Jessie Farnum's old place, which they heard about from Dwight himself whenever he came up weekends to try to make the place livable by spring; not to mention the onrunning quarrel between Bob Cressman and Lester Marcotte, on one hand, and Gene Linquist, on the other, over how the town tricentennial drama would be staged, and by whom, and Gene's new ally against the Marcotte forces in the person of that De-Marco woman. At this point the comment was always made that they couldn't keep track of the marriages she was supposed to have ruined, or come close to ruining. Although, they gave her credit, once her own marriage had broken up she had seemed to calm down a bit, as though married life itself had somehow been the cause of her being out a lot at night.

"Old Gene's safe enough, though," Tolman said in his garage, sitting on the back seat of a car he had set up against the wall of his small office and drinking coffee from a greasy mug.

"It don't matter how much those two get together late at night to figure out ways to do up poor old Lester Marcotte, she likes the young fellows, and that leaves out Gene and a lot of us other good-looking, gray-tipped men."

"Well, that Gene thinks he's good enough for a young fellow," Bob Cressman said.

"But," said Tolman, "is he good enough for a young girl?"

"I always thought he could go either way," Tommy Lehoux said, laughing at his own joke until he had to blow his nose.

"He sure *acts* like he thinks he is good enough," Cressman said.

"Acting won't be no help with anything like Pete DeMarco's wife" (for they could still call her that), Tolman said. "Jesus, but don't she carry herself like a rattrap set on a hairspring and full of the oldest kind of store cheese. Oh, she's got to have the real thing all right."

"If you ask me," Bob Cressman said, "it's that Penelope who had better watch her boyfriend. That DeMarco woman sure likes to have coffee with old Dwight over at the Green. Don't they get together, though, talking about psychology, philosophy, religion, Shakespeare—ever hear them at it? You can't tell me she doesn't have her eye on him."

"Well, if he's going to live out at Jessie Farnum's place, at least Gene's daughter will know how he'll spend his summers," Tolman said. "Cutting firewood to keep warm all winter!"

"Seems to me that fellow would rather have coffee with Jessie Farnum," Tommy Lehoux said. "Or with you yourself, Bob. So he could find out some more about the old way of doing things."

"Or so he could tell us some more about how we used to do them," Cressman said. "He must know more about how my granddad lived his life than I do. Or thinks he does, anyway."

"And tells you a lot more than you'd want to know about how he lived it, too," Tolman said.

"I guess!" Tommy Lehoux said.

But Cressman wasn't the only old-timer Dwight had flattered or amused with his intense interest in the old jobs done with the old tools in the old ways. So that one evening Maurice Dube, peppered with sawdust and excelsior from cutting cordwood with his chain saw in the woods all day, and giving off that gasoline-kerosene smell of his, said on the porch of Roscoe's store, "He's some fellow, that one. Wanted me to plow those old, grown-over fields of Jessie's when he got them clear. No, sir, not with those ledges out there at Farnum's, I told him. Why, by Jesus, I never heard such a thing. The plow would ride on them ledges and turn the tractor over. I told him why that land wasn't ever meant to be worked by no machines."

"You'd think that would have pleased him," Roscoe said.

"By Jesus, didn't it please him, though? Better get yourself a team of horses, that's what I told him. Now, that's an idea he went for. Said he could use the horse shit for natural fertilizer. He didn't want to use any of that artificial stuff."

"He'd be better off with a pair of oxen," Roscoe said. "He could use them to pull up the stumps and drag off the timber before he yoked them to the plow. And that's cow shit. Good stuff for the organic vegetables he's going to grow once the stumps are pulled."

But it was still the news of Winnie's ghost that could create the most talk in the most circles. And fresh news it was these days, too. Because if the appearance of the ghost out in the pasture had been nothing more than an inexplicable mistake, as Winnie herself had come to believe, it was apparently a mistake that was being made again, repeatedly. Because, according to Gene, she had seen that same familiar but faceless ghost—or at least had convinced herself she had, Gene had once admitted, depending more on intuition this time than on any evidence from even so untrustworthy a source as her senses. Saw him, though, just as Gene said she had some time ago, inside their barn. Naturally the news spread. And if anyone had yet to hear it, he had only himself to blame, he had stayed that long away from any conversation with his fellow man.

Even the schoolchildren came down with ghost fever, which wasn't so hard to foresee, given all the supernatural and monster shows they were watching nightly on television. At recess they stood about in little secret groups against the rear of the school building, their hands in their pockets with the cold, and talked about the haunted graveyards and their grandfathers' haunted barns, or whispered knowingly about their town's only certain haunted house, the old Hoitt place out there in the country somewhere, which some of them claimed, against the denial of the others, they had actually seen. They pointed out the Linquists, too, whenever they saw them in the stores in town, as the people who lived out there with the ghost. Small gangs of children could be encountered taking long walks out into the countryside to see any of several abandoned houses or barns that had recently gained the reputation for being haunted, or they could be seen before the door of such buildings, daring one another to be the first to enter.

One windy night a house that had been in the Chase family for nearly two hundred years—and had been abandoned for the last thirty because, with an unclear deed, it could not be sold—burned to the ground, leaving only a still-standing brick chimney and a shallow smoking cellar hole. Recently there had been rumors of its being haunted.

In the morning the fire was the talk of the Village Green, where the volunteer firemen, worn out from the long night of standing around their water trucks and watching the house burn, forsook the smoke of the fire for the smoke of those booths. There they stripped to their nylon down vests, or un-zipped those snowmobile suits and removed those helmets that made them resemble jet fighter pilots or astronauts and that were often decorated with the stars and stripes.

"Damned if those boys on the Mountain Road didn't set it, though," Murry Holland, the oilman, said. "Gladys Chase said they've been saying they were going to do it since Halloween."

"First time I come across three separate fires burning all at one time in one house," Dicky Beers said. "Two upstairs and one down, and all in different rooms, too!" Didn't they all laugh at that, though.

"Still, it's a goddamn shame we had to lose a fine old house like that one," Bob Cressman said. "It had some nice Christian doors, had some nice old latches. Still, the way it was, it was bound to fall in someday."

"Should have been pulled down long ago," Dicky Beers said. "Some kids could have been playing inside it and fallen through the floor, or have a piece of it fall on their heads."

"The fire department should have burned it years ago," Tommy Lehoux said.

"Now, Gene," Harvey Deming said, at the door of his kitchen, "you don't want to go burning down that barn of yours to get rid of the ghosts. Because you can't burn them things up anyway." And didn't everybody in all the smoky booths, all down the line, laugh at that, too.

But when Gene had left, Murry Holland said, "Say, Bob, I been out there to Linquists' place delivering oil half a dozen times, and I couldn't locate that stone you said marked the place where that young fellow from Canada was killed."

"Well, where the oil pipe is was just about where it used to be," Cressman said.

"I figured it was," Murry said. "It must be buried over, like you said."

"Well, that roofer don't worry me so much as those Mountain Road boys do," Cressman said. "I just hope to hell they don't catch the fire bug from watching this one go up."

It worried Gene, too. He was afraid that his place, although inhabited, with the reputation it had for being haunted, might well be next. He kept a light burning in the house and on the barn all night.

It was in the barn that Winnie had caught through the slit

of the barely opened sliding door—how many times she couldn't tell—a movement within the gloom against the far wall that suggested a man crouching, or sometimes caught in the act of ducking. Once, as the sunset shone through the rear window and illuminated the rise and fall of the ancient dust and chaff, she had glimpsed some old clothes or horse blankets hanging on a hook balloon out with the beginnings of a body, which, if she had stayed at the door to watch, would have become a complete man suspended in the air.

Then she had begun to hear the noises in the barn. Brief, sharp, unexpected noises. Like a jack kicked out from beneath a car, or the swift and explosive deflation of a tire. Or the slamming of a trunk or hood. Heard them when the car was gone, or parked outdoors, and the wide aisle between the horse stalls was empty the length of the barn.

It had never been a place that Winnie cared to enter. A great cavern of hand-hewn timbers, it was always dark, or half-dark. In the time of Mamie's older, half-wit brother, it had become no more than a garage for his car, and in Mamie's time a storehouse for her most worthless things. The Linquists had never cleaned it properly, and it was still a mess. Old auto chains hung high up from the timbers, and several oil-saturated toolboxes stood along the walls. On the half-rotted floorboards that still showed the oil stains where Mamie's brother had parked his car were tufts of wool from the sheep that had been kept there before even Mamie's time and the sweepings of the hay stored there when Gene and Penelope had briefly kept a pair of horses, all intermixed with the old postcards, canceled checks, and electric bills that had once belonged to Mamie, and the droppings of swallows and bats. More often than not, it seemed that whenever Winnie entered the barn some unseen animal scurried off.

She could have ignored the barn entirely, cut it off, so to speak, from the rest of their place, if it hadn't been connected by that Cape Cod ell to the main house, which meant that anyone inside the barn was only the width of a door away from being inside the house. So she took to keeping the door between the house and barn locked, and to scolding Gene if he failed to draw the bolt or, God forbid, set the latch on the striker plate. Once he answered back—sharply too—that, closed door or open door, it made little difference to spirits, who preferred, if anything, the closed door, since it gave them the chance to show us mortals what they could really do. She was not amused. For it was no longer a ghost that she feared but, strangely, a real man. With bone and muscle, who could not only make you see and hear him but *feel* him, too. A local drunk who slept it off in their barn. An escaped convict. Some runaway kid. And any one of them a madman or pervert, who intended when the time was right to accost her. Or so she took to imagining.

She no longer cared to stay inside the house alone, and accompanied Gene whenever he went to town, sharing his morning newspaper over coffee at the Village Green. She even tagged along to the meetings of the theater group at night, watching at a distance the early preparations for the tricentenninal play. But here was what was odd about this new behavior: despite the terror the mere thought of a real man lurking in the barn could make her feel, she would go out of her way to persuade herself, even if it meant misinterpreting and doctoring the evidence, that what she saw and heard was real. What a long way she had come from those days when she had been known to shade the truth and stretch the powers of her senses beyond their limits in her claims that what she had seen was no man but ghost.

While Gene kept a wary eye on the road for any strange cars or strolling gang of boys, Winnie watched the road, for what, exactly, she could not say. One afternoon she saw an old delivery wagon, hearse-sized and painted black all over —a young kid's or hippie's car, she guessed—drive past the house and disappear into the dead-end wilderness ahead. Only to return in reverse and pull into the driveway before the barn. The door on the driver's side opened, but nobody got out, nor could she see anyone inside the car. Then the door closed—she couldn't hear it, though—and the car backed into the road, turning to face not the direction of its exit toward the town but the dead end again. But then it stopped in the middle of the road as though studying the house. Odd that she couldn't hear the motor running. Odd, too, how she seemed to notice most of all the silver paint that showed in the dented places through that slapdash coat of black. Then the car drove off, disappearing behind the trees. This time it did not return. She had just begun to think of throwing on her coat and walking after it when she heard the noises in the barn, coming through the ell into the house. As though someone wanted something buried beneath a pile of tools he had to toss about to find.

She told Gene about the car, how whoever was in it had looked the place over, before parking it out of sight down the road, working his way back on foot through the woods to break into the barn. Gene telephoned the town police. "I'm sure it's nothing," he said. "But all the same it ought to have a quiet looking into."

Winnie knew, as he did, that any police or fire call could bring out more than just the deputized volunteers, including half the idlers at Tolman's Garage and the Village Green. Their call was no exception. Within fifteen minutes a caravan of half a dozen cars drove into the driveway, followed a moment later by several stragglers racing to catch up. She recognized most of the men gathering in a party around the cars. There was Dicky Beers and Junior Cressman, in their blue uniforms with the American flag patch on the shoulder, and wearing their heavy black-looking sidearms; and the younger Donald Woodly, who was wearing something of a cowboy hat. And Harvey Deming, with a parka thrown over his white ducks; and no less than Lester Marcotte, a friend of Junior Cressman's, searching about with his shy but nervous birdlike head; and Hank Silva, a newcomer to town and a real-estate developer of sorts, who in just the year he had lived here had become thick with both Bob and Junior Cressman and Ben Tolman, with all of whom he was presently involved in land deals. He in turn was in the company of several of his friends. They had arrived in Massachusetts cars that were as wide as the Old Crown Road. Underdressed for the weather, they were soft but ugly-looking men, wide like their cars, who looked as though only minutes earlier they had been drinking beer and watching television in someone's house trailer. They did seem apologetic about their being there, but only vaguely so, as though they acknowledged they were trespassers and vigilantes all in one. Winnie was unhappy with their presence, and she could see how it infuriated Gene.

"Do you know what make of car it was, Mrs. Linquist?" Dicky Beers said.

"I don't know how to tell those things."

"Then I suppose you wouldn't know what year it was?"

"Just that it was old."

"And the license plates?"

"I didn't think to get the number. They weren't New Hampshire plates, though."

Meanwhile groups of men trooped in and out of the barn, prying into things and banging about, shouting back and forth and joking. Some men walked alone around the outside of the barn, looking in the windows. Others did nothing, just stood around their cars in groups, smoking and talking. Dicky Beers went into the barn and Junior Cressman took a carful of men down the road in search of the parked delivery wagon, leaving Winnie and Gene in the company of Donald Woodly. A graduate of the university who had never lived outside the town and whose forefathers reportedly owned the first farm in town, he had a reputation for being tolerant, well-read, and shrewd in a way some people would say was wise.

"We wanted to be careful," Gene said. "We've heard there's been so many break-ins lately."

"Crime's moved from the city to the suburbs to the country," Woodly said.

"That's not surprising," Gene said sarcastically, "when city and suburban people have moved to the country." Winnie knew he meant Hank Silva and his friends.

"When we first moved up here, we never even locked our house," Winnie said. "Now I just don't know. There's so many drifters and hippies in town these days."

"Now, back in the old days," Woodly said, "any theft or murder committed in the neighborhood, they always suspected a tramp first thing. You read accounts of old crimes and they were always looking for some stranger. Some tramp who had been seen around on foot, a day, a week, maybe a month before, looking for food or work. Yes, sir, they were always looking for the outsider. Of course, it nearly always turned out that somebody local did the crime. Some neighbor, or member of the family. Scared half to death out there in their isolated farmhouses that some crazy stranger was walking around the countryside when all along the murderer was their neighbor or sweetheart or hired hand."

"You don't think this barn business of ours is the work of a stranger?" Gene said.

"Well, Gene, if you're not haunted after all, most likely it's some local kids. But then again, it's a whole lot different than it used to be. As I said, used to be if a girl was molested, or somebody robbed of their savings, after the tramp scare died down and no stranger was found you could pin it on, you knew it had to be somebody local. There weren't any strangers around back then, except the rare tramp, because there wasn't any way to get around the countryside. There weren't any cars. By Jesus, today I'm afraid to have my kids walk home from school down my deserted country road. Some fellow in a car that just drove in from California could pick them up and then drive straight off to Nova Scotia without so much as stopping along the way. Why, anybody in the country can be just about anywhere he wants to be at any time. And it's the automobile that's done it, too."

"Makes it tough for the police officer," Dicky Beers said, having joined them. "An awful lot of suspects."

"Now in the old days, anybody would remember a stranger he saw walking or riding a horse down his road," Woodly said. "But you wouldn't take any special notice of any cars passing your house, now, would you? Except maybe you and me, living way out in the country like we do. But we're the exception these days."

The car that had gone in search of the delivery wagon now came back, Junior Cressman claiming they had gone about as far as they dared go. They couldn't find the car, couldn't see where it could have pulled off the road anywhere, either. That was some rough country back there.

"Then the car must have come by again on its way out," Winnie said. "Only I didn't see it. . . . It must have been when I was telling Gene."

Donald Woodly said, "If it was an old beat-up car like you said, Winnie, maybe they drove it all the way through to the other road. They would have been fools to do it, though. Could be done, though."

When they left, Winnie felt foolish, felt guilty, thought she must be a great burden. Fortunately Gene was fair-minded enough to direct his anger at them instead of her. Although he did say later that night in gentle reproof, "Don't you think it was just your ghost again? Because it just occurred to me that it would be impossible for a real man to be around here and not have old Pierce here barking his fool head off."

This relieved her only until she could persuade herself that Pierce had shown a recent interest in the barn, sniffing at the door and along the sills, and barking more than usual at whatever he saw or heard inside.

"Who's to say," Gene countered, "that Pierce doesn't smell, see, and hear him, too? All we know for certain, it seems to me, is that whatever it is, it isn't a man. Of course, if it's not the ghost it could be a raccoon. Or another porcupine."

The next day, after he had a long look around the barn, he showed her the quills he had found, and suggested she come in and see the fresh white wounds of a windowsill the animal had gnawed to get the salt a century of human hands had left upon the wood. She said she would take his word for it, remembering how she had once seen far back in the barn, in a small dusty ray of a wintry sundown and on top of a pile of moldy mattresses, the thin white skeleton of a lone chair a porcupine was eating.

But even if she could become convinced a second time that the man she saw was just an apparition, she remained as frightened of him as she had been earlier when she had persuaded herself that he was real. Because—well, she had to face the facts—hadn't she been unreasonably optimistic about her ghost? About ghosts in general? In spite of what Dwight said about them never strangling you or dragging you off to the underworld, who said they necessarily wished you well? What made her ghost any different from the real man she had imagined skulking in the barn, except that whereas the man had been waiting to do her some physical outrage or injury, the ghost was already at work menacing her mind and nerves?

"I wonder what will make him disappear—for good?" she said one night to Gene, surprising both of them. Which caused Gene to remark sometime later that he was amazed that, having wished so long for the appearance of an apparition and apparently having got her wish, she could wish that it would go away.

CHAPTER 10

ONE DAY Winnie, in Penelope's faded army fatigue jacket, found herself walking in her fields on an afternoon when it was spring in name only, with the grass yet to green and the trees as bleak as they had been in winter. It had been her custom to celebrate the first bright spring day after the snow was gone by tramping through her woods and fields on an itinerary that made the two Hoitt graveyards the highlights of the walk. But this year she had let the good days slip by until today, of which she might have said, had she thought about it, that it differed from the usual pilgrimage in that "something special had called her out." She was heading for the graveyards first thing.

The Frenches' graveyard was halfway up a wooded slope so steep she had to use her hands and was in danger of sliding back through the deep-lying slippery leaves as though down a wall of ice. The graveyard had once stood beside an orchard, in the middle of a hillside pasture, but now the original apple trees had been replaced by a thicket of their own wild stunted offspring, and the pasture by a sunless forest of white pines already so tall that they thinned out their slower-growing neighbors. The few graves, with their slanting, broken, or sunken headstones, were overrun with vines, and small oak trees poked up from the acorns buried in the moldering leaves. She had always found this a lonesome place, and that inscription on the Frenches' gravestones, "We hope to meet again," too moving an experience to indulge in often or, when she did, for very long. Today, however, she felt no melancholia, no pathos. Her eyes were wet only from the force of the dry wind that smelled of pine and nothing else. She was fearless, heartless. How she would have liked to behold the shadows of those long-dead Frenches walking in the gloom between the pines, passing behind the dead branches that stuck out like spikes from the trunks, their legs lost to the carpet of pine needles as far as their knees, he in his beaver hat and cane, with a great scarf wrapped several times around his throat, his free hand made into a gaunt fist held behind his back, while she, in bonnet and shawl, was at his side, steadying his arm. But her feeling for them—that special empathy of hers—was not strong enough to renew their lives; she saw that now. She had no signal to send to them, and no honest way of receiving theirs. Nor did that melancholic bond of friendship between the doomed siblings, as evidenced by Amy's diary, appeal to her with that same longed-for perfection as it had before. She was too down-to-earth for such a fantasy.

In the open field again, she walked first through the orchard and then along the ridge. High in the adjacent field was the second Hoitt cemetery, used only after the Civil War, where Belle Hoitt was buried, her grave site indicated by that giant Baldwin apple tree that was the only tree in both graveyard and pasture, and determinable from half a mile across the field. She made her way inside the tangle of gnarled limbs that had cracked under the weight of the fruit they still provided every other summer even though they sprawled upon the ground. She put her foot up on one of the branches and looked down. It seemed that the roots of the tree must embrace the remains of Belle herself, breaking her open and sending up her passion to feed the living tree. That was what was meaningful, that was what was powerful—the woman's passion. She could imagine it in all its far-ranging and erotic variations, and sympathize with it entirely. The woman had been strong and selfish, so much her own self, and if there was a ghost about her grave, it would not be that of some forlorn local lover but her own. The man that she, Winnie, had seen, had nothing to do with Belle Hoitt.

But just as she was stepping over the wire strung between the granite posts that fenced the place, she had a premonition: a man was sitting on the highest bough of the tree overhead. He was gazing down at her, swinging his legs. It came upon her like a sudden loss of breath, like the wrong connection between two nerves. But when she forced herself to look up, no man was there. All the same, it frightened her. Only when she was halfway back across the pasture did she catch a glimpse of what might have made her think she saw him. In the patch of sumac trees just beyond the fieldstone wall there perched a flock of evening grosbeaks with the density of blackbirds in a larger tree. How incongruous they seemed, those fat silent black-and-yellow birds squatting on the forked branches of such small and fragile trees. It was the black markings around the birds' eyes that troubled her, and the way the birds refused to move, while, Janus-like, they appeared to look as a flock in all directions. These are not real birds, something told her, but the souls of dead men.

She was certain a spirit was in the air, on the verge of manifestation. She felt the same sense of menace, and that same disorientation and dizziness, like *déjà vu*, even though she could name the time and place that triggered it: exactly here and on the day the man had disappeared upon the wall. The house, too, gave her that same sense of alienation she had felt before. The place was so much by itself, so much of another time than now. She could discover nothing to date the moment, nothing to relate the buildings to the landscape. They were like a clump of toadstools that had sprung up in the pasture in the night. Graveyards, she thought, were more familiar and friendly places than that house. Once again she had left the door wide open, could not remember opening it, could not remember going out. Now she knew why there was no man to be seen. It was because he had yet to be seen. He was inside the house. He had transformed himself into something small and dark and fluttering, and had darted like the shadow of a chimney swift flying across the fields and lawn and through that open door, vanishing upstairs where it was trapped, beating its wings against the walls.

No car was in the driveway, no light was on inside the house. Why had Gene gone off without consulting her, without telling her where he was going? Why hadn't he at least offered to take her along?

Inside she made a second, then a third circuit of the rooms downstairs, unable, having discovered where the supernatural thing was not, to bring herself to search upstairs where, by the process of elimination, it had to be. The house itself did not feel unnatural to her; rather, it was the other way around. She lacked a context with the rooms, and felt this keenly even though she had sanded every floorboard, rubbed every piece of paneling, had puttied every light in every sash, must have painted every other clapboard, nailed on every other shake. But now she roamed from room to room like a stranger who had found the front door open and was searching for the household in the unfamiliar rooms.

She did not pause to switch on the lights, did not leave lamp after lamp burning in the rooms she wandered through, even though the rooms—with their few small windows, most of which were covered by the Indian shutters that slid out from behind the paneling to shade the sash—were always dark regardless of the weather or the time of day. There was a reason why she didn't, too. Light would reveal her presence in the rooms and at the foot of those stairs she could not bring herself to climb, along with whatever else was there, that presence less intrusive than her own. And she would have the furniture just as indistinctly seen, all those museum pieces that had come before her and would outlast her, that did not serve her half so much as she served them, possessions and creations of another people of another time to which she had imparted no portion of herself, neither taste nor need.

She had only begun to climb the stairs when she heard the noises. Not from above, either, but from the barn, the barn again. Just the dog, though. Just the porcupine again. But when she passed into the ell and faced the door between the house and barn that she made certain was still locked, she knew the wishfulness of such thinking. Someone was moving lumber, walking on the loft boards that were not nailed down, opening cupboard doors, whispering.

From the window she watched the two women come out of the barn, slide the barn door closed, and stand together in the driveway, talking. They lit cigarettes, letting them bob in their mouths as they talked, hiked up their dresses, beat their purses against their thighs. They were older women, careless about the way they looked, the thin one looking as though she had thrown on whatever oversized coat and dress she had found at hand, the fat one as though she never removed her dress at all. It could have been their house for all their nonchalance; they could have merely gone into their barn to see their horses.

Then they walked toward the house and out of sight, knocking at the door, which Winnie—acting on instinct alone, because she knew she would never get the courage for a second chance if she acted otherwise—so suddenly replaced as the barrier between indoors and out, taking a position on the threshold as though to block with her body any violent rush into the house, that the women took each other by the arm and stepped backward off the stoop in unison onto the grass.

There the thin one was saying—saying what? An explanation and apology of some sort. No car in the driveway and a dark house and no one to greet them when they drove up, and so they had decided the house was owned by summer people, and that it would do no harm if they had themselves a look around the barn. Then, of course, when they had heard those noises coming from the house—*Coming from the house,* Winnie thought, putting her hand to her head—they knew someone was home after all and that they had better knock.

She must have invited them in. Either that or she had offered no resistance to their self-invited entry, for the three of them were now together in that little room where old harnesses and saddles and other leather articles were stored, reminders of those days when Penelope had been enamored of riding and she and Gene had owned horses. The thin woman leaned back against the tack with her head tipped forward to avoid the low beam, while the fat, ruddy-colored woman shut the door Winnie had not thought to close.

Now she recognized the women. She had seen them several times before, at antique shops and country auctions and once at the Village Green, where they had asked her if she had any antiques up at her house, and she had answered that she had indeed, but not to sell. They came from just over the border in Maine, and were country women of the old stock they called "swamp Yankees." They had a reputation for being characters, and were known locally as the "quarter sisters," ("qua-tah," in local pronunciation), a name they had earned from the twenty-five-cent bids they were famous for making at small auctions for kitchen chairs and cardboard boxes heaped with rusty cutlery, mason jars, broken lamps, and incomplete appliances. In the parlance of antique dealers they were "pickers," small-time dealers in antiques who worked out of the battered station wagon that was now parked in the driveway, loaded down with those heavy bureaus and presses and kitchen tables they were the masters of piling on and lashing, when they had to, to the carriage rack on top. They went to country auctions and called at the out-of-the-way antique shops and at old houses on the back roads, buying pieces they would in turn sell to dealers who owned shops. In the hierarchy of antiquedom they occupied the bottom. The thin one was called Abby, the chubby one was Maude.

Abby was explaining, "Mrs. Cressman told us she heard you might have some old furniture to sell."

"I don't know where she heard that," Winnie said. "We did have a number of things—my husband's great-aunt's estate—but that was some years ago."

"Mrs. Cressman must have been confused, poor thing," Abby said. "She's so old, you know. Still, I don't much care for coming all the way out here for nothing."

As though responding to this cue, Maude said to Winnie, "You never know what you might have that's an antique and worth an awful lot of money." And she looked as though she possessed at once a deep well of good cheer and a small spirit that was shrewd and mean.

Winnie had nothing to sell them, had nothing they could afford to buy. But she wanted them here all the same, looking on them as a godsend. If only, she decided, she could keep them here until Gene returned, the mysterious energy behind that apparition she had yet to see might wear down in the meantime, as it had when the man had disintegrated on the wall.

"Let me think for a minute," she said. Then after the two sisters must have despaired of learning the product of her thoughts, she said, "Maybe you could come in and tell me if there is anything I have you think is valuable. . . . Maybe I don't know as much about my chairs and things as I should. . . ." And a look passed between the two sisters that could have been a reckoning of plunder.

But once inside the parlor Abby looked suspicious. "Did an old woman used to have this house?" she asked.

"Yes, Mrs. Hoitt, my husband's great-aunt."

"Oho," Abby said, "old Mamie!"

"Then you've been here before?" Winnie said.

"Many's the time," said Maude.

"You've changed it a whole lot since then, haven't you, dearie?" Abby said.

"We tried to buy a few things from her once upon a time,"

Maude explained, and a glance passed between the sisters that appeared to recall some past piece of dickering, if not deceit.

"But all we could get her to part with was an old iron stove," Abby said. "Mamie was as nice and sweet an old lady as you want to find, but she just liked to get us to come in to talk to, and tease us a little, but she didn't want to part with nothing except for ten times what it was worth. Thought just any old piece of junk was an antique and worth something." The implication was that Winnie would not be so obstinate and misinformed as all that.

"Of course what she thought they were worth then, they're worth that much and more today," Maude said, winking.

"I guess you could say Mamie was ahead of her time," Abby said, laughing. And what a jolly pair the sisters were, always on the brink of laughter. But their eyes squinted while their mouths laughed, searching the rooms. They were at once nervous and tough, the result of living off a small margin of profit and of having to make a dozen cheap bargains a day.

"Mamie must be dead by now, I suppose," Maude said.

"Oh, yes, these many years."

Abby gave a jerk of her head. "It isn't her who's . . ."

"Who's what?" Winnie helped.

"You know, kind of *come back*?"

Winnie turned to Maude for some explanation.

"Isn't this the haunted house?" Maude said.

Winnie started and gave a look around, as though suspecting the women had seen something she had not. "Do you have a reason for asking that?"

"That's what we heard in town," Maude said. "Didn't we?"

Abby said, nodding, "It's old enough to have one, ain't it, though?"

"Well, it doesn't have one," Winnie said. "I never heard of such a thing." She even placed her hand reassuringly on Maude's back. "And I ought to know, I live here."

"People do talk an awful lot of nonsense, don't they?" Abby said, moving, like Maude, around the parlor, seeking out the furniture and bric-a-brac in the gloom.

What they saw made them uncomfortable, Winnie saw that much immediately. They were accustomed to bargaining in barns and attics and not in rooms that were more properly the showplaces of a museum. They had no taste or knowledge outside the Victorian country pieces of native pine they traded in, and if they had been offered a Pilgrim chair of native oak for fifty dollars they probably would have been terrified and offered ten. Why, Winnie knew more about the native furniture than they did, and was more sensitive to it, too. And yet with their heavy local accent that you almost never heard anymore and in their dresses that looked as though they were discovered on the bottom of their own "quarter" boxes, and their large cracked and dirty hands, they seemed so much more the inheritors of this house than she could ever hope to be, and she felt theatrical and guilty, as though she had unfairly dispossessed them of their own. Among such pieces she was no more at ease than they were, and she saw suddenly that their jocularity was nothing but a show and that they were prepared to leave. "Will you sit down?" she said, sitting down herself.

The women did so reluctantly, as though if they could not leave, they preferred to be on their feet nosing about.

"Now," Winnie said, "if you'll just tell me what it is you're looking for."

But they were hardly women who would give their price before the seller or buyer, as the case was, had given hers. "What do you think," said Abby, "you might like to sell?"

"I'm trying to think," Winnie said.

The two women watched her think. Abby in that ladderback behind the tavern table, sitting as though she had to violate a museum chain to reach the chair, Maude in that thronelike chair beside the window, more in the cold light of the approaching sundown than in the firelight of the room, while Winnie sat by the fire, her shoulders sagging and her hands folded between her knees as though they held a damp handkerchief they had twisted into a knot. What an awkward trio they made. They could have passed for sisters just back from their father's funeral, which few relatives and fewer friends had troubled to attend, only to sit in the uneasy silence of that empty house they had equally inherited, a place they had not visited since they had run off as children and gone their separate ways.

But when Winnie in desperation tried to speak, Abby, who had been studying the ceiling, raised her hand for silence.

"Those timbers?" Winnie said. "They're oak—is that what you want to know?" She turned to Maude. "Imagine the work adzing oak—"

"Shhh," Abby said. Then, as though a welcome thought had just occurred to her, "Look here, dearie, you don't have squirrels in your walls—"

"Sometimes," Winnie said, puzzled, "they get in in the fall."

"Ah," Abby said, repeating ominously, "in the fall."

"In the fall," echoed Maude.

"Have to watch them, don't you?" Abby said. "They'll gnaw through them nice old beams, foul the plaster, and open up the clapboards to the weather."

When no more conversation followed this remark, Winnie jumped up, saying, "Why don't I stir the fire? You must be cold." She put on some firewood, but it only smoked, smothering what little fire was left in the coals. "I seem to be making a mess of it," she said, throwing up her hands.

"I suppose . . ." Abby began, rising, looking at Maude, who closed her purse.

"Can I get you a cup of coffee?" Winnie asked.

"Just had some at the Village Green."

"A cup of tea, then?"

"Well, we just had coffee."

"Perhaps a glass of sherry? A can of beer?"

"I suppose," Maude said, looking at Abby for some guidance, "we could have ourselves a quick look around."

"Of course you could," Winnie said before Abby could say otherwise. "And be as long about it as you like." She led them into the dining room and switched on a dim lamp placed inconspicuously in the corner. Here the furnishings were the equal in age and value to those in the parlor. Maude pretended to examine the pieces while Abby stared out the window as though taking a sudden interest in the weather.

"What's for sale?" Maude said.

"Oh," Winnie said, throwing out her arms, "everything, I guess. Everything has its price."

"What would you want for this, dearie?" Maude said, running her hand along the surface of a harvest table.

"Oh, I couldn't part with that," Winnie said. "That's been in my husband's family for over two hundred years."

She had just given the same answer to another piece that Maude had indicated with half-hearted interest when Pierce, after running through the house, tags jangling, raced into the room and slid across the wooden floor, rumpling up the Caucasian rug that finally stopped his slide. Ignoring Winnie, he ran to Abby and, jumping up, put his paws upon her legs.

"Pierce!" Winnie ordered. "Get down!"

Abby laughed, cooing at him, and pretended to pet him, then, when she thought Winnie was not looking, pushed him down.

"He always jumps on people," Winnie apologized. "We could never seem to break him of the habit."

"Step on his paws when he does it," Maude said, winking, "that will put a stop to it." And when the Schipperke jumped up on her, she warned him first, saying, "If I have to put my big feet on your little paws, you'll end up with feet as flat as a duck," then demonstrated what she meant. The dog yipped and got down.

Winnie stroked his ears while he wagged his tail and looked over his shoulder at Maude. "Where have you been?"

she said, glad to see him. At least if she lost the women she would have the company of the dog.

"You don't suppose he was upstairs just now?" Abby asked.

"I don't see how," Winnie said. "He just came in through his own door from outside. I'm sure I heard him."

After an investigation of the walls and furniture, the dog ran out of the room before Winnie could grab hold of him or order him to stay, exiting, presumably, through his special door. Winnie went to the front door and whistled for him, but he wouldn't come back.

Abby eyed a dry sink that held a philodendron, the least valuable piece in the room. "I guess I could offer you twenty dollars for that," she said.

"Oh," Winnie said, "I couldn't part with it for that."

"Now, I don't blame you one bit, dearie," Maude said, jolly with sympathy. "You must have done an awful lot of work stripping and refinishing it."

Abby had passed on to an old kerosene store lantern with a tin shade and glass bowl. "I think I know where I can get you one just like that to make a pair with," she said.

"I don't know," Winnie said. "I haven't got around to cleaning up that one. . . . What would it cost?"

"Forty-five?"

"Too much," she said.

Maude had strayed into the hallway where she stood at the foot of the stairs. "Have you anything up in your attic, dearie?" she said. "Oh, you must have. Everybody has some worthless something in their attic that's worth a whole lot to someone else."

"No," Winnie said reluctantly, "there's nothing upstairs."

"And a good thing, too," Abby said to Maude, "because I'm not up to climbing stairs—not those stairs."

There was nothing left to see now, and the women trailed their fingers along the furniture as they drifted into the kitchen and toward the door.

"Maybe I could buy something from you?" Winnie said,

following. "Maybe I could have a look in your wagon and see if you have anything I need."

The women looked at each other, uncertain, it seemed, whether they preferred the possibility of a sale or the certainty of being gone.

But Winnie was already at the window, pointing to a country dresser of pine, a common and popular piece, on top of the wagon, and mentioning that she had always wanted one for her daughter's room.

"You can have it for thirteen," Abby said.

"We just paid twelve for it this morning," Maude put in. "But it's worth it not to have to tote it around wondering when we'd sell it."

This was cheaper than Winnie would have paid for it in a shop, and although she neither needed nor wanted it, she said, "It's just what I want. Come back into the parlor and I'll write out a check."

From the disappointed looks on the faces of the sisters it was apparent they had not foreseen that, having come this close to their exit, they would be sent back into that house they had managed only now almost to leave.

At first, Winnie could not find her checkbook. Then where were her glasses? Where was a pen? And they never work, those ballpoints, do they? And so she had to find a decent pen. While Maude collapsed in a chair, apparently surrendering any hope she had of leaving, and Abby in her nervousness picked up the tongs to rearrange the smoking fire that Winnie had abandoned, only to drop them with a clang upon the hearth. "What on earth was that?" she said, still stooped over and looking at the ceiling.

"Yes, what *was* that?" Maude said, looking up, too.

"What was what?" Winnie said, holding her breath.

"Why, that noise. You don't mean to say you didn't hear it?"

"It must have been you-know-who," Winnie said.

"Who?" both women said in unison.

"Why, the dog. That's all it was, the dog."

As though to confirm this explanation, the Schipperke once more tore through the house and skidded into the room. For a moment he stood panting, with his legs splayed, looking like one of those small, bug-eyed, insane-looking dogs in a primitive painting that is just about to devour a bird. Then he circled Abby, but jumped up on the seated Maude before retreating pell-mell from the room. "Well, I guess I didn't teach him his lesson after all," Maude said, laughing, brushing her lap.

Using a ruler, Winnie tore the check along its perforations, and handed it to Maude, because Abby was still staring at the fire tongs as though she expected them to rise up and walk. Then Winnie escorted the women into the tack room, feeling about the twilight for the door. She said, "I'll come out with you and give you a hand taking down the dresser. We'll put it in the downstairs bedroom for now."

Hearing this, the women made a little involuntary movement toward the door, which Winnie quickly moved toward first, putting her back against it as though she could not let them go just yet. The women spoke with their eyes that silent language they had developed over the years of bargaining in the presence of someone else.

"You want it *moved in*, then?" Abby said. She made it seem like such an unexpected request. Unreasonable, too.

In the long silence that followed, it seemed that all three women were willing to acknowledge that some secret and sinister collusion was taking place somehow in the very air between their minds and nerves. Winnie retreated into the shadows until her elbows touched a saddle while Abby shifted impatiently along the wall and Maude slid her hand along a bunch of hanging reins. Sleigh bells were brushed against by someone, and all three women reached out at once to still them, seizing straps and bells and other hands.

"And what about *Mr.* Linquist?" Abby said, breathless and

as though she must be clutching at her heart. "Won't he give us a hand?"

Winnie's head swayed back and forth before the small window beside the door. She said, "I don't understand."

"It's not so difficult," Abby said. And then repeated, "Won't he give us a hand?"

"He would, I'm sure he would," Winnie said. "If he were here."

"Ah," the voice said. Not Abby's voice, but Maude's. A tremulous and drawn-out whisper that Winnie did not like the implications of at all.

She was willing to tell them something more, tell them anything at all to calm them if she could, but Abby had her hand up as though to tell her she was listening to something else. So in the silence the three of them listened against their will and with a kind of horrible and embarrassed fascination, as though to love-making in the room beyond the wall.

"Then will he—or she—help us, then?" It was Abby breaking the silence she had herself imposed.

For a moment Winnie thought the woman must be mad. Nor could she say who panicked first, inciting the others, only that the panic was infectious, so that in that small, cluttered, darkened room where the sense of touch was so exaggerated, they could have been on the deck of a badly listing ship the way they threw themselves against the same wall, wrestling ineffectually against their own desperate crush to exit through the outside door.

"Who do you mean?" Winnie said, giving up for the moment, like the others, her attempt to open the door, unaware of how much time had passed between Abby's question and her own. "He . . . she . . . help . . . what on earth?"

"What do *you* mean?" Abby said. "I know it's none of our business, but surely you won't stand there and tell us no one else is here?"

"But I have to tell you that. No one else *is* here."

Maude said, "Upstairs, she means."

Winnie said, "I mean upstairs, too. . . . Oh, now I see—you mean the dog."

"I mean," said Abby, "before the dog came in the house—the first time, even."

"You won't tell us," Maude said, "you didn't hear it?"

"Hear what?" Winnie said.

"What I've been hearing on and off since I stepped inside this dreadful house," Abby said.

"What *we've* heard," Maude corrected.

"I didn't hear anything," Winnie said. "You didn't by chance see . . . ?"

"Only heard, whatever it was."

Instead of asking more, Winnie eased in beside the other two so that the three of them stood with their backs against the door, staring ahead at the gathering dusk that seemed to keep pace with the acclimation of their eyes to the failing light, as though having gotten as far away as they could from what it was they feared inside the house, they were now re-solved to meet it face to face. She smelled the women now, a sour woody smell. And smelled also the saddle soap and leather and a trace of that bitter reek of horses and their manure. Something masculine about these smells, and obscene, too. Something to do with knotted whips, leather boots, and sex-crazed and hobbled stallions mounting wild-eyed but unwilling mares.

Then: "Footsteps," Winnie said, "was that it?"

The three women looked up together at the low wooden ceiling they could have touched, as though following the course of footsteps along those boards.

"No, not walking," Abby whispered. "More like—sleeping. Turning about, maybe, on an old spring mattress, rustling the covers and every once in a while—"

"A loud breathing," Maude explained. "Like a snore—"

"Or a cough," Abby said.

"But not like he was hurting anywhere," Abby said, narrowing it down further yet.

"Good Lord," Winnie said.

"You know what we mean?"

"I have an idea."

"I thought someone—some relative was in the house and sleeping."

"Or trying to," Maude said.

So he *was* in here, she thought. In the house, as she had thought. And this time others had heard him, too. And it was the sounds of the bed, because that was where he was, sick or dying, cursing and death-rattling behind the crewelwork curtains of the high canopy bed. And he had sent the message to her only to have her, unbeknownst to her, pass it along to Abby, who had in turn passed it along to Maude.

Then she found herself in the driveway, guided out perhaps by the two women who were now themselves outdoors. She watched them busy with ropes and blankets, unloading the bureau from the station wagon, and then lugging it with her help into the house, but only as far as the tack room, where it was put down, and even then only far enough inside to close the door. For a moment the three of them leaned on the bureau, listening.

"Well, at least you didn't hear it," Abby said. "Maybe it was my imagination after all."

"*Our* imagination," Maude corrected. "Still it don't seem hardly likely that you and me could *both* imagine such a thing—"

"Don't seem likely?" Abby repeated. "It don't seem possible!" And then, beaming with the thought that had just come to her, she said, "Or maybe this dear lady here has a secret?" And she came close to Winnie and took her by the sleeve.

"By heavens, yes!" Maude said, catching on from the wink and the elbow she received from Abby. "But she can't hear him because she don't dare let on to us and give away her little secret."

"Believe me," Winnie said, "I'd let you know if I heard something that sounded like a ghost."

"Of course you would," Abby said. "Ain't that just what we're saying, too? And if it's not a ghost—why, then don't it have to be the real thing?" She drew closer to Winnie, suggesting, "A secret visitor? Oh, you know!" As though this were the clue that would compel Winnie to admit the truth.

Maude said, "Oh, don't mind us. Mum's the word with us. Still, you could have told us, though. Here we were, scared to death with all that talk we heard in town about your ghost—"

"Let's hope," said Abby, giving Maude the elbow again, "that he's a young corker with a fresh face. Because these old fellows hereabouts aren't much, are they?"

"Nothing like a young man," Maude agreed. Adding, "Or so they tell me, anyway!"

"Now, Maude here," said Abby, "she doesn't need anyone to tell her anything about the old ones!"

And they snickered until they doubled up with laughter, jerking their heads with a motion that said, Wasn't that a good one, though? It was a laughter, Winnie realized, that was like their smells. It was what you heard after a dirty joke and smelled in the beery air in those mill-town cafés where the women are treated like the men and the linoleum that is on the floor also patches the walls and doors and overlays the bar.

When they reached their car, Maude said, "What beats me, though, dearie, is how come you wanted us to hang around?"

"Ho-ho!" said Abby, her coat open and her hand on her hip and a cigarette hanging by the paper from her lip. "Don't you know, you old thing? She couldn't go back yet—she had to give herself a breather!"

"Oh, yes," Maude said, waving. "Them young men."

Winnie watched them drive off in their lumbering, over-laden wagon, dragging the tailpipe over the outcrops of ledges in the road that also banged against the frame. Alone in the house, she watched the gloom that was the ceiling overhead. It didn't take her long to convince herself that she could see the floorboards depress like the mattress of a bed.

CHAPTER 11

UPSTAIRS THE BATTEN DOOR of that museum-like bedroom stood ajar, the long, tapered flat-black hinges looking like arrows directing her to enter. She ducked her head beneath the frame and peered into the boxlike room of plaster walls. The shutter was closed across the only window; the room, scrubbed and dustless, was doleful with a century of dusk, the only light coming from the low and narrow corridor in which she stooped, and that less light than gloom. That high fourposter bed stood in the center of the room, bed and posts hidden from floor to ceiling by the drawn dark curtains, ragged and faded, with their silken medieval-looking crewelwork of fanciful designs faintly phosphorescent in the gloom.

She tried to whisper Gene's name, in case somehow, unknown to her, he was inside the house and for some strange reason slept behind the curtains in this room. But she only breathed hoarsely, as though about to choke or cough. She actually stepped into the room, her hand raised toward the separation she thought she could make out between the curtains, and was surprised how close one step had taken her to the bed. So surprised she stepped back again, and kept on stepping back until she was in the corridor and no longer able to see inside the room. She was afraid to pull those curtains apart and discover what, if anything, was on that bed. It was not that she feared to find another apparition, a new one or the same man she had encountered in the pasture months before, now clad in pajamas, bug-eyed and bloody or still saluting in his death or sleep, but a real man, alive and sleeping naturally, a man who was not her husband, not Gene. Naked, too, lying face down upon the bedspread as though upon the flesh of an unseen woman, a naked, heavy woman. Or what was worse, no man there at all, but the depression of a body in the wrinkled bedspread, and the traces of the body heat rising from the bed against her outstretched hand.

And linked to this fear of discovering the man upon the bed was an even greater fear: that if she tried to pull the curtains of the bed apart her fingers would not feel the cloth, nor would prevent her from going farther, too, pushing in her flesh and bones were light, would pass between the weave and vanish on the other side, her hand a stump at the knuckles pushed flush against the cloth. And if this happened, what would prevent her from going farther, too, pushing in her hand up to the wrist, up to the elbow—the shoulder, even? She might even throw in her other arm and then her legs, might even quarter and then decapitate herself right through the cloth. She backed down the corridor, away from those black hinges and that heavy open door. So who is the ghost now? she asked herself. And who, God help us, has become the flesh?

She crept down those steep dark stairs enclosed with paneling, the patina as dark as coal, the steps so narrow she had to walk sideways, the ceiling so low she had to duck her head. In the sharp turns her shoulders brushed against the walls—she didn't like such touching in the dark. Her hands, which trailed along the paneling, suddenly grew warm and wet and sticky, as though passing through some pulsating, plasmic substance. . . . Had she the space and agility, she would have bolted down the stairs; she would have fallen if the narrowness of the walls had not served to keep her upright. People, she felt, were in the stairwell. People from the olden days. They were loitering against the walls, sitting on the stairs. In the pitch-black confinement they overlapped each other like circles on a piece of paper. And her own body —if it was a body now—was passing through them, feeling nothing obstructive and substantial in the pathway of her senses, only the abstracted warmth and wet of flesh.

Her restlessness persisted in the living room, where she circled aimlessly like a woman impatient for an appointment she had no wish to keep. She avoided the fire. Faces— cheeks and ears—were on the verge of materializing within the smoke and flames. She wondered if the thing, when it came indoors, hadn't gone temporarily into the fire. She was afraid to touch anything. She walked around the Pilgrim furniture, the wood natural and dark as English oak. Like an odor coming from the cooking in the kitchen, the smell of life—real life—came to her from off the wood and plaster walls. Again she imagined people of another time leaning up against the walls, sitting in the chairs, staring out the windows, ignoring her, and muttering into their hands and arms. Or standing at her shoulder, touching her, overlapping some portion of their invisibility upon her own flesh and bones. Or pacing back and forth along the wall and passing through her, as if she were herself no more than an image imposed upon the air.

Hypnotically, she focused on a single spot in space. It was where a beam of fading sunlight slumped across the threshold of the doorway to the dining room, transforming the light and shadows there into an atmosphere of drifting haze. This, she knew with certainty, was where the man would soon appear. And she was right about it, too. Except that he did not materialize in the doorway by gathering his image from the hazy light and shade. Instead he appeared ready-made, pausing there while in transit between the rooms, the pause explainable and entirely natural, reminiscent of someone who had just remembered something he must say or do. At least his posture was one of recollection. Although he could have just as easily paused from apprehension, sensing in the room ahead a forgotten and formless memory he might not wish to recollect or meet.

Thus far she could only make out the buckles of his shoes, silver rectangles floating stationary in the uneven and smoky light above the floor, and directly above them, the white bowl of a clay pipe a foot below the beams. In the space between the pipe and buckles, streaks and dapples of the light and shade gathered and dispersed and then regathered once again. Then the buckles glinted, grew bright, grew brighter yet. Smoke wrapped around the white clay bowl, passed in and out of the flecks of light, then drifted up into the darkness between the beams.

Then the man remembered what he had forgotten, or else determined he had nothing to fear inside the room, and his portion of the light and shade began to move. The buckles advanced, one at a time, up and down, until they reached the range of firelight where she could discern also the knee stockings and dark breeches, the gray blouse, open at the throat, with billowing sleeves, the gray hair pulled back and tied behind the head. Surprisingly the man was short—but wouldn't he have to be in such a low-ceilinged house? He was heading for the hearth with one hand held behind his back and the other pinching that long reed stem inserted in the bowl, coughing and discharging long strips of smoke like cobwebs as he came.

At the hearth, he leaned his forearm on the bricks and stared down into the blazing logs until his face became the color of the bricks. How strange that it would be his face, that same face she knew she had seen before in the flesh but could not say when or where. And strange not because she had not expected it—because she had— but because this time it was not imposed upon that lanky, long-legged body that had disappeared upon the wall, but on the squat and sturdy body of what she would have called a solid burgher type. But although it was the same face as before, it was heavier now, and she could see the creases in the jowls, the stubble of the graying beard, the weather lines about the eyes, even the clumps of white hair protruding from the ears and nose. It was too real a face. In contrast she could not feel her own. Her hands, when she put them to her face, could have overlapped inside her head for all they felt of skin and bone.

She read the implications in all of this: in this seeing him, in this lack of feeling to herself. They were to play the game again. Only this time with the roles reversed: she would be the apparition, he would be the man. Which was not unreasonable. After all, it was *his* house. But was it equally *his* time, that of the earliest period of the house? Because wasn't it far more probable that she had gone backward in the spirit than that he had come forward in the flesh?

Now the man took a pewter mug from the mantel and sat down at the tavern table in the middle of the room. The chair creaked beneath his weight and the legs wavered, digging into the soft pine floor. Gothic finials rose above each shoulder. He set down the mug, which he guarded with a forearm, and continued to pull upon the pipe as the firelight danced across the table.

The same light played upon her shoes—thick hiking shoes —and flashed up as far as her knees. Pressing deeper against that wall she could not feel, she wondered what he would do when he first caught sight of the stranger standing in the darkest corner of his room. After he had sorted out from the corner of his eye the kerchief she had not remembered to remove and the bright blue ski pants and liver-colored jacket, and concluded this was no human intruder but an apparition of some woman coming not from the past or present but a future too far away for him to comprehend, just what would he do? Cry out, no doubt, upsetting the chair and table in his flight. Or maybe he would be both brave and curious and approach her with his arm outstretched, feeling for her face and compelling her to draw away from him until she vanished backward through the wall.

But she didn't have to stand there, waiting on him to make the first move. She could step out of the shadows and walk slowly toward the table, letting the firelight play upon her as it would on any other piece of matter that stood at that time in that place. But before she reached his table she might turn and walk away from him only to vanish as silently as she had come, her light dispersing to pinpoints that squeezed between the atoms of the closed door, revealing only at her departure that she had been an illusion, and nothing more. But —and think of this—just before she vanished shouldn't she make some pronouncement with an air of profundity and intimacy and certainly mystery? Shouldn't she wave and say, at the very least, "Hello, again"?

But the truth was she didn't know what she would do. Nor what the man would do, either. Nor what she would do in reaction to the man. She knew only that despite the change in roles she was again ignorant of the rationale behind the scene. She had not the slightest notion why she had been made to manifest herself inside this room, nor who this man was she had appeared before, nor what the bond was between them that was so strong it could make her image overrule the laws of time and space. The man, however, did not appear to share her ignorance. With his chin resting on those fat forearms he had crossed upon the table, and apparently dozing off except when, without opening his eyes, he woke just long enough to draw upon his pipe and keep the tobacco burning in the bowl, and smiling all the while as though he saw something comic in his thoughts or dreams, he seemed to manipulate through the power of his mind the stagecraft of the scene: who would play which part and why, and what would happen when and where. Man or ghost, he was still the unknown factor, and it was as unnatural for him to be the man as it had been earlier for him to be the ghost. Just as unnatural as it was for her who was alive this morning to be this afternoon, without any recollection of her death, the ghost.

But wasn't this sense of herself as an apparition, as something that was not, or no longer was, as much an illusion as the man she had seen disappear upon the wall? Because now there was something painful about her numbness, something thickening about her formlessness, as though the effects of a strong pain-killer were wearing off. She heard her heels bump against the paneled wall, felt them sink and settle in the rug; felt the dampness of her hand where it gripped her wrist, searching for the pulse, her fingers digging deep enough beside the vein to find the bone. She was flesh and blood and bones. It was the man who was the apparition after all!

Because before her very eyes he had begun to wear out, come apart, dematerialize. She watched the clay pipe burn up to smoke, and the buckles on the shoes beneath the table return to shadows. The head, grinning with a self-satisfaction that bespoke omniscience at the shadows where she stood against the wall, detached from the borrowed body and drifted like a lost balloon above the table through the smoke surrounding it until, grinning and then winking one sleepy eye at her, it vanished into the dark world between the beams.

No man sat at the table now; the pewter mug was on the mantel. This time it didn't matter if she had really seen the man in space. He had come back, in any case. And the glimpse of that disappearing head as it had winked its eye at her had been a true touch she could not deny. She had recognized the face.

The man was Sneevy, her first husband.

Sneevy, all along.

CHAPTER 12

OH, NOT SNEEVY as she had known him thirty years ago, or as he necessarily looked today, but Sneevy as she might have reasonably imagined him to look at his present age. But if it was in some form the face of Sneevy, it was hardly the character of Sneevy. Not the Sneevy she had known. What a joker the fellow had become in his middle age. "Hello, again," indeed. "Mrs. Sneevy, I presume," would have suited the darkness of his new-found bitter humor better. (*Mrs.* Sneevy: once upon a time, she had answered to that name.) What a joke to masquerade with his brand-new face inside those Colonial clothes. What had he to do with this house, or with the Hoitts—or with New England, even? What had he to do with history? . . . But then again, what had *she* to do with it? Because wasn't that his point? Think upon the past, his mime as good as lectured her, but not so far back as these old clothes. No, not so far back, my dear, as you might like. No further back than your own history, your own beginnings. She had never suspected he had the makings of an actor, would never have guessed he had a gift for slapstick, insult, irony.

Why else had he refused to appear before her in a costume more appropriate to where and when and who he was? Just before the moment of his manifestation the air should have reeked of fresh plaster, axle grease, grape soda, smoke-stained car upholstery, chewing gum. Followed by the ghost itself in the soiled coveralls of a grease monkey, and on his head that oily mechanic's beanie she had cut a sawtooth border on with her pinking shears, bearing in his hand some unrecognizable engine part dripping crankcase oil. Or in the outfit of a plasterer's helper, the ghostly dusty white pants and T-shirt, and that white peaked, billed cap that Russian workmen wear. Or in the orange pin-striped uniform of a driver of a soft-drink truck. Or in his softball uniform, that sweatsuit-shaped affair with luminous stripes along the arms and legs, and that duck-billed cap he wore backward whenever he played catcher, which was most of the time. Or in his sailor uniform, the navy-blue peacoat and white cap he had worn as they walked arm in arm on the weekend of his first leave along the neon-lit downtown Chicago streets so crowded with soldiers and sailors it seemed the war must be only miles away, and he had saluted all the passing officers and she had had to take small flurries of steps to keep up with him so rapid had become his stride. That same uniform he had been wearing that grim November morning when she saw him for the last time in her life. The coldest November morning in almost thirty years, the radio had reported at breakfast after the news bulletins delivered in awesome tones on the fighting at the Russian and North African fronts. She had waited for him just inside the gate of the Great Lakes Naval Base—where he had taken basic training, and in whose hospital he had lain ill with pneumonia for the past month—stamping her numb feet with the cold, her hands burrowed in the pockets of her cloth coat. He had seen her first, picking her out of the crowd of mostly wo-men she stood among, and she spotted his arm waving sig-nal-like above the other sailors' heads. He had run to her and attempted to sweep her off her feet and swing her about him like a child, and she had hung limp and cool, her purse dang-ling from her arm, until she could no longer tolerate the false impression of his embrace, and had pushed him away as she might have some pawing, drunken stranger at a roadhouse dance. She remembered those gusts of wind that blew off the dustings of fresh snow from the frozen patches and whirled them about the earth like spray, like smoke, and that yard before the complex of battleship- or gunmetal-gray buildings that looked as though milk had spilled and frozen over it, where squares of men in navy-blue peacoats and convoy caps and white leggings were drilling to the bark of brutal voices beneath a gray sky so full of sea gulls it seemed there must be a large dump along the lake close by, and remembered how he looked drawn and gaunt and freshly shaved, his ears rosy-pink and "lowered" beneath the cap tipped forward almost to his eyes. For a moment they faced each other with a small stretch of ice between them, hunched over and doing a little skipping dance to generate some warmth, he with his palms already muffling his frozen ears. It was too cold to stand and talk, too cold to pace back and forth along the fence, and she had warned herself beforehand that she was not to let him take her anywhere. In that brief frozen moment before the end, she wanted only one thing: to be back in the warm coach of the electric train that had brought her northward and that she had had to force herself to leave, exiting into the wind that whistled off the platform of the Great Lakes stop and through the open door. She had a sore throat that morning, had had it all week, and she clutched it now, giving the appearance that she was strangling herself. She had a cough drop in her mouth, too, a small hard black bitter piece of licorice that she moved around her mouth as she spoke, saying in a rasping, painful whisper, losing his face behind the outburst of her breath, "I can't take it anymore. . . . I'm all through. . . . We're all through . . . that's what I came to tell you. . . . It's all over now. . . ."

She had turned and fled, coughing into her glove, and had not looked back, not even when she was past the gatehouse and back into the world she knew he could not enter. He had

not run after her, had not wrestled dramatically with the pro-
testing sentries at the gate, had not so much as shouted out
her name, her knife-blow had been that swift, his surprise that
great. On the electric train back to Chicago, she had been dry-
eyed the whole trip; seated in the empty car, on the cane seat
with its heater beneath, her handkerchief wadded in her fist
and poised against her mouth, her forehead hot and thick with
sweat, she had gazed sleepily out at the roads flying past always at a right angle to the tracks, and at the random tree-
clustered houses set out in the flat snow-covered fields. She
had done what she had to do the only way she knew to do it.
My God, though, he should have seen it coming; that's what
she told herself. He should have known it had to happen someday. If he hadn't known it, or had known it and refused to
believe it, he had only himself to blame.

Apparently he had seen no such thing. Had not so much
as guessed at the possibility of her leaving him. Or so his
best friend, Rollo, had claimed when she ran into him a year
later in a tavern in the Loop. He had passed along and sec-
onded Sneevy's complaints against her, the worst being that
she had broken off with him when he had not seen her for
three months and just when he had been discharged from
almost a month in sick bay, and had not once in her many
letters and phone calls given so much as a hint that she con-
templated such a move. She wondered what Mary Lou,
Rollo's steady girlfriend of several years, who was with him,
would have to say about what she had done, but she must
have just quarreled with Rollo or else was so upset with Winnie that she meant to slight her, because she kept busy talking with the army lieutenant who stood beside her stool,
chewing gum even as she drank. Rollo, however, looking at
his highball, cut her in a different way. "You made him bitter,
Winnie," he said. "I mean it's getting so I don't even like to
go out with the guy anymore. He's got too short a fuse and,
uniform or no uniform, he's always looking for a fight."

She placed the dissolution of the marriage in the hands of a lawyer, and kept it from her family, his family, their friends. When the divorce was granted, they had been married not quite three years.

In the months and years ahead, though, how he haunted her. She grew to dread a surprise encounter with him on a busy downtown street, or in a crowded subway as she came home from work, or worse, as she was out on the town in a nightclub or tavern, feeling good and loose and happy in the company of one of the soldiers and sailors, or the older married lawyer in her office, and finally Gene himself, all of whom she had dated then. She was afraid, too, that he would discover her new apartment and would loiter in the street below her window and accost or follow her when she went out. Long after she had married Gene and moved out of the city, she had feared the letter in the morning mail, the telephone call in the middle of the night. But all her worries had been for nothing in the end. She never saw or heard from him again. She never even heard *about* him. Even Rollo, when she saw him last, this time in a neighborhood grocery near her mother's flat, had not known where he was or what he was doing, and that was less than a year after the divorce. And some time later she ran into Mary Lou, and she had not even seen Rollo for the past six months, never mind Sneevy or any of their old friends.

Now whenever she got a moment to herself, which was often with Penelope gone and Gene busy with his play, she took to wondering what had become of him. What had he managed to make of himself in the past thirty years? Just what had been the limit of his heights and depths? In her scale of up-and-down—in which tradition triumphed over innovation, stability was valued over mobility, and the cultural scored a notch above the purely social—it hardly seemed likely he could have traveled far.

She was only too well aware that Gene had gone exactly nowhere, that he had never wanted to be otherwise than where he quite comfortably already was, and then, when the chance came, to retire to his beginnings at the family home of his happy boyhood summers. He had not pushed on ahead, nor farther west, nor further up. For her purposes this had been exactly right. Because how difficult it would have been for her had he not presented a stationary target she could set her sights upon and slowly travel toward, but had been a star instead that always rose at the pace of her own ascent?

Sneevy, she concluded, had been too hard a worker and too fond of money to have failed in life completely. How the man had loved to work, welcoming the chance to work overtime with the enthusiasm other men reserve for their paid vacations. How he had lived for those Friday nights after payday, too. He had cashed his paychecks at the local currency exchange with the pleasure and belligerence of a man who held the winning ticket on a horse. (He liked a thick wallet, you could tell by the way he weighed it in his hand.) With money in their pockets, they would spend Friday evenings on the town, calling at several taverns where they were known, with Sneevy treating himself to a shot of whiskey and a big cigar along the way. Or they would merely stroll through the neighborhood in pairs or four abreast with Rollo and Mary Lou, smoking cigarettes and feeling as though they owned the sidewalks and the world owed them a living, while Sneevy and Rollo and sometimes Mary Lou addressed with friendly arrogance the strangers they met along the streets. What a cock of the walk that Sneevy was on Friday nights! And if he had failed at all in life maybe it was because he had become a hard drinker or a compulsive gambler. Hadn't he had a fondness for penny-ante poker and an occasional bet on the horses, and for a bottle of whiskey on the weekends if he could afford it? But then again, he had controlled these small vices as much as he had enjoyed them. No, she couldn't see him owning a bankrupt business, cashing a welfare check, or wandering about the inner city as a bum.

Surely if he had continued on a payroll he would have a title of some sort by now. Like foreman, supervisor, superintendent. Even manager. The manager of a good garage that serviced foreign cars. She could imagine him in his blue smock, approaching her with clipboard and pen in hand. Or the owner of his own gas station—an overworked but happy man in a mechanic's suit with "Sneevy" sewn in script upon his breast—who wiped the windshield of her car. He had once spoken of going to barber college, persuaded more by his friend Rollo, who was himself a barber, than by his own inclination, which was for work more physical than the use of comb and scissors in either hand. Maybe he and Rollo were partners in a barbershop in a north-side Chicago neighborhood, or in some Illinois or Wisconsin small town. She remembered seeing Rollo in white tunic, with his wavy hair and pencil-stripe mustache and his scissors going snip-snip in his hand, working in the barbershop on the balcony of a dime store, and she could imagine Sneevy, bald like most barbers with the years, and with his own mustache, working at his side. There they were, for want of customers, side by side in their own barber chairs, listening to daytime radio, thumbing through their stacks of dog-eared magazines for the hundredth time.

She couldn't see him staying in the navy; he was too independent for that. But, come to think of it, he would have been eligible for the G.I. Bill, and wasn't it possible that he had seized this as his one opportunity to turn his life around and gone on to college as so many of his generation had? It could have made the difference in him, especially if the war had changed him first. Why hadn't she seen that possibility before? She supposed he would have become an engineer of some sort. Although she suspected he had never gone further than a correspondence course on radio or television repair taken from one of those schools that advertised on matchbook covers and on the inside back covers of comic books.

If he had become successful, it would be because, primarily, he had wanted to make money. Try as she might, she could not picture him working for any other reason than the making of money, good money. He had never been one to save it, though. What was it Rollo used to call him, "the last of the big spenders"? There was no limit to the amount of money he might have been driven to make in order to have all the money he wished to spend, and perhaps no limit, either, to what he had made of himself while earning and squandering such fantastic sums. She supposed if he had earned a fortune it would have been the outcome of a mechanical inventiveness of the sort that designs a better jukebox, or slot machine. Or maybe he had been lucky and gotten in at the beginning of a new industry after the war, like plastics, electronics, defense equipment, frozen foods, swimming pools, computers, duplicating machines—oh, any of a thousand things. There he was, the boorish self-made millionaire, with sunglasses the size of goggles and the yachting cap of a commodore covering his bald head, bare-chested and in Bermuda shorts that should not have fit a human waist or revealed such knees, and a cigar in his fat, ring-laden fingers, sipping at a can of beer on his white yacht moored in Miami Beach, his American flag flying from the fantail. Given his interest in machines and willingness to work hard and change jobs and gamble, too, and given the changes that had taken place in the world in the past quarter-century, it was not impossible. If he had acquired any social or cultural prestige, it would be the by-product of his wealth, like the illiterate Texas cowhand who makes a billion dollars in the oil fields and thereafter hobnobs with English earls while amassing the largest collection of French Impressionistic paintings in the world.

In her desire to understand who he had become, she took to remembering who he was. In the beginning it was to be a game, a feat of memory. Afterward, although she could not say why, it became an act of desperation. Her first attempts resurrected very little. Only with a great effort could she begin to bring back his face. That sandy hair combed straight back that looked plastered down and wet, the broad face and flattened freckled nose, the high cheekbones, the touch of buckteeth with the gap between the two in front, the protruding ears. He had been strong but not athletic, and his glasses had given him an intellectual look his interests and outlook belied. His forearms were larger than his biceps, or so they appeared, and his friends had nicknamed him "Popeye" in consequence. The forearms were always tan, while his upper arms, like the rest of his body below the neck, were snow-white, for he wore only long-sleeved shirts he would roll up to the elbow. In his bow tie he looked like a soda jerk. He had chain-smoked cigarettes, had smoked a pack a day since he was eleven, and the fingers on both his hands were yellow. He liked soft drinks as much as beer.

He had been fond of swimming and bowling and, most of all, of roller-skating. Some Saturdays he would play golf on the public golf courses with Rollo, the two of them sharing an old bag that held half a dozen clubs, and she remembered how once she had washed the mud from the battered heads to surprise him. He was fond of dancing, too, and could jitterbug with both an older and a younger sister. His passion, though, had been his car. How difficult to imagine him without that car! An old black Studebaker coupe he loved to work on and sit in, alone if he had to, as much as he did to drive. He was always waxing it, tuning it up, jacking it up to rotate the tires. Once he seemed to spend a month on what she now recollected to her astonishment he had called "dropping the pan." Saturday mornings when she did the grocery shopping he would hang out at the automobile-parts store on the next block, talking cars with the men in the greasy uniforms behind the dirty counter and buying, when he could afford it, seat covers, a secondhand radio, and replacement parts for his car. He had a special affection for hubcaps and hood ornaments, and would point them out to her on the cars along the street, and his mother had once shown her an assortment of both that he had collected and polished as a boy.

It was the car that had prearranged their marriage. It had

been their first house, a cramped but mobile home of their own, which, when they were sheltered within its doors—in their own minds, anyway—aged them by a dozen years. They could have been shut up in an airtight diving bell submerged beneath the sea for all the outside world interfered or mattered. If she pictured Gene best posed against the backdrop of this almost three-hundred-year-old New Hampshire house, she pictured Sneevy with a foot on the running board, or behind the steering wheel, of that first car, winking, with his thumb raised.

It was hard to remember the time he did not have a car. And yet when they first dated they had traveled on streetcars and on the el, holding hands as they sat on the hard cane seats. Two years ahead of her in the same high school, he had wooed her with heart-shaped boxes of chocolates, a cashmere sweater, a pair of nylons, a rhinestone necklace, and at every prom or dance he was sure to greet her at her door with an orchid corsage. He had sent her secret notes that had made her laugh, made telephone calls in which he pretended he was someone else, and she had pretended in turn that she did not recognize his voice, for he liked to think that he had fooled her, and he would recount these conversations endlessly, laughing all the while. They had both been something of loners. For her part she had not been able to define herself within her family, or with her girlfriends, and she was no good by herself. She supposed by the simple process of elimination she was to find herself with a man.

Somehow she had slipped into marriage with the inevitability of night following day. There had never been any dramatic moment of decision when she could have said yes or no. And it was not so much that she was in love, either, as that she had acknowledged she had reached a moment in her life when she was expected to pass on to something else. They had honeymooned at a cottage on a lake in Wisconsin that was owned by one of Sneevy's many uncles. . . . My God, how young they had been! Penelope and Dwight had never been so young!

She could not recall their talking much in the marriage, for what had they to talk about? What had he said to her in their private hours together? Indeed, what *could* he have said? They had said it all in the wisecracks and small talk they had traded when they were dating, sitting side by side on the running board or bumpers of his car. The marriage had been so visual, she saw that now. Not like a silent movie so much as an album of snapshots that touched her with nostalgia if they did not embarrass her first.

Their apartment (they had lived with his parents for the first three months of their marriage), which she had maintained after he was drafted into the navy, returned to her with a clarity that made her present environment seem unreal. There had been only two rooms, the bedroom and the kitchen, with the elevated tracks running close to the windows of both rooms, and they had spent more time outside of them than in them, and she, because of the long hours he chose to work, spent most of her time in them alone. She couldn't believe how real that kitchen was! The glossy pea-green pantry and the cream-colored linoleum with the black-and-red flower-like designs upon the floor. The red-and-white metal table and matching set of metal chairs, the red-and-white checkered oilcloth, the tomato-shaped and tomato-colored salt-and-pepper set, the set of white porcelain pots and pans with their bright red rims and handles, the thick coffee mugs trimmed with a green stripe just below the rim that had once belonged to a local diner, the cheap dishware in aquamarine and tangerine that had a high Mexican glaze, the juice glasses circumscribed with alternating green and orange stripes. She could see herself inside that kitchen. She was busy making sandwiches for their lunches on a dark winter morning to the smells of perking coffee and toasting bread, or frying veal patties for supper and opening the window to fetch in the milk and let out the smoke. She could see Sneevy, too. He was leaving for or coming home from work—she could not tell which. His work shirt was rolled up to his elbows, his lunch-box was in his hand, and a cigarette was stuck behind his ear.

The bedroom she did not remember quite so well. It seemed the place had always been so dark, the shades always drawn. There had been the shiny veneer headboard and footboard of the bed, the same veneer exactly of the square nightstand on skinny legs that held some tall rectangular Japanese-looking vase.

She recalled the nights so much better than she did the days. It seemed they had gone out every evening that Sneevy did not have to work late or at his second job, with Rollo making a threesome, and often Mary Lou making a foursome. Usually they went to the movies—weekdays or weekends, it didn't matter—sometimes every night of the week, it seemed. Their favorites were tenement melodramas in which tough-talking young men and women made a go of their jobs, got married, and moved out of their families' cold-water flats; and those café-society comedies of the superrich who wore evening gowns and tuxedos to dinner parties given nightly in English-looking mansions of palatial staircases and unseen ceilings. But best of all she remembered Sneevy slouched down in his seat with his knees pressed against the back of the seat in front, the light from the screen flickering on and off his face as he chewed the popcorn he emptied from the box into his mouth.

Sundays they spent at his parents' house. After dinner, Sneevy and Rollo, who was often there, and Sneevy's father and his uncles would drink beer and play pinochle on the back porch, while she would listen for a while to Sneevy's half-blind mother and his aunts in the kitchen and then move into the living room, where she would read the comics and the true crime stories and the short pieces of romantic fiction that were featured in the Sunday papers then, and listen to the Sunday afternoon radio shows. Eventually, Sneevy and Rollo would join her there, and she would have to listen to Rollo promoting the trade of barber and the partnership in the barbershop, arguing that there were only two things in this world that people could not avoid, haircuts and death, and Sneevy proposing that they move to Alaska and work in a salmon-canning factory instead, which would earn them a small fortune in hardly any time at all, for he had gotten it in his head somewhere that good money was to be made in Alaska but few people were willing to move up there to make it. She remembered one Sunday afternoon especially, although even now she could not say why, exactly, so small a scene had proved so important. Sneevy, who had just finished with the want ads he read faithfully every Sunday, suggested to Rollo that they place an ad in the personal column asking anyone who read it to please send them a penny in the mail. Such an ad wouldn't cost much more than a dollar, which was a hundred pennies, and there were several million people in Chicago, which was several million pennies, and anyone, he didn't care who he was, could afford to part with a penny. Rollo was enthusiastic. Why, if everyone in the city sent them a penny, he reckoned, they would be rich. And without putting a single person out of pocket, too. How they had congratulated themselves on the simplicity of their scheme. So simple, they maintained, that that was why up to now it had been overlooked, and weren't the big fortunes always made by people with the common sense to see what was right before their nose? Through all of this she had sat in a well-lit corner, darning a sock on a lightbulb, saying nothing even though she saw immediately, as they did not, that not everyone in the city bought that paper, and of those who did buy it not everyone read the want ads, and of those who did read them not everyone would see that ad, and out of those who did see it who would be dumb enough to answer it when it would cost them three cents' postage and an envelope to send a pair of strangers a penny through the mail? She could not believe they could be so stupid. So what if they had been drinking beer? So what if they never placed the ad, never so much as mentioned it again? It did not excuse them from being stupid. They were *different* from her. They lived in a different world entirely. That was the only way she could explain it. Funny how she had not seen that before. Sneevy had been older, more experienced, so much more certain of himself, and until now she had merely gotten in step behind his swagger, letting him lead the way.

With Sneevy gone into the navy, she had been given a breathing spell that, unknown to her at the time, would turn out to be her second chance. Left alone, she had felt not loneliness but freedom. She was becoming, before her very eyes, herself. What an exhilaration it was to see herself, in her mind's eye, by herself—in the round—alone. She didn't need him, and did she even want him? Why hadn't someone told her she could do without before? In the meantime she gave him every opportunity to show what he could do and, in her dissections of him, gave him every benefit of the doubt. She tried to imagine what his ambitions were (which, she had been quick to realize, was another way of asking what *hers* had been). Ambitions? They didn't deserve the name. They were little wants, unfocused wishes, petty fantasies, day-to-day biological desires. To him—and she had made a point to bring this out from him in a kind of test—the ending of the war did not mean some new direction in their lives but only that his would be one of the first names on the waiting list for a new-model car.

She could not foresee him becoming someone other than he was, nor her life with him in ten years' time as being significantly different from what it was. Instead she saw herself doing nothing, being nothing, going nowhere. She didn't need any special vision to foresee only more of the same. It was something like her moral duty to leave such an unimaginative man and thereafter to make the best of the opportunities that came her way. That was how she must have seen it then. He had let *her* down, he would continue to fail her. That

was how it was. And somehow he was morally culpable in
all of this, as though he had unexpectedly renounced the
church in which they had both been married and confirmed,
and in which she worshiped still. What choice did such a
man leave a woman? She could not commit her whole life
to a single experience (she never went so far as to call it an
error) committed in the overheated innocence of youth. To
do so would be to admit to a predestination that was no
better than imprisonment without hope of pardon. Why, one
would have to be suicidal, or simple-minded, to surrender
without a fight to such a doom.

But wasn't it odd, though, how she had been so quick to end
her freedom, satisfied with Gene? She supposed she had
judged him near the bottom of the high rungs, and even
this at first had simply overwhelmed her. Surely anything
higher would have constituted too great a risk, would have
made her feel too out of place, too ungrateful, too much in
the wrong. In the years following her marriage to Gene, she
had been of fond of assuring herself that in this world one
moved up or one stayed down. Or else contrived, as she had,
to step outside the race, surrounded with a stable atmosphere
that gave one the dignity of family and history.

But was this really how it was? she grew to wonder. Because
wasn't that the very lie the ghost of Sneevy had only to show
itself to disprove? Surely he had only to show his face to tell
her not only who she had been, but who she was. In him
how easily she saw herself! In that suburban village as she
stood behind the counter of the travel bureau and pointed
with a pencil at an item in a travel folder on the Aegean
Isles and explained about the "throwaway" in the package
tour, and at the real estate agency as she spoke into the phone
with a cigarette in her mouth and enumerated the terms of the
buy-and-sell agreement on the big imitation Tudor, and at
the country club as she begged out of the doubles match because she knew, as her partner did not, that she was so inferior to his game, or actually played in the women's golf

tournament with her preposterous handicap, and at the
P.T.A. meetings where, because of her long residence in a
village half of which was noted for the transiency of its
residents and because of her husband's popularity, she was
certain as often as not to have the last say—in all these places
she had been a ghost. (No more substantial than a ghost,
she told herself.) And no less a ghost as she stripped the
paint and oiled the antique furniture or merely lived from
day to day inside this, her husband's house. She belonged to
neither here nor there, to neither then nor now. Nor to Gene
and Penelope, if it came to that. She had insisted Penelope
was more his daughter than she was hers, excusing their
special fondness for each other as the natural state of things.
Well, it was unnatural, and had been her own doing from
the beginning. She had set about to make them into something different from herself, and then had kept herself apart
from them by claiming they were something else. All these
years, she had been a part of their lives but had never let
them become a part of hers. She had never shown them who
she was, nor let them find out on their own. Why, she had
lost her life in their lives! Had been swallowed up! Erased.
No better than a shadow—a ghost! How perfectly she had
buried herself beneath what she, and she alone, had determined were the demands of her role. And it was not what
her husband and daughter had demanded of her, either, but
what she believed they had demanded of her, or worse yet,
what she believed they *should* demand of her, for the truth
was they were self-inclined and demanded very little.

What an actress she had been! Gene would have to give
her credit. He wasn't the only one in the family who knew
how to put on a show. How adroitly he had maneuvered on
the apron of his little stage with his small role of high school
teacher in that wealthy suburb, turning it into one of the
principal roles, which was only what, in her judgment, he
deserved to play; this much she had known from the beginning. But only now did she see how all along she had been cast

at his elbow, with his performance bringing out the best in hers. Because that had been her job for all those years, to do her best beside him in the role. But who she really was, or would have become had she not taken that irrevocable step on that cold November morning, her imagination could not begin to satisfy. She suspected only that at one time her possibilities must have been unlimited, and that had she surrendered to them instead of marrying Gene, she would have become someone of whom the Winnie of today would disapprove.

Then Gene had been right in claiming that long-buried sin and a long-forgotten curse were the powers behind the manifestation of a ghost—her kind of ghost—her ghost. Only it was a not-so-long-buried sin or even a forgotten curse, and it was not at all what he had in mind. It was the curse of having no real home, no village—no real family, even—of not having been on one piece of earth for enough generations and centuries to have any values other than getting on and moving on and climbing up and keeping up. It was the sin of the ruthlessness you needed in this rootless, wind-swept place to become someone other than you really were, or even *who* you really were; it didn't seem to matter much, because you had to move on from your starting point to become one or the other in any case. Small wonder the younger generation had acknowledged the curse but would not assume the burden of the sin, and were taking to the roads with packs upon their backs. In this country we were all hobos and peddlers, and only money made the difference in the way we traveled, and with whom. And her Sneevy was no ghost of antique houses full of antique furniture and ancient history. He appeared instead outside the picture windows of ranch houses, or on a superhighway before your speeding car; spoke as an echo on telephones wires; slept on the stripped-down beds of last night's motels; sat behind the wheel of cars in junkyards and used-car lots.

But such diatribes as these would always yield to memories

of the man that, with the passing of each day, grew more and more involuntary, coming out of nowhere and so often at such awkward times and places. One sunny morning as she arranged a bouquet of flowers in a vase. she remembered the old habit he had of winking at her. It had never meant that they shared secrets, only that he liked her. Liked her a lot. And he would whistle at her, too, what they used to call a wolf whistle. He would follow her down the street with his hands in his pockets, or only from that small bedroom into that small kitchen, whistling. And when they danced he would sometimes croon in her ear, mocking the leading man's outburst of romantic serenade on the marble dance floors of those silver-and-tinsel films they saw.

She saw him sauntering down the midway of a carnival in his sailor whites, with the blue-and-red revolving lightbulbs of the Ferris wheel behind him, a plaster-of-paris Kewpie doll in bell-bottoms and sprinkled with glitter held, unknown to him, like a baby in his arms, and several leis around his neck. His white cap was pushed back on his head and his shoulders were thrown back so that he seemed to strut. He was wearing a sleepy grin, and he was winking, and there was lipstick, a cherry-colored impression of her lips, across his cheek.

She saw him on the small lake they went to on their summer holidays, where his parents owned a cottage called suits us and there was a raft and giant water-toboggan slide and rowboats for rent—green boats with yellow numbers painted on their bows—and a large white pavilion where there was roller-skating every night. She was in one of the roofless cabanas in the trees just beyond the shore, and he had scaled the wall and was leaning over it with his chin resting on his forearms and, in a quivering voice interrupted by much swallowing, making small talk about the weather and the drive up and a new song he had heard on the radio and what was playing tonight at the movie in the nearby town as he watched her remove her clothes and squeeze into the one-piece rubbery swimming suit. Then he was in his large boxer trunks and sitting on the dock. He was kicking the water with his white, hairless legs and drinking an orange soda through a straw. And then, at night, he was swimming toward her in his splashy crawl, throwing his head from side to side to keep his face out of the water. (When he jumped into the water, he always held his nose.) He caught up to her, pressed against her, and bid her step upon his feet. No one else was in the water. So they kissed once, and their lips were wet, tasteless, cold. Behind them the pavilion and its veranda were lit up like a great ocean liner in the middle of the sea, and the organ music and the grinding of the roller skates upon the wooden floor and the laughter and the droning conversations of the skaters floated out across the lake with a melancholy that suggested even then that the time could not be now but that of a long-lost time in a never-to-be place. Only their heads were above the water, and the moonlight, which lay in long crooked bars of gold across the water, seemed to break in ripples against their faces. They were waltzing now, her body rising on those feet he lifted—one, two, three—from the sandy bottom. She seemed to rise and fall and float without control, going where he went, feeling as though she were he, and he were she, as though together they were some exotic, aquatic, love-making beast.

Then she saw him inside the pavilion on the roller rink and skating toward her. He was shouting, "Come on, Winnie! I'll hold you up. I'll show you how." Shouting it out above the din of roller skates and childish laughter and the circus-sounding organ as he floated toward where she sat behind the wooden railing. He was coming faster now, his legs held ramrod straight in those polished white roller skates that seemed to her like gladiators' boots, rolling effortlessly on the steel bearings of those wonderful and magic shoes, his arms outstretched toward her, his palms upturned and ready to take her own extended hands.

CHAPTER 13

WHATEVER SNEEVY HAD MADE of himself in his lifetime, she was later to realize, he could be dead. For all her communication with his friends and relatives he could have died as long ago as the war, lost aboard a torpedoed ship. It was possible. There was no reason for the War Department to notify a divorced and childless wife. Still, it was far more likely that he had died naturally in the intervening years. And more likely yet that he had only just died, or was in the act of dying, which would explain the appearance of his apparition now and not before. But if that was so, wouldn't he have appeared before her only once, and then only long enough to say goodbye? She had seen him for certain only when he had masqueraded in the parlor in Colonial clothes, but was fairly certain she had seen him also in the pasture and possibly as many as a dozen times inside the barn, and this, along with her strong premonition that she was to see him yet again, suggested to her that if he was dead he had not come to say goodbye but to haunt her with his deathless outcry for justice and revenge.

Still, it didn't seem likely that he could continue to hate her after all these years, and surely he was incapable of such a passion as revenge. Wasn't it far more in character for him to have returned for the old-fashioned reasons of sentimentality and nostalgia, hoping he could let her know that he had forgiven her, and that he, her first choice, had come round to his first love again?

But this question, like all others, depended on her knowing first of all if he was alive or dead. One day after she and Gene had helped Dwight load up his borrowed pickup with the boxes he had stored in their barn and was now moving to the Farnum place, she said to him, "I remember your saying once that you didn't think it possible that telepathy could come from someone who was dead. It just struck me that you hadn't said it was *impossible*, and I was wondering why you hedged."

Obviously this took Dwight by surprise. Winnie had said nothing of her ghost, or of ghosts in general, to him, or to anyone else, for some time now. "Well, I know there are case histories which, if true," he said, "could only be explained by the information having come from dead men."

"The long-dead thief appearing and telling some young girl where he buried the money," Gene offered.

"Or," Dwight added, "someone sees a ghost and its description turns out to fit exactly that of a man the person seeing him has never seen before. But some of these cases may be explained by the telepathy coming not from the dead man but from a living third party, who had known the dead man when he was alive. I'll admit, though, there are some cases— not very many, though—you just can't explain. That is, if you believe the evidence."

"But, Dwight, what's your own feeling about this?" she said.

"My own feeling?" he echoed. "Well, I'd seriously doubt that any message could come from a man *after* he was dead. As he was dying, sure. If someone sees the ghost of a dying man after the man is dead, it probably means that the message, for some reason, stayed dormant in the receiver's brain.

Then something triggered it—who knows what?—and it popped to the surface, and the receiver saw it there in space."

Her own reasoning must have already taken her close to such an explanation, for the new understanding came to her immediately, and she said, "Then the message could stay dormant in the brain, could still be present there—could be in here!" And she tapped her forehead. "It could be waiting to be made visual even though the brain doesn't have the power, or the key, or whatever, to make the picture at the moment. And—yes, of course—that would be true whether the message came from a dead man or not."

If Gene, who had been only half listening anyway, looked confused, Dwight looked impressed. "I hadn't thought of that," he said, "but of course you're right. If one is possible, so is the other."

In the end she may have mistaken her logic for evidence, and her wishfulness for intuition, and let herself become persuaded that Sneevy was not dead but very much alive. From this she went on to determine that *he* alone was responsible for the apparition, and that he had returned not to haunt or harm her but to woo her back instead. He was to do it all over again. Only this time with the promise of a new adventure, with a different ending from the one before. And he had returned to her only now after so many years of staying away because his wife had just died—that could be the reason, couldn't it? Or maybe she was still alive, and their children, who had kept them together all these years, were now grown-up and married, so that they had finally been able to go their separate ways. Now he was returning to court his first—his only—love. It was easier, wasn't it, than finding someone new? That would explain his repeated presence. He was like a kid hiding behind a tree outside the house of the girl he had a crush on, or walking (innocently) back and forth along the sidewalk before her door. Remember: he had not said goodbye, but hello—hello, again. And come to think of it, hadn't there been something mildly flirtatious in his greeting? He desired her, pure and simple. His desire was as strong as it had been in the beginning. It drove him on. And he was driven by it to see her in the flesh as much as he was driven by his nostalgia, if indeed those two feelings could be separated in him. Perhaps one forced the other, and perhaps this was as true of her as it was of him. Because most of all he hoped to greet her in the flesh. He had only made contact through the mind because, unable to discover where she lived, he could reach her by no other means. Telepathy was the last and primitive resort. It was something to be used only in the interim. Because at this very moment, as she stood gazing into the fire or doing dishes, he was busy tracking her down; she could count on it. Whenever the telephone rang, she anticipated his foggy voice on the other end of the line, and especially when she was home alone, or was the only one awake at night. She expected a letter, too, scrawled in his rough hand ("I am writing this letter to you Winnie because I don't know how to say this to you but here goes anyway. . . ."), and whenever she saw the red flag on the mailbox no longer up but down she ran up the road to fetch the mail. That she had not seen his apparition lately, nor heard it in the barn, she interpreted as a sign that the real man, or some real message from him, was already on the way.

Of course when he did come, he would show up in a car, a brand-new car—expensive, too. He wouldn't feel right about himself, she knew that much about him, if he arrived in anything less. So she took to standing in the window facing the road a strange car traveled down no more than several times a week, anticipating his arrival in every car. First she would hear the engine as it came down the hill, or see the headlights shining through the trees at night. Presumably she would hear him honk the horn, or slam the door. She would have to be ready to run out and greet him, though, and possibly to wave him down, for he might mistake the house and turn around and not come down this way again. Still, she needn't worry, she told herself. He had his antennas out; his detectives were everywhere. He would find her somehow.

But he did not find her and, exasperated, she concluded she would have to do her share. She would have to discover where he was and get in touch with him. So she said yes to a shopping trip to Boston, and while Polly Fisher and Helen Slim were having their hair cut she went off by herself, supposedly to spend the day at a bargain sale in the basement of a department store, but really to consult the telephone directories from around the country that were kept in the public library. As they drove down and Polly and Helen chattered in the front seat about town doings, she composed the wire she would send him as soon as she discovered where he was. She would phone it in as early as tonight. HELLO AGAIN YOURSELF, it would say. And she would sign it, BOTH SORRY AND LATE. Or NO LONGER CERTAIN. Or that pseudonym she decided she liked the best, WAITING FOR MORE. It was suggestive. It kept up the mystery.

Although Sneevy had often insisted he would never leave the Chicago neighborhood in which he had been born and raised, she reasoned that as he became better-off, and as his old neighborhood changed for the worse, he would have moved out to the suburbs, to one of those developments of several thousand houses in what were once farmers' fields. And if not to such a suburb outside Chicago, then to one outside some city in the West—the far West—with California the likeliest place. She could see him in California better than almost anywhere. As she ran her finger down those long lists of names, repeating to herself, "S-n-double e . . ." she could imagine the network of telephone lines strung out across the continent by a series of turns and straight lines to a single house that contained a phone that would be answered by him. But she could not find his name in the Chicago and Milwaukee phone books, nor in the Los Angeles, Seattle, Denver, or Phoenix phone books, either, nor anywhere in the suburban directories she could discover for the areas outside those cities. She couldn't find his parents' names, either, which convinced her they must be dead. Nor those of his two sisters, who, she was certain, must have married long ago. No Sneevys at all were listed in the Chicago directory anymore. She could not even find Rollo's name, which was Moetzne, the only old friend of his she thought would have a chance of knowing where he was. How strange that he could have become so lost. She could not believe it. Among the two hundred million people living on this vast continent, he had simply disappeared. It wasn't right, somehow. Why, if he had lived in Switzerland or Belgium, he would not have managed to disappear like that.

As a last resort she attempted to reach him down the same mysterious channel he had used to reach her. If he could appear before her, why couldn't she appear before him? All she had to do was force her passion into her mind and then, by means of concentration, generate that message, which was herself as she appeared in space. This she would transmit like radio beams broadcast in all directions from a large radio tower throughout the world until it found him, overwhelmed his mind, and stimulated a misfire of his senses. For this she needed to be alone, sometimes for hours at a stretch, and in her quest for privacy she often resorted to secret and deceitful means, which convinced her that what she was attempting was a kind of intercourse that was forbidden. This in turn made her feel unfaithful, an indictment against herself she came to like. She went so far as to contrive to send Gene on errands into town, or to ferry some unimportant parcel down to Penelope at school, while she, who was too busy or too ill, had unfortunately to remain at home. Rid of him, she would sit alone in the darkened parlor or, more often, stand at the window and stare out at the darkened landscape as though to provide her spirit with an access of escape. There she would shut her eyes and press her fingertips against her eyelids and concentrate, concentrate, concentrate. Let her spirit leave her flesh! Let it go forth into the world! All she needed was the deathless passion, the dynamic will. And sometimes it seemed to work. She could almost persuade herself that she had seen her image superimposed upon vaguely familiar Chicago streets that ran beneath the el. Wasn't that the neon sign of a tavern —was it the 1111 Club?—she had neither seen nor remembered for thirty years? And there the small shoe-repair shop where she had taken Sneevy's steel-toed shoes and her own white semi-high-heeled summer pumps she had worn with ankle-length socks rolled-down. Other times she was certain she saw herself on the unfamiliar, palm-lined, smog-bound boulevards, swollen with speeding bumper-to-bumper cars, of a city she took to be Los Angeles. And then among irrigated orange groves, and over highways that wound along cliffs that overlooked the sunlit ocean, and along brilliant desert wastes. And there she was walking over suburb after suburb of block upon block of boxlike villas or bungalows she looked down upon as though from the window of a plane. If and when she saw him, and he saw her in turn, she would speak her address in New Hampshire—or write it down on a piece of paper that was handy, or, if she had to, write it with a finger in the air. Sometimes in these attempts to let her spirit wander, she lost all track of time and place, and would fall asleep from the trauma of her efforts, waking exhausted in an hour, or in the morning, as though from the embrace of a deep trance and the rigors of a mighty trip.

But despite her superhuman efforts, he sent no message in reply. Nor did he appear before her again, either in the spirit or in the flesh.

One day she searched the attic under the guise of looking for things to send to the church rummage sale (or so she felt she had to make a point of telling Gene). She went through old boxes and pieces of luggage that had belonged to her before her marriage to Gene, hoping to find a letter, a photograph, anything at all that had to do with Sneevy. She even shook old books and albums by their bindings in the hope that something had been pressed accidentally between their pages. If only she had a piece of concrete evidence to weigh upon her hand! Maybe, like a clairvoyant, she would only have to feel it with her fingers to envision where he was living, or to make him come before her, or she before him. The search was hot and dusty, forced on her by a frustration that was not unlike an urge for sex that would pass before it could be satisfied. But here where she had discovered Amy French's diary and that box of daguerreotypes and photographs of ancient Hoitts and near-Hoitts, their toothless and wrinkled faces staring out at you with eyes that looked evil or insane because they had been blue, she found nothing that related in any way to Sneevy. A quarter of a century ago when she had thrown out or returned everything that had had to do with him and their short-lived marriage, not so much as a piece of paper had she overlooked. Why, she had set out to rewrite the little history of her life. Had set out to destroy him—and, equally, had destroyed herself.

He was always on her mind now. She couldn't shake him off. How he liked to keep her at a high pitch from which he would not let her come down. Eventually she fought back against the unrelenting, if still exhilarating, menace of his presence. She took herself out of the house and to the movies, driving over the mountain to the next town where there was a small theater. Fortunately she got to go alone, since Gene, who did not care for films anyway, was busy evenings with the town's tricentennial play, if not at the house of somebody in the drama club then at his desk at home. She treated herself to popcorn and didn't care what film she saw, a black detective killing drug addicts in Harlem or a planet inhabited by manlike apes. She took to going early, too, and to sitting in the parked car beside the theater, listening to the radio, and to stopping for a coffee and a small dish of ice cream in a diner afterward.

She would stay up all night reading those historical novels and romances with New England settings that the town library owned in great supply. How she tried to lose herself inside those literary worlds. But what had once seemed as real to her as this house and all its furnishings now read like fantasy, an alien landscape and the doings of a strange people set in an improbable time. Nor could she escape the reach of Sneevy in those pages. Everything she read seemed to speak to her directly, addressing her peculiar problem. Repeatedly she encountered what she remembered Dwight had called "echo phenomenon." My God, it was uncanny. Finally she gave up entirely and read not to escape him but to encounter him thinly disguised within this unlikely setting, looking not only for the "echo phenomena" but for hidden messages that would tell her that he always thought of her, was still looking for her, was on his way.

One passage that touched her deeply came from a novel called *The Luxury of Tears.*

. . . Her face, susceptible to the fallibility of his memory, appeared to him in the center of some mental candle, the face more flame than flesh. Only the buns and tresses of her auburn hair swirled free of this distortion. Even in his middle years Eban Coriander would practice the recollection of her face, nursing the image to perfection. The ability to reconstruct her had been his talisman, resisting age and distance, even the implacability and insult of her hate. For as long as he could recall that face he was not without the hope that time would not exceed a point where it was no longer retrievable, at worse, adjustable, with nothing really lost to him in the so-called years between. But long ago his memory had begun to lose the face and, as if she were lying in the church-yard, nothing but her hair remained. Indeed, it even seemed to grow. How the clarity of that hair, the color, sheen and strands, even the light seen through the loose hairs exasperated him! And now so many years had passed since he had recalled her last that the youthfulness of what little he could recollect astonished and shamed him. Timeless within his memory, she remained a girl, and he was powerless to touch her flesh with that same span of time that had altered and corrupted him. He felt it was as unnatural to recollect her as it would be to dream lovingly of the child, even the grandchild, of some contemporary. . . .

Moved to tears, she underlined the entire passage, marked it with a dried flower and reread it nightly for a week. How wonderful it was. How much it told her about herself. It told her that Sneevy had been her youth—which she saw now as being something like her only chance—and that in losing one she had lost the other. Surely she would never grow so old that she could no longer take the false step back. Surely as long as Sneevy was at her side, or on his way, she need not abandon hope. All she had to do to countermand the turning of the clock was to welcome Sneevy back, taking him as he was. "Oh, Sneevy," she wanted to cry out at times, "could you really have been my lover? My husband, too? What a stranger I've been to myself. What a silly girl I must have been. Whatever must you think of me?"

These days she could not be bothered with Gene, Penelope, their circle of friends, the house. She served them all with a perfunctory diligence that masked the excitement and the not unpleasant guilt of her well-kept secret. Now whenever Gene approached her with manuscript in hand—which was not so often anymore—his glasses on the tip of his nose or pushed up on his hair, cigarette holder held upright in his hand like a candle, asking her if the language in this or that speech sounded authentic to the Puritan period, or if a wealthy farmer in Revolutionary times would wear a wig, and should Empire furniture be the stage setting for a certain pre-Civil War scene, she answered yes or no, I don't think so, as the fancy took her, without listening to what he said. It was an attention that would have flattered her and kept her busy searching for the answer in the days before she saw and recognized the ghost.

Some of the women began dropping in on afternoons: Helen Slim, Polly Fisher, Gladys Chase, that bunch. They didn't see much of her these days, they said, unaware that if it were left to her they would see her not at all. They said she had changed, too, and she supposed she had. She had thinned down a little and was careful to keep herself looking nice, even to wearing make-up again after all these years, so that at first the women would apologize on seeing her, believing they were calling on her just as she was stepping out. She had taken up smoking, too, cigarettes and those small Danish cigars, which she did not breathe in and out so much as puff, and there was always an ashtray of stubbed-out butts on the sill of the window she liked to stand before. She had smoked during the war, and then only rarely, and had not smoked at all since the time of her sore throat when she had said goodbye to Sneevy. She had taken to humming to herself, too, alone or in company, and to tapping her feet to some unheard rhythm or tune. The women were concerned about her, and said so, although they could not bring themselves to tell her why. She knew the reason, though. They wanted somehow to relay their fears that Gene was seeing far too much of this DeMarco girl. Or perhaps by now it was no longer fears or even suspicions that they had but certain knowledge of a passionate affair, they having heard the gossip she would never hear, how the two were seen sneaking out of rehearsal early night after night, and how Dicky Beers or the Mountain Road boys or somebody had caught them in a car on Cooper Road. She knew, too, that they had not banded together to exact some collective feminine revenge on a feckless, cheating husband, but that most of them, even though they had always liked her, sided with Gene. Or, at the very least, they attempted to understand him. This was because they wanted to forgive him. They did not mean to tell her that she should leave him, should divorce him, should throw him out so much as they meant to tell her that because of her recent inexplicable distractions she was losing him, and that she had better look to her business if she hoped to woo him back. They were certain, you see, that she would want him back. Oh, they only hinted, and then reluctantly, at all of this, waiting to say more, although not much more, if she had let them. They thought that they knew everything, that she knew nothing, that, like all wives, she would be the last to know. But if she had become one-tracked, it was not because she was blind. What did she care about Gene? What if he was running around, making a fool of himself at his age? Who could blame him, given what she was up to? And didn't it justify her own interest and insure her own privacy by keeping him out of the way?

One day she said to Helen Slim, whose concern for her could sometimes reach her, and who would often come alone, "Did you ever have a girlfriend, Helen, a good friend, when you were young?" It was a question that not only interrupted Helen, but changed the subject.

"Why, yes, of course I did," she said. "I guess I had several. One was very special, though. . . ."

"Who was she?"

"A cousin. We were the same age, almost."

"Tell me about her."

"She died when she was in college, Winnie. I guess today I can say she died of an abortion. We called it pneumonia in those days."

"What did you do together?"

"Talked a lot, mostly. . . . Slept over a lot at each other's house."

"I never had a real girlfriend," Winnie said, drawing on the thin cigar. "Oh, girls who were friends, but never one to hang around with and tell secrets to. Oh, maybe when I was a little girl. And it's true of Penelope, too."

One evening Penelope came home unannounced in the middle of the school term for a reason Winnie made no attempt to learn. The girl went directly to her room, where Gene reported she was lying down in the dark with the door open. "Best leave her be," he said.

To Winnie she had looked, in passing, as though she had just absorbed an emotional beating, as though she had experienced something more than mere disappointment, something closer to humiliation, the breaking of her spirit, outrage.

In the early hours of the morning Penelope came downstairs to the darkened parlor where Winnie kept vigil at the window. They couldn't sleep, they told each other, had given up trying. Thereafter they stood in silence, with Winnie hoping that Penelope would take the hint and go away.

Then: "It isn't working out the way I thought it would," Penelope said at last. "Things aren't so good between us— Dwight and me, I mean. . . . He's not exactly what I thought he was—and there are so many things I don't like about myself."

"It never works out, does it?" Winnie said, keeping her eyes on the moonlit landscape beyond the window.

"Oh, don't say never."

For a moment Winnie offered her a kernel of concern. "You just don't want to go so far in one direction that you can't return, especially if you've taken the wrong way in the dark."

"But you and Dad made it. You can't deny you're better, stronger, for being together, and that it was the right way."

"There was nothing about it that was right."

"You mean you don't remember when you used to call him 'Mr. Right'?"

"He was never that," Winnie said. "No matter what I said."

"But you were right for him," she said at last, sounding as though she might be crying. "You helped to make him, and that counts for something, that counts a lot."

"I made nothing," Winnie said. "I only *watched* him, wherever he was."

"But you must have helped him, must have given something of yourself up to him, and that was important, too."

Oh, so that was it, Winnie told herself. That was what *she* wanted to do with *him*. Maybe she had figured it all wrong, and it was Dwight and not Penelope who was weak. Maybe it was her weakness to give herself up to dominate him. Maybe the same had been true of herself and Gene. "Why give up anything to anyone?" she said at last. "You're free, aren't you?"

"Oh, I'm liberated, if that's what you mean."

"No, I mean free. Free to make as many mistakes as you

like. Free to become nothing. Free to suffer, free to become a damn fool."

"Maybe I'm not such a fool as you think," Penelope said. "I know I don't want to tie myself down so much that I can't make a change. I don't want to give up too much of myself. I know I'll never have children—oh, maybe one. Did you want grandchildren?"

Winnie didn't think she had ever thought about it. She did not need grandchildren, though, just as she had not needed children. Not even this child who stood before her. She could have lived her life without children, just as she could have lived it without Gene. "You know, you need a man," Winnie said, her voice sounding tough, as though it had been burned out by whiskey. "I thought maybe you wouldn't, and I don't mean you ought not to *have* a man. Only that you wouldn't *need* one." And then, realizing that Penelope might misunderstand her and think she meant she would need a man for sex, she said, "For yourself—to be yourself. Although that's false, isn't it? Because how can you be yourself if you need him to be yourself? Doesn't make sense, does it?"

Penelope shook her head.

Winnie went on: "You see, I thought you would be like your father. But you're like me. You can't see yourself—can't be yourself—or be by yourself. You have to have him."

"Who?"

But she turned away and threw up her hands with the futility of it. "Anyone," she said.

Later she said, "But you're right about not having children. If I had it to do over, I wouldn't have any children."

"Have I been that great a disappointment?"

"Life," Winnie said, "has been that kind of disappointment. It just hasn't added up to very much. It's just been one mistake after another. I mean if they aren't mistakes but what were always the right things, then life is awfully strange, awfully cruel, and it doesn't make an awful lot of sense."

"Then if you feel like that and you were me, Mother," Penelope said (and how seldom she called her that), "and you had my problem, what would you do?"

It was a question Winnie remembered she had asked before, only then her tone had been playful, her problems hypothetical. Now she was sincere, pathetic, desperate. And for a moment Winnie came close to working free of her obsession and giving her the comfort of her arms. Because wasn't that what she wanted of her, the backing of a mentor who was a friend? But Winnie was worthless now, she had always been worthless, she had been alone too long. She knew she was required to ask first exactly what the problem was, but she didn't want to hear about Dwight's obstinacy, destructiveness, perversity, his continuing infatuation with this Lisa, whatever the problem was. Oh, she had been willing to talk intimately for a while, but with reticence, and only then about herself and Gene—and mostly about herself. Penelope and her affairs with Dwight were not her concern. How much more convenient it was to step into the role of the scatterbrained and innocent mother, pretending ignorance of the darkness in her daughter's invitation to confess. How much easier to do as Gene did, dispensing the platitudes of a philosophy that supplied no map and tolerated every false start and lost way. All she had to do was to deliver them as he did, in the sympathetic voice of the exhausted traveler. After all, she told herself, Penelope was entitled to her own mistakes. She had her own affairs, her own secrets. They were her business. "You do what you have to do," she said. "Don't you? I mean you have to, because no one is exactly like you. And no one—believe me, no one—can put herself in your place and know what you're feeling, really feeling, or what goes on inside your head. . . . But we learn from our honest mistakes, don't we? Learn who we really are. . . ."

In the morning, without any further attempt at conversation, Penelope returned to school.

There was no way Winnie could tell her that Sneevy took all her time now, that she had to save everything for Sneevy.

He was beginning to hang around. She thought she could hear him whistling after her as she went on her errands from room to room. She had only to sense his presence and it was as though he had put his hands upon her thighs. He was always after her, trying to date her, begging her to go away with him. If she wasn't careful, he would take to ringing her on the telephone at all hours, slipping her obscene notes. He was shameless. He wouldn't take no for an answer, wouldn't leave her alone, wouldn't keep his hands off her. Christ, he was persistent! Rough, too! If he insisted on behaving in this manner, he would have to learn to be more discreet. As it was now, Gene, who was trying his best to be discreet, was bound to know. She would just have to keep Sneevy out of the way as best she could. She might as well have kept a real lover in the attic for all the cunning she was forced to use in her deceit. She passed her days light-headed and nervous, ready at a moment's notice to put on her best face and brazen it out if suddenly confronted with the truth.

Thank God he was coming. She could feel his messages; they were all sensations she read with her nerve ends. She could have passed for a young girl on the eve of her elopement, with her few things packed and a note left on her dresser, waiting at the window for her lover, frightened of discovery by her father, who was very strict and easily enraged and would shout at her in German. She would escape him, though. She would vanish like the day into the night. She would leave it all behind her—house, family, everything. She saw Sneevy and herself running hand in hand into the night. They wouldn't stop until they were as far away as Oregon, or Alaska. They would lose themselves in a remote corner of the continent where they would confront the endless challenge of new frontiers. There they would lose themselves a second time, in the opportunities of each other's arms. It would be just the two of them against the world, with nothing but their brains and willingness to work hard, trusting in the luck that was bound to come and turn their lives around.

At the window she could imagine him coming toward her through the night. Walking, walking, never sleeping, never resting, always walking. Haunted, wasted, lovelorn Sneevy, wading streams and fording rivers, trampling fields of corn and wheat, unconscious of what grain or soil was underfoot. There were stickers in his socks, burs on his trousers, dead leaves on his back, water in his shoes. He would walk the breadth of the continent if he had to, from west to east, homed in on a straight line that took him through and over anything that lay across his path. He was silent as he came. He was determined, too. She could hear his footsteps and his heavy breathing from all his walking. She could see the long shadow he cast across the silver landscape of moonlight and night, passing before the silhouettes of barns and chimneys, grain elevators, silos. . . .

Then she received a premonition that contained the message that he was about to come. It was the worst of mud season, when the mail had not reached them for several days, and Gene, when he had tried to drive out in the afternoon, had been forced to abandon the car a mile down the road, mired in mud. He had tried to call the garage in town, but the phone was dead, the lines down no doubt in the recent high winds and heavy rains. After stripping off his muddy boots and trousers in the tack room, he went upstairs to take a shower before he went to bed.

Alone, she leaned her head against the window and watched the raindrops break against the panes and then race sideways in the wind. Bubble-like and wavy imperfections were in the tinted glass, making the distorted sight through each unique. By now the sun behind the clouds had set below the ridge, and she watched the stone wall merge with the woods, and the orchard on the ridge merge with the heavy clouds. No light in such a landscape, no moon, no stars, no window of a neighboring house, or the headlights of an approaching car, only that dim lamp behind her on the mantel that reflected on the glass, creating the illusion that it emanated from out-of-doors. The wind picked up, howled against the barn, and the glass rattled in the rooms upstairs. The drizzle turned into a downpour and splashed in gusts across the soaking ground. Upstairs in the shower, water drummed against the plastic curtains, roared through the drains and pipes.

Then the lamp on the mantel that reflected on the window only inches from her eyes went out, and all the panes went dark. No gradual dimming of the current had signaled the loss of light. She listened to the shower stop upstairs, caught the patter of a few drops, the gurgle in the drain. The house, already dark, grew still. Somewhere the lines were down. Now they had no power, no telephone, no mail, no cars. They were cut off. Nothing could get in or out. Now the ancient conduits of communication were open.

She could not say when she first saw the light out in the pasture. All she knew was that the landscape had been dark and then, without the forewarning of an aura on the horizon that a brighter light was soon to follow, there was this light. Flamelike, it leaned this way and that, flickering in the wind and rain that, strangely, could not extinguish it. It was moving, too, jerking left and right as though it were itself walking at a height upon the window that approximated the orchard on the ridge; and it was the size of a man, and not a lantern, if he were seen from this perspective, walking on the ridge.

But no outline of a phosphorescent and flame-licked man could be distinguished within the blue-and-yellow arrowhead of fire that was this light. Nor, oddly, did the light send out a beam that searched the landscape, nor did it even so much as illuminate the head or arm of the man or thing that carried it. Just the darkness and that single light. As though the light were only superimposed upon the darkness illuminating nothing but itself.

It was enlarging, too. It was coming down the ridge and closer to the house—toward the very window in which she stood. It was Sneevy—surely it was Sneevy—come at last! Any moment now and she would see him through the wavy, rain-blurred panes, standing only the width of the glass away from her, shining in his fiery light and warming her like sunlight, inside the room. There he was! she told herself. She could make him out within the brilliant center of that light—she was sure she could. He was wearing an overcoat and a soft cap, and his shoulders were hunched with the wet and cold. His hands were in his pockets and a cigarette was in his mouth; he hadn't shaved for a week. God, but didn't he look driven and grim and a bit green? But the hard times hadn't dulled his boyish humor, and right away, she could tell, he was going to put the best possible face on things.

Good to see you, kid, he said. I sure missed you, missed you a lot.

Oh, Sneevy, she said. I missed you, too. You just don't know how glad I am to see you back. Gee, I'm awfully sorry about that time—oh, you know, honey—

Aw, forget about it, he said. It was nothing, Winnie. I probably had it coming. But if I'd let it bother me would I be standing here in my wet feet and with this lousy cold?

Oh, Popeye, she said, starting to cry and leaning against the window in her desire to reach him.

Hey, what's the matter? he said. Don't go all mush on me now. We've got to get a move on. . . . Say, where are your things? Aren't you ready to go?

Well, that's just it, she answered. I'm only taking the clothes on my back. I want to start from scratch, like we did before—remember, Sneevy?

You bet! he said. But tell you what, let me pick you up some things along the way. Because you deserve the best. Okay?

Okay, she said, drying her eyes. I guess I'm all set, then. Where do you want to go?

Anywhere you say, he said. Just so long as it's you and me and someplace where we're all alone.

That's just the way I feel, too, she said. We know what we want, don't we, honey?

Then why are we standing here, he said, shooting the breeze?

Where's your car? she said.

Out there, he said. Just over there. And he jerked his head and then his thumb to indicate the dark windblown world at his back. You should see the way I got it to shine, and just for you. And when I get it on the highway, just wait until you see what it can do.

Gosh, she said, will you give it the gas?

Why, I'll put it to the floor, if that's what you want, he said. You know I'd do anything for you. You know I'm crazy about you.

But then by some miracle the light was not halfway down the slope, which was where she had last reckoned it to be, but already right before the window, looking in. Only the light was not itself the apparition, nor did it encase the apparition, but rather the apparition was itself carrying the light—a small flame—in the wax-heavy saucer that seemed to be its hand. The left side of a human face shimmered in the reflection of the flame. A cheekbone, an eye, a clump of damp hair curled around an ear took shape. Not the face of Sneevy, either, but of a man or woman she had seen before but could not immediately recognize. The flesh rippled on the imperfect surface of the glass she saw it through, and wavered from black to sallow with the flicker of the light, so that, like an unfocused film, each feature of the face was a quiver of duplication: three overlapping eyes instead of one. Something repressed about this thing before her that demanded to be acknowledged, as though it were the manifestation of an unhappy dream she had mercifully forgotten upon waking years ago. Something unnatural in the force that generated it, too, some sublimated guilt or evil, far removed from love. But then she cried out as the face of the apparition at last came together in its given shape, becoming unmistakably familiar. It was Gene!

"Winnie?" he was saying.

She whirled about, as though to defend herself. He was

there before her, not as a ghost but in the flesh, wearing a bathrobe and sandals, his long hair and goatee freshly combed and
dried, holding up a candle melted to a saucer. He smelled
like—like nothing.

"How you jumped," he said. "Sorry if I frightened you."
And the evenness of his voice contradicted her own desire to
scream.

"What are you up to?" he asked. And when she did not
answer, he said, "Wouldn't you know I'd get caught in the
shower when the lights went out?" He held up the candle on
the saucer. "Look at the torch I rigged up in the bathroom."

What madness, she told herself. To think she saw a light
outdoors when all along the light was indoors, his candle
reflected on the window as he came down the stairs and walked
across the room, coming up behind her. Thank God she
recognized him when she did. In the thrill of thinking he was
outside, and was someone else, who knows what foolish,
passionate thing she might have said?

She skirted him where he had seemed to plant himself with
his candle and went into the bedroom where she lit a kerosene
lantern. Her hand was shaking. The light shuddered against
the walls as she fiddled with the wick. Pierce, she noticed,
had followed her in. So had Gene. "I don't suppose you're interested?" he said. At first she could not make out his meaning.
He was smiling, but cautious, uncertain of himself. He held
the candle out before him so that she might see how his robe
was open, and how—although he might not have known it—
he was only the smallest bit aroused.

CHAPTER 14

A WEEK BEFORE CHRISTMAS the Linquists always had their biggest get-together of the year. By then the Bromley brothers would have the Christmas lights on the big spruce tree in the front yard of their funeral parlor and the spotlights would be on the white steeple of the Baptist church, and we would have had our first big snowstorm, our first below-zero temperatures, so that when we passed Crazy Corner and traveled down the Old Crown Road, the snowplows and salt trucks would be out, as would the snowmobiles, and the snow itself would lie deep upon the fields and in the woods, looking wavelike where it was caught in drifts against the fieldstone walls. On the Linquists' roof the snow lay melting, puffed up like thatch, while smoke poured from the great center chimney and the aroma of the apple wood they were burning sweetened the sharp air. The freshly plowed driveway was already full of cars, some with their motors left running and the exhaust blowing out across the snow, and numerous bootprints overlapped each other in the inch or two of new snow on the shoveled path that led to the wreath of spruce boughs and pine cones hanging on the door. Electric candles burned with a yellow light in the center of the smaller wreaths hung out in every sash, and now a piano could be heard playing an old tune, a sentimental tune, that made a man happy with melancholy, the right hand stumbling with the melody as the left hand pounded out the strong major chords louder than the lyrics being sung in the church-hymn harmony of many untrained voices. Then faces in the window, fogging up the panes, and our host, Gene Linquist, in an Irish knit sweater and a Santa Claus cap, at that open, wreath-hung door, shouting, "*Willkommen,* friends!"

In the dining room there would be the harvest table laid out with what seemed half a hundred dishes: a ham, a turkey, a tongue, imported cheeses, the German breads and coffee-cakes Winnie had learned to make from her father displayed on brightly decorated Swedish breadboards, open tins of meat and fish, pickled dishes of every sort—melon rinds, onions, smelts—a chafing dish of meatballs, and, on the cobbler's bench in the parlor before the fire, a steaming pot of fondue. The fondue was a tradition they had acquired from their neighbors during their sojourn in that Chicago suburb. The *smörgåsbord* itself was a tradition of Gene's father's family. So was the hot spicy punch called *glögg* that they heated and served us later in the evening when we were heavy with that food and already light-hearted or half-asleep with the bottles of wine and spirits and the stacks of canned beer that were set out in the kitchen. We would gather around Gene as he prepared this *glögg,* pouring the purple wine into the large silver cauldron with handles like the horns on a Viking helmet in which he always made the brew. This particular recipe, he told us, he had learned from his father, and he and Winnie had made it every Christmas since they were married. It was an important part of the Christmas celebration in many a Scandinavian Chicago household, he explained. For the wine, he preferred claret, although burgundy would do as well. The French cognac, which he would add later after he had warmed and sweetened the wine, he considered second-best. "What you really want," he said, a gallon of wine gushing into the cauldron from the glass jug beneath his arm, "is *aquavit*. Which you can't get around here."

Winnie said, "Remember how some of our friends around Chicago would use bourbon?"

"You can't use bourbon," Gene said. "This isn't an American drink."

Penelope explained to us that when she was only two she had helped her father make the *glögg*, throwing in the raisins and the blanched almonds and candied fruit with such a determination that the wine had splashed all over her new holiday frock.

This Christmas, Gene's and Winnie's friends and neighbors were not their only guests. In what we supposed was an attempt to bridge the generation gap, Penelope was there with Dwight and a crowd of friends their own age. Most of the men seemed to wear full beards and spectacles, and arrived either in ski clothes or in the greatcoats of some country or other's army of fifty years ago. The women, including Penelope, who was wearing her hair in thick Saxon braids, wore granny glasses and granny gowns and hiking boots. Two of the men and one of the women lived with Dwight (and Penelope, whenever she was in town these days) at the Farnum place. The girl was from Oregon, one of the men from North Carolina, and the other was, oddly, Ben Tolman's youngest son. Some of the others we recognized as newcomers who were hoping to establish themselves in these parts as potters, carpenters, or smiths.

Gene had also invited his theater group, most of whom were also young: schoolteachers and their husbands, a commuting university student or two, along with a few locals who, although older, must have possessed what Gene had determined was a youthful outlook on life. To our surprise Dionne DeMarco was among them, although since she was so much Gene's partner in his plans for the tricentennial production, she could hardly be denied an invitation. Still it was—to several of the women, anyway—shocking that she would come. Especially when, instead of taking the opportunity to be inconspicuous among such a large group of guests, she had taken pains, it seemed, to be the most striking woman present in the most striking dress. Small-boned and white-skinned, and something of a Nefertiti, as Warren T. Fisher had once said, she wore an evening gown of black satin, which, she said, was a nineteen-forties model she had found tucked away in the attic of her house. There was something worn and dusty and even wrinkled about the dress that contrasted with the rich shine of the cloth and the porcelain quality of her skin. Her lipstick was a bright cherry color with a high glaze. She was one of those women who look at once ill and passionate. Or, as Gene himself had once said about her when he first met her, someone whom the excitement of the intellect alone can make passionate. She seemed to ignore Gene, who was favoring the company of his daughter's friends and his own theater group to that of his old friends like the Fishers, Yarrows, Chases, and Slims. Perhaps this was a sign that whatever had gone on between them had run its course, and there was still some dispute as to what form, exactly, their friendship had assumed. Some thought it was only an innocent infatuation because—well, hadn't they been seen at the university some afternoons last fall, sitting on the lawn, beneath a shade tree, holding hands, beaming, blushing? The men said an affair on the order of what most of the town gossip had conjured up would be impossible for a man like Gene. To which the women always said, "What makes you sure?"

We suspected that the DeMarco woman was in good part responsible for Winnie having become so nervous and withdrawn of late. Afraid of her own shadow, we might have said. Winnie, however, had blamed her ghost again, confiding to us in passing that she had been through a difficult period when the mischief of the ghost had nearly worn her out, keeping her awake all night. Fortunately the ghost had not been heard for some time now, and she had almost returned to her former self. No question but that she was looking better. But she still looked like a woman whose husband had just walked out of the house to take up with another woman without giving her a clue to his intentions. Or who had herself just experienced the smash-up of an affair into which she had thrown herself without any forethought of retreat. She seemed as though she were often remembering to put on a happy face, or to brace up under the obvious strain.

The house had suffered, too, during the period of her distress. Nothing looked as well kept as it had in times before. None of the natural wood of the paneled walls and furniture had been recently oiled with that old Colonial recipe of a sixty-forty mixture of linseed oil and turpentine that Winnie swore by, nor had the floors been waxed for months. Much of the furniture, including many of the best pieces, was missing. Now whenever the backs or legs of chairs came undone, as often happens with such antiques, the chairs were set out in the barn with the others waiting to be mended. They did not return.

Naturally Penelope's change of plans couldn't help but contribute to Winnie's gloom. After insisting that she wouldn't return to college, she had gone back, but just to earn a certification that would enable her to teach in a local school. She saw Dwight only on weekends and vacation periods. What astonished us was how easily Winnie had reconciled herself to such disappointing news. Apparently she had prepared herself for something worse, and could now console herself with the observation that Penelope had been cautious enough to keep a portion of her life, if only a poor remnant of what may have been Winnie's grand ambitions, divorced from Dwight.

The bleak forecast Winnie had once made from her reading of Dwight's character seemed to be coming true. He had developed an obvious fascination with the religions of the East, and his hair and beard, although longer now, were kept trimmed and neat, the hair tied in a braided ponytail. It was said that he had become the skillful devotee of one of those

Oriental sports that seem to be a combination of imaginary self-defense and a strange ballet, and that he could become trance-like and break into a slow-motion solo and lengthy performance of its ritual at any time and place. Before helping himself at the *smörgåsbord*—vegetable dishes only, we noticed—he stood over the table and prayed silently, hands folded Hindu-fashion. Some of his friends, however, were reported to be enamored of the doctrine of some fundamentalist Christian sect, in which, paradoxically, he was also interested. Around the liquor table in the kitchen we overhead a conversation between Dwight and his circle of friends on the merits of astrology. Dwight agreed with a silversmith from Brooklyn that there was something to it, explaining that it was only another way of looking at the stars and how they influenced men on the planet earth. After all, hadn't the ancient civilizations reconciled science and religion all in one? Penelope supported him in this, adding that archaeological studies had proved that the Egyptians and the Stonehenge people, just to name two, had believed in a religion in which astronomy was indistinguishable from astrology. The silversmith then repeated a theory that perhaps the early earth civilizations were founded by visitors from outer space.

Apart from it being Christmas, Gene was making a special celebration of tonight. The historical society had finally asked him to direct the pageant it had earlier designated him to write, and he was in a gay and mischief-making mood, although he was unusually magnanimous to Lester Marcotte, whom he had bested.

It would be a cavalcade, he told us. A scene from each decade of the town's three hundred years of history, with the authentic costumes—cocked hats, wigs, bustles, blazers, flapper skirts, whatever—appropriate to each. Enough parts to satisfy a Hollywood extravaganza—so many parts they would have to bus in the neighboring towns if they hoped to play before an audience. "And I've a good mind to stick in some fireworks for the big finale," he said. "Something that ties the olden days up with the new." And as he poured himself a large plastic glass of California Chablis he peered at us with that mask of theatrical menace he must have remembered from a Japanese film. "And what does a better job of that than *our* ghosts? The ghosts that have been here in every decade and that still return to haunt us, no matter how modern and scientific-minded we think we are. Imagine the special lighting effects, the sound effects, the hidden wires, the smoke bombs, all the gimmicks we could use."

We agreed that it sounded like it might be fun, although we winked at one another that this passion for the supernatural should work its way even into a play about the history of our town.

"But," he continued with an air of putting us on, "I'd like to focus on what I call 'The Secret of the Old Hoitt Homestead.' You know, this secret hometown lover of Belle Hoitt, the fellow who seduced little Belle and sent her on her wanton way to all the best bedrooms of Europe. Who was the fellow, anyway? Who did Belle return home to see when she was dying? Who broke her heart, not once but twice? Which family in the town can lay claim to such a cad? Those are the questions I want to answer. And I say we ought to have an actor for each of the old families as a suspect on the stage. Or better yet, cast real members of the families in the roles themselves. And we'll have the hottest young thing in town play the part of Belle."

"Oh, *they* won't like that," Helen Slim said, by which she meant that *we* would not like it, neither the idea itself nor the typecasting for the heroine's role. It seemed such unnecessary mischief.

Having found a sore spot, Gene had to make the most of his little joke. "And don't think I don't know who it is," he announced. "The play, however, will reveal the truth! Not even the actors will know who until I give them the lines for the last scene only minutes before the curtain call."

"But, Dad, if we really want to find out who the ghost is," Penelope announced suddenly, "why, we can—with the help of J.T."

"Of course!" cried some of her young friends. And the cry went up like a football chant: "A séance and J.T.!" Apparently they had all witnessed J.T.'s attempts at something of this sort before.

J.T. was a tall girl, over six feet, who had just opened a health food store out in the country somewhere in a neighboring town. She had arrived wearing a feathered fedora of a sort that only Indians of the last century, corrupted by the white man's fashions, would have worn.

"Can you really get in touch with the 'dear departeds'?" a doubting Major Bill Yarrow said.

"I'm still not sure," J.T. confessed, loosely flapping her hands, one at a time, palms up, as she spoke. "But I think you can. At least, I can't think why you shouldn't. It's only a matter of learning how to use a faculty you've always had—as Dwight here has often said—and crossing over into the other world, or letting the other world cross over into you. And that means deep concentration, deep sympathy, and pure thought. You have to empty your head, free up your senses, and just hope you're worthy of the wonderful experience of joining forces with the other side."

"Super," Dionne DeMarco said, winking at Major Bill Yarrow, and speaking in a tone of voice that might just as well have said, "What crap."

Dwight turned to Winnie. "Who do you want us to try and get in touch with first?" he asked. "Old John French or the lover of Belle Hoitt?"

Winnie said, "I don't want you to get in touch with anyone. Not on my account. Besides, does it really seem right to play such games at Christmas?"

But Penelope and some of the others were already ordering us, young newcomers and townspeople alike, to take our drinks into the parlor where J.T. would conduct a séance around the card table they were setting up.

"Now, don't go away, Mother," Penelope said as Winnie made as though to see to other guests and chores. "It's no good without you being there."

"Right on," Dwight said. "After all, you're the one with the contact. You're the only one he cares about. That's been proven by the fact that you're the only one who has actually seen him."

"And," Gene put in dramatically, "has seen him again and again. And to this day is still seeing him. . . ."

"I'm not, either," Winnie said. "I saw him once, maybe twice. Now he's gone for good. He won't come back. . . . Sometimes these things appear; they come back, do what they can, say what they want to say, and then they just go away. You can't explain it. They don't have any effect on us. They don't hurt anyone, they don't change anyone. And in the end, they just go away."

"You couldn't be more wrong about that," Gene said. "And the rest of you are wrong in thinking that Winnie was the only one to see him. I've seen him—oh, yes, I have, too— seen him several times. How could I miss him, the way he hangs around the house?" Just then he might have winked at Winnie. He was staggering, pouring from the green wine jug he held in one hand into the glass he held in the other. "I'm onto your little secret," he said. "You can't have him all to yourself, you know."

We watched the color sink in Winnie's face. It was like watching a sheet of water running down a windowpane, it was that observable.

He wasn't looking at her, though, wasn't aware of the depth of her feelings.

"No," she said matter-of-factly, keeping herself under control, "you haven't seen him." Then she turned and indicated us, as though inviting us to take her side, saying, "Everyone here knows how you make these stories up. Sometimes they're even entertaining. Some people, I know, think so." We had never heard her contradict him before in such a cutting tone of voice.

It was the same hour and setting as those entertaining evenings we had spent here in the past. The roaring fire, the Revere lantern, the exposed timbers, the dripping candles, the Pilgrim furniture, all the atmosphere and trappings they had used before to create their spectral moods, and yet there was before us now only a man and a wife and the makings of a subtle quarrel.

"Now, see here, Winnie," he all but protested, "you know that isn't true." But what he really seemed to say was: Why ruin the little show I'm about to put on before our guests?

"Tell me where you saw him, then."

"Well, in the kitchen, to start with."

"And he was wearing—?"

"A bandanna around his neck—to hide the scar, of course. He'd probably had his throat cut from ear to ear. Or maybe it was to hide the rope burn made by the noose. He'd probably been strung up for murdering some young girl—anyway, that's how I'd figure it." We could almost see his mind working as he spoke. "All I know is that every time I've seen him he's had a muffler or a scarf or his collar turned up to hide his throat."

We could see the color return to Winnie's face. With a faint ironic smile upon her lips, she gave him such a look then, like the look a strong and silent parent might give a naughty child. "I guess you've seen him after all," she said.

Meanwhile the young people—along with some others, including Bonny Yarrow and Gladys Chase—had filed into the parlor and taken seats around the table in anticipation of the séance. The Indian shutters were slid across the windows, and the lights were all turned out, the only illumination coming from the fire and the doorway in which half a dozen of us clustered, looking in and making noise. J.T. instructed them to hold hands and close their eyes and concentrate.

But then Penelope said, "Oh, look, you people, we'll have to close that door."

"You must either come in or stay out," J.T. warned. "And if you come in, you must be quiet."

Just then the telephone rang. Gene gave a fillip and raced across the dining room to answer it, saying as he maneuvered through the crowd, "Ooooooh, don't I know who *that* is!" Into the phone he all but shouted, "What do you mean, guess who? Guess nothing! Darling, I know who! I knew who with the first ring. It was *your* ring, I'd know it anywhere. . . . Merry Christmas to you, too, dear. . . ." Then with his hand over the receiver he called out, "Hey, Winnie! It's Sheila! Come over here and say hello!" But Winnie, who looked at him only once before she turned away, did not go near the phone, nor did he appear to expect her to, for immediately he continued into the receiver as he had before. "I was just thinking of you myself tonight, and was thinking I would call *you*, except that we're having a party here—and how we wish you were with us, too!—so I planned to give you a call to-morrow. . . . That's right, it's the old telepathy at work again —we've got something going, you and me. . . ." Then he shouted out, looking in vain for Dwight, who was closeted in the parlor, "Hey, Dwight, how is this for proof of ESP?" Thereafter he sat hunched over in the corner, with his back to us and his hand over his free ear, talking confidentially, throwing down the drink.

After a while the participants in the séance came out of the parlor, blinking in the light. "It's no good," J.T. said. "Too much horsing around. We can't get ourselves on the same wave-length."

But Penelope had just located the ouija board the Chases had given the Linquists as a joke some months ago, and was ushering as many as she could back into the parlor. "Who we really need is Mother," she said. "She can make him come."

Maybe Winnie's recent confrontation with Gene had given her a new confidence, because she merely shrugged and accompanied us into the room. No one could persuade her to take a place at the board, though, and so she stood behind the table, along with Penelope and Dwight, looking over J.T., Gladys Chase, and the Brooklyn silversmith, each of whom had touched their fingertips to the frozen pointer on the board. Then, before anyone could put the first question to the board, the pointer began to move, as though it preferred not to be interrogated but to make statements of its own. And moving so fast, too, that at first it seemed the table must have tipped, with Gladys Chase and the rabbinical-looking silversmith rising in their seats in an effort to keep their fingers on the pointer that was sent sliding pell-mell across the tabletop.

"Who's doing it?" Gladys said.

"Not me," the silversmith said.

"Be quiet, both of you," said J.T., the sweat already heavy on her brow.

Someone called out the letter s, which had been indicated first, and thereafter the n and e. Then the pointer left the e only to return to it, spelling out, thus far, SNEE.

At this point Winnie looked as though she might be sick. She had clapped her hand to her forehead so tightly that you might have thought she was trying to keep some thought contained within.

Then, after a pause, the pointer moved again, this time lazily, adding a z and then another e, spelling SNEEZE. Dwight seemed disappointed; Penelope, like the rest of us, appeared confused. Winnie was managing something of a smile now, but still looked like an ill woman who hoped she could be brave.

SNEEZE was now followed by an almost reluctant spelling of GESUNDHEIT.

Then HANKY was spelled out, followed very quickly by PANKY. After that the pointer refused to budge, and the three participants removed their hands and slumped over the board. Gladys Chase looked exhausted. J.T. complained of a headache.

Someone recollected what had been spelled. "Sneeze—Gesundheit—Hanky-Panky."

"From a head cold to adultery," said Warren T. Fisher, "and in just three words."

"But there must be a message in there somewhere," Penelope said. "It can't have been such a failure as it seems."

Dwight just shook his head, not so much to contradict her, it seemed, as to confess how much he was confused.

As we went into the living room, Penelope said to Winnie, "I'm just sorry we couldn't make him come."

"But I don't want him to come," Winnie said, showing us just how far her position had changed. "Not anymore I don't. I couldn't make him come if I wanted to. And besides, if he were here I would want him to go away."

"But, Winnie," Dwight said, smiling, "you never gave us a clue that it was like that. Still, I suppose I should have known. Because it isn't a good spirit, is it? And it never was, was it? It's an evil force—I should have known."

"But why didn't you tell us it was evil?" Penelope said. "We could have done something about it."

"We still can," Dwight said. "Broken Wing will make him go away."

"And just how will Broken Wing do that?" Major Bill Yarrow said.

"Exorcism," Dwight said.

Major Bill Yarrow hazarded the guess that Dwight and his friends probably knew a whole lot about exorcism.

"I know something all right," Dwight said. "I've done some reading and research into it."

"Funny your being interested in exorcism," Gardner Slim said.

Broken Wing McGoon was sorted out of the crowd and introduced with the claim that he had recently performed a rite on a friend's sick calf over in Maine with what appeared to be a limited success. Tall and heavyset, with almost red-colored long hair and beard, he looked, in his bare arms and leather vest and leather wristbands, like some wild Gael standing on a mountaintop in heavy weather. On a leather strap around his neck he wore an unwieldy crucifix, the size a Greek Orthodox priest might carry, which he fingered while he spoke. Some said he was a dropout, others a graduate, of a divinity school, and allegedly he had married a young couple or two in town. He was called Broken Wing because of a withered, shortened arm that was bent at the elbow, giving the appearance of his hand being on his hip. He was from the north country and had a milk goat, which he sometimes carried about in his car, the back seat having been removed for that purpose.

Immediately he was encouraged to perform his rite upon the house not only by Dwight and his friends but by the rest of us. However, like a bashful singer, he had to be encouraged and coaxed while he steeled himself with apple wine. We seemed to have gone about our business, drinking and talking and sometimes shouting, until the next thing we knew a good many of us were trooping outdoors into the arctic air and snow—not even troubling to bundle up against the cold—led by Broken Wing, who was holding up that heavy crucifix from around his neck as though to destroy an approaching fiend. We were to line up in a procession behind him, he informed us, and to shout or chant whatever nonsense came into our heads. The important thing was to make a mighty noise while he pronounced the magic words. This combination of noise and adjuration would celebrate God and terrify the evil spirit so much that it would have to leave.

Now he delegated the crucifix to one of his friends, who carried it before his face in both hands, while he himself splashed water from an antique wineglass of Winnie's onto the clapboards of the house, where it must have immediately frozen. Perhaps two dozen of us followed, most of us the drunks of either group, young people and townspeople alike, including Warren T. Fisher, who had his arms around the Brooklyn silversmith he had sentimentally befriended, and Gardner Slim in his bow tie and well-worn cardigan, for despite the lean Protestantism of our lukewarm faith, we had cast our lot in that drunken moment with the good fun of sorcery and superstition. There we were, stumbling and wading through the deep snow, collapsing only to be helped up by those following behind, if we didn't first bring them down upon us, while Pierce leaped about us in the drifts, barking and jumping into us as though intending to knock us down. Some had taken pots and pans from the kitchen, which they beat on, or wore foolishly upon their heads, and which were then beat on in turn by the pots and spoons that came behind, while the dog took to howling, Gene bringing up the rear and mumbling to himself, putting a spoon to a bottle of Scotch.

Such a racket must have been heard in the next town over the hills. Even a good spirit would have sought the silence of his grave. And through it all we could hear Broken Wing, who in that beard and shoulder-length hair, a raccoon coat thrown over his shoulders like a cape, resembled some youthful Greek Orthodox patriarch of the far north, commanding the evil spirit to be gone in the name of the Father, Son, and Holy Ghost. . . . "Go into this, your servant's house . . . sanctify this hearth. . . . Grant us that between these walls malicious ghosts will never show themselves again by sound or sight. . . ."

Then we tramped indoors and warmed ourselves before the roaring fire, watching the snow melt from our pants and sweaters and a flush come to the other fellows' faces, as though we were some ski party that had just come from a moonlit slope into a warm, narcotic den. "Well done, Broken Wing," a drunken Warren T. Fisher kept repeating, following Broken Wing about and clapping him on the shoulder. Gene was heating up the *glögg* at last, stirring in the sugar, and the infusion of heat, alcohol, and spicy wine lay in heavy fumes upon the air.

Now Gene carried the great silver cauldron by its hornlike handles into the parlor, where he set it ceremoniously upon the table. From the sideboard Winnie took down those special glass mugs they had imported, they told us once, from Sweden, and that they used only for the *glögg*, which was once a year. He poured in a fifth of cognac, stirring it into the brew. Then a second fifth, which he allowed to float undisturbed upon the surface. We bunched up around him, summoned by the aromas and the spectacle of the impending rite. The lights were ordered out in all the rooms, and the only light we had to see by came from the fires in either room.

"This," Gene declared, indicating the steaming pot, "is witches' brew." Through the smoke and vapors that rose before his face, he pointed, with the large wooden spoon with which he had stirred the brew, at the swaying, sleepy Broken Wing, who was somewhere in the crowd across the pot. "And, Broken Wing," he said, "or whatever your real name is, your magic is . . . poppycock! The ghost is still here. In this bubbling, frothing cauldron before your nose. He will soon be with us, once again in this very room."

"Oh, Father, don't be silly," Penelope said. "We've made him go away, and here you are, trying to bring him back."

Even Broken Wing's smile seemed to say to Gene that surely he did not expect to make *him* appear? Oh, something else, perhaps, but not *him*. That thing—whatever it was— was gone. It would not return.

"A battle of wills, is it?" Gene said in his theatrical villainous voice, shakng the spoon at Broken Wing. "Then you're on, my boy." He rolled up his sleeves and, striking a footlong wooden match, put the flame to the *glögg*. Immediately blue-and-yellow flames danced in a low circle on the wine as Gene leaned over until he must have seen the reflection of his own frowning face wreathed in flames. With his goatee and long silver hair he could have passed for a mad German scientist, syringe in hand and electricity leaping about the laboratory in the background, in an early monster film. "Fair is foul," he chanted, "and foul is fair."

"A drum, a drum," Dionne DeMarco said, "Macbeth doth come."

Gene held his hands above the flames as though to warm them. No one spoke. Everyone tried to lean through the crowd to catch a glimpse of the dancing flames. Then Gene held out his hands as though to bless us, or perhaps only to indicate the curvature of an imaginary crystal ball. "He is here!" he announced, throwing out his arms like an Old Testament prophet. "He has joined us at the cauldron—make him room!"

We glanced apprehensively from left to right, at each other, at the empty Pilgrim furniture, at the empty spaces along the paneled eggplant walls, at the empty cup he raised, priest-fashion, in both his hands. "Can't you feel him?" he said, his finger to his lips.

We felt something all right, each man by himself and all together, too—no question but that we felt it. The chill of another world that, despite our being warm and dull and weighted with the food and liquor, penetrated to the bone. We could have been drinking pots of tea freely laced with sugar the day long on an empty stomach for all our sudden attack of jumpy nerves.

Then Gene, to save the remaining alcohol of the cognac, slammed down the cover on the pot, putting out the flames and startling us with the sudden clatter. As he ladled out the *glögg*, careful to put a few raisins and blanched almonds in each cup, he started on another of his stories. Up in the attic this time. Overhead. A skeleton in a moldering uniform. Hear him walking? Left, right, left, right. All night long. Night after night, too. The attic door—does it stop him when he wants to ramble? It does not. Why, he walks through it as though it were just another slice of empty air. He comes down those steep attic stairs, a bundle of bones sailing through the dark. Left, right, left, right. Now all the way down the first-floor stairs. He pauses just beyond that closed door over there— right over there (indicating with his eyes as he is busy ladling). His hand rests on the hilt of his rusty sword. His hair, which has grown in his grave, is long and wild and stringy and mat- ted and green-colored and windblown on top of his skull, and his nails are as long as knives. . . .

At this point we would not have been surprised by a sud- den clap of thunder and the blowing open of a pair of French doors, with the drapes dancing out like ghosts, and a dark wet mass taking shape in the lightning-lit threshold of the open and banging doors.

Instead the supernatural and, for some of us, terrible spell was broken. We could not say who laughed first, only that the laughter infected others, for it was not long after that first solitary outbreak that we all joined in. Nor was the laughter hysterical, or maniacal, in the beginning. Someone, you see, had turned on the lights.

It was because of Pierce, the Linquists' dog, that we were laughing. "Look at Pierce, will you?" the cry went up. "Oh, everybody come and see!" We couldn't help but laugh at such a sight. But it was a laughter that sounded perverse and cruel even to our own ears, as though it was our response to the stoning of a toad, or a fat lady falling on the ice. You would have thought it could not come from us, but rather from the inhuman timbers of the ceiling or the panels on the walls.

It had begun with the dog barking, rapidly in a combina- tion bark and whine and growl the like of which we had never heard before—and not just from him, either, but from any dog—as though he were confused about his own instincts, which were telling him to be at once protective, playful, and afraid. Next he had taken to running in a circle around a por- tion of empty floor, snapping in a manner that seemed to us more bluff than viciousness, his head turned back as though to bite his tail.

"Stop him, someone, please!" the girl from Oregon shouted, her hands to her face. "He's having a fit."

"Let him out of the house," Norman Chase cried. "Someone—open a door!"

But no one dared to catch hold of him. And no one could stop laughing long enough to do so much as try to shoo him toward the door.

Now he put his chin to the floor and his hindquarters in the air and, crouching in this manner and wagging his tail, scooted across the floor. But before he reached the window he uncoiled and leapt forward, not to land in a heap, or on all fours, but to a stop almost in mid-leap, with only his hind legs touching the floor. At first he just stood, shifting the weight from one hind paw to the other. Later he walked. What a surprised and sickly look he had about the eyes, though, walking forward and then backward as though dancing, while his front paws, to keep his balance, batted at the air. He kept it up for so much longer than you would think a dog could walk. You might have thought, too, that he was trying to jump on somebody's legs the way he boxed and batted with those paws. Or that someone had taken hold of them and would not let go.

"I'll be goddamned," Gene said, frozen with a ladle of glögg poised above a cup, "he's put his feet up on people so often he's gotten so he can walk by himself on his hind legs. What does he think he is, anyway, human?" Because wasn't he acting just like one of those little circus dogs dressed in its little jacket and conical hat, with ruffs around its neck and paws?

Winnie stood clutching the back of a chair, looking like an invalid who must use a chair to walk, and we half expected to see her and the chair together begin to scrape across the floor. She was staring not so much at the dog as at that piece of space he seemed to battle with his paws. My God, she was white, though. Trembling, too. What is she seeing? we wondered. We always said that she was the one to watch.

CHAPTER 15

IN THE END, the play Gene had written to celebrate the town's tricentennial was staged by Lester Marcotte after all. Even if it had been under Gene's direction, it was hard to see how it could have amounted to much. It was without plot or character, without point or surprise, and dragged interminably. We submitted to it as we would to any of those end-of-the-year programs the Sunday schools think they have to put on. Sorry to say, our local actors were either too stiff and stage-struck to deliver or recollect their lines—although a number of them simply read from a piece of paper as though reading an official proclamation to their fellow actors, an effect that was heightened if they were costumed in frock coat and Ben Franklin glasses—or else were too relaxed, breaking into laughter in the middle of a speech, or stepping out of character to wave at someone they recognized in the audience. The crowd was noisy with children, and there was the feeling in the gymnasium of a movie theater during a Saturday morning special cartoon show.

The play itself—that cavalcade of the town's history, as Gene had preferred to call it—turned out to be a costume epic of unrelated tableaux and vignettes of such historical events as the famous early Indian massacre (one settler killed, a farmer's wife by the name of Mrs. Little tomahawked in her doorway by a drunken Indian, Tobias Wright); the march of the local farmers, under the command of Major Woodly, down to fight at Lexington (they had arrived in time only to do some sniping at the British on their retreat to Boston, although some doubt had been cast on even this much); the opening of the turnpike through the center of town in 1798; the opening of the town academy in 1879; a typical Fourth of July celebration of the eighteen-nineties. There were no ghosts. Or if there had been any, they had been exorcised by Bob Cressman's counsel and Lester Marcotte's fountain pen.

The truth was, we guessed, that in three hundred years nothing much important had really happened in the town. Once upon a time there had been a few hundred farms, and later a few shoe factories, and a single railroad track, and now there were no farms, and no shoe factories, and a highway ran along the railroad bed. Maybe our lives had always been as Roscoe claimed they were in answer to someone in his store who had drawn the conclusion after the telling of a particularly nasty piece of gossip that we small-towners were a wild-living, backsliding, secretly scandalous, corrupted lot. "That's a bunch of nonsense, if I ever heard it," he said. "Because, Jesus, it's boring living here, and dull, and there's no secret about it, either. Doesn't it make sense that if the things they gossiped about really happened they wouldn't have the time, or the interest, to talk about them? They'd be too darned busy doing them. Oh, sure they want all sorts of things to happen, but that's only because nothing ever does."

He was wrong about Gene Linquist, of course. We were all wrong about that man. Not that what he did wasn't done all the time in town, by women as well as men—and by the newer people, mostly. But it shocked us, no doubt about it, the way he ran off with Dionne DeMarco in what amounted to the middle of the night. We had known that Dionne had sold her house and accepted a teaching position at a college in the

Midwest, and some of us said it was probably a good thing, too, that she was leaving town (and some of us seemed to recollect that Gene himself had said as much), but we didn't know then, as he did, that he was to go along. Apparently they had planned it all for months. Because they drove right through Ohio where Dionne had her job and straight through to Nevada, where she had taken a position teaching summer school at a local college, and Gene had only to sit in the sun in a poolside chair establishing the residency he needed for the divorce. "I guess all those months," Gladys Chase said, "they didn't spend so much time on writing the play after all." Which was only what the production of the play had demonstrated.

Sometime during that first year they were gone, Penelope went out to Ohio to visit them for a week, and what we knew about them we learned directly from her, or indirectly from Dwight. They were living on the campus in a small university apartment in an ultramodern dormitory-type building that Penelope said resembled—if you could imagine it—a cruise ship made out of yellow brick. Gene liked it there, he said. There was always something going on—plays, concerts, recitals, lectures—and the hordes of young people were so active and stimulating. (Can you imagine the difference for him between living here and in some trailer park in Florida? he asked.) He liked the local people, too; they were real in-the-heart-of-the-country people, he said. But he complained of having little enough to do, other than working an evening or two a week helping to catalogue some collection in the library and substitute teaching whenever he could at the local high school. Both he and Dionne had originally expected that with his experience he would be able to teach theater part-time at the college, or at least become involved in some way with teacher-training, but it was said not that he was too old but that he was unqualified. We suspected he would have preferred this reason to the other. Penelope had been reluctant to discuss Dionne with us. According to Dwight, she had not exactly gone out of her way to make Penelope welcome, and had been curt with her when she hadn't tried to ignore her presence entirely. Fortunately she was too busy with her profession to be around the apartment much. A professional, that was the best word Penelope could find to describe just who she thought she was. Which, in Penelope's opinion, meant she tolerated neither nonsense nor a sense of humor, and was self-centered, hard-working, and just plain hard. Everything she said and did was like a boomerang, Dwight had reported Penelope as saying. It always came back to her. She could not spend fifteen minutes without talking about herself.

But after that we didn't hear of Gene again for some time, and as far as many of us were concerned he had as good as disappeared. Penelope had taken a job teaching school up north in the mill country, with its polluted air and rivers and nine months of winter, and she came down to visit her mother no more than once a month. At first she had stayed with Dwight and whoever else happened to be living with him at the Jessie Farnum place, but later, even while Dwight was still living there, she stayed with Winnie in the house. For a while Dwight was, perhaps, the most active member of our town. He went to town meetings and spoke out against house trailers and in favor of a comprehensive zoning law, circulated petitions against the pollution of our ponds, and taught mountain-climbing and swimming without pay at the summer program at our grammar school. But then suddenly he returned to California, supposedly to visit his family and friends, but the strange young people—who resembled Appalachian mountaineers in some postcard cartoon—now living at the Farnum place had reportedly told Roscoe that it was their house now —Jessie Farnum said so—and that Dwight was not coming back. There was some talk that the girl from Oregon who had lived on and off at the Farnum place had gone with him. A strawberry blonde with frizzy hair and the paleness of a medieval maiden, she was thought to have answered to the name of Erikson. The only impression she seemed to have left with people, including her young friends, was her repeated references to the big raspberries that grew in Oregon.

Just before Dwight left, he had said something to Roscoe at his store that might in some unknown way explain his decision to leave us. "You New Englanders never really shared in the frontier," he said. "That's the difference between you and the rest of the country. And you never knew the melting pot, either. You weren't the settlers and immigrants who really made America, the modern America. You may be the first Americans, forgetting about the Indians, but you're not the *real* Americans, like the rest of us." These remarks had nettled Roscoe and he had remembered them, although Dwight could have been telling him how robins lay their eggs for all the passion or rancor the monotone of his voice betrayed. It seemed, though, it must have been a conclusion he had just come to from some unknown observations or evidence he had gathered on his own.

We heard nothing more of Gene until the next winter. It was the Saturday morning after the first good snow of winter when a bunch of us men—fathers and sons, mostly—were gathered in Tolman's Garage in small groups around those snowmobiles that were all the rage in our small part of the world and that were being repaired on the oily concrete floor, now pooled with snowmelt. Gathered as in an earlier time they would have at the smithy's to exchange small talk and watch the blacksmith work his fire; and later at this same garage around the early cars, which, like these snowmobiles, had then been the rage. Old-timers and newcomers alike had become good friends in their pursuit of these machines, and some already owned and wore their special bright yellow or lavender snowmobile suits, even though they could not yet afford to buy the machines. You could overhear them talking above the loud rapping of those engines indoors about which models were best, what they cost, what they could do.

"You mean you fellows haven't heard yet?" Tolman had hollered out to us above the awful racket of the machine he was working on, kneeling on its seat as though upon some wild calf he hoped to brand. "That friend of yours, that Linquist fellow, he's back in town. Looking for Warren Fisher, and maybe you fellows, too."

"Not come back to move in with Winnie, has he?" Norman Chase said.

"Hell, no, he hasn't. He's got Pete DeMarco's wife with him, and—guess what—a new baby besides."

"Theirs?" Norman said.

"Don't you mean 'his'?" Tolman said. "Because it's bound to be hers."

"His, then?"

"Sure—if she's taken to acting a lot different than she used to!"

Major Bill Yarrow said, "What's he done, come back to rub our faces in his scandal?"

Old Bob Cressman said, "He never did have any taste or sense. Of course his family wasn't really from around here, anyway. His father, or grandfather, was just a Swede lumberjack or stonecutter up in Maine someplace. Out on Vinalhaven, I think."

We found Gene where we were told we would, in the Village Green. "Did you look who's here?" Harvey Deming, who was lingering over his cash register and smoking, said to us, as he said to everyone who entered. Gene was holding court in one of the booths, and minding the baby, a dark-haired, dark-eyed girl in bunting, until Dionne, who was off on business, returned. They were staying, he said, at the motel down on the lake, the only one open this time of the year. He in no way seemed guilty or ill at ease. Nor did he mean to show off to us his new baby, his young wife, his new life at his age—that much was certain right away—although within himself, given those feelings he used to express in favor of youthful energy, he must have been mightily pleased. It was difficult to imagine him as the father of that small child, though. Baby-sitting, changing diapers, making formula, pushing a baby carriage down the sidewalks—all jobs that, with a working wife, would have been his. But then again, it would have been just as difficult to imagine him as a much younger man and the doting father of the young Penelope. Even now, as he cooed and fussed over the baby whenever he had to amuse her, he seemed like an old bachelor who only that morning had been given a child to mind. Or maybe like an actor who had been given the baby as a prop with which to do a scene. He was wearing a great jersey sweater, amazingly loose at the throat, with the sleeves pulled up to his elbows, and one of those black visored caps that students had taken to wearing in imitation of their counterparts in Holland or somewhere, which made him resemble a barge captain with long hair. He sprawled in the booth, with his long legs stretched out on the seat, looking over the back at the rest of us and talking. He enumerated the changes that had taken place in town, changes we no longer noticed. The new passing lane on the hill, the many new house trailers along the highway, and the lack of trees—the big elms that had been cut down because of the Dutch elm disease, and the sugar maples because of the use of salt on the roads in winter. "God," he said, "I certainly don't miss your winters. I don't think we had a day below fifteen above last winter. And I don't miss your black flies in May, either. And there is something to be said for living in a small place, a new place, and in an apartment, too. It's so much easier to heat and keep up. And that leaves you some time for the more important things in life, because there's no way that time isn't running out on you, is there? Now, my old aunt's old place out there, I was a slave to that house."

"Gene, that's what we were telling you for years," Harvey Deming said, winking at the rest of us.

When Dionne came in, she spoke to no one, looked at no one, only sat down and picked up the baby as though it had been deliberately ignored until that moment. She could have been working late at her job and come home to find her husband in the middle of a drunken poker party for all the icy anger that you thought she was feeling. Gene turned about to face her and they talked quietly while she drank a cup of tea.

When they left, Harvey Deming leaned over the counter and whispered with his hand cupped around his mouth, while the waitress, who was his wife, pretended to punch him in the arm, knowing before he spoke what he would say: "Maybe I shouldn't tell you fellows this, but I always imagined her busy on top of a fellow and smoking a cigarette at the same time—coming off and puffing away all in one!"

Dionne had come East at this time, which was her between-semester break, because of the final work she had to do on her doctorate at the university. Gene had returned, we soon found out, in an attempt to persuade Winnie to move out of his house so he could sell it. Whether he ever talked to Winnie directly on the phone or at the house, or had even written to her on the matter, no one knew. He had talked with Warren T. Fisher, though, who handled Winnie's end of the divorce, and according to Warren he was outraged that she should be living in his house, victimizing and robbing him of what was his. He wanted her out. Immediately. He promised her one-third of the sale price.

"It's a matter of his ego, I suppose," Warren had told us. "He hasn't any money of his own, and no way anymore to make any, and his young wife is the breadwinner—and a professional to boot—and probably holds the purse strings. He's dependent on her. But he thinks if he had some money—and a nice piece of money at that, because two-thirds of a place like that with all its furnishings and acreage and no mortgage is worth quite a piece of change these days—he could hold his own. He probably feels like a gigolo, like less than a man. I don't think Dionne has gotten after him about it. She hasn't had to. He's been after himself."

The house was still in his name, and his name alone, and he paid all the taxes and insurance on it, and had to, because although he could not legally sell it so long as Winnie continued to live in it, he could not afford to lose it, either. In the divorce settlement the house had been ignored. He had not offered to share its ownership, much less to give it up entirely, and Winnie could not be persuaded by Warren T. Fisher and others to demand a portion of it as her own. "It's not my home," she would always reply to any counsel that she should fight for it. "It doesn't belong to me. And I don't belong to it, either. Believe me, I don't want the place." That was not to say, as we were to find out, that she ever planned to leave it.

Gladys Chase had said to her once, "If you feel that badly about the house, why don't you let him sell it, take the lump sum, and move into a trailer in town you can take care of? You'll be a lot closer to other people, too."

"Believe me, I wouldn't live here if I didn't have to," Winnie said, then went on to explain, "I need the address." As though to her the house was no more than a post office, or letter drop.

Penelope had also attempted to persuade her to leave, but without success. "She hates it there," she told us once. The paint was peeling on the clapboards, revealing a battleship gray beneath, and the corner posts and roof lines gave what was probably only the illusion that they were sagging. We didn't know how many rooms she had shut off—the whole upstairs likely.

She rarely left the house, rarely went outdoors. We never saw her at country auctions anymore, and we were never invited to her house. To earn some income, she ran a typing service in her home, typing manuscripts for professors and students at the university, and the bills and accounts for the local doctor and several small businesses, including Tolman's Garage and the Village Green. Usually the typing had to be delivered to the house and then picked up when it was done. Those who went out there for some reason said there was never more than one light on inside the house, and never the outside light on; the sound of typing went on late into the night, and they had the devil of a time raising her with their knocks. Pierce was no help, having gone deaf in those few months before he had to be destroyed. She would not replace him, either. Apparently she didn't like to listen to the radio or watch television, and Chet, the mailman, said she never sent out a piece of mail.

Once Helen Slim had suggested that she drive to Florida with Gardner and herself. Warren T. Fisher would look after the house, just in case Gene heard about her leaving it and got it into his head that it was abandoned. Once in Florida, she could go her own way if she wanted to. They planned to stay about a month, and would miss the worst of the winter. A change of scenery, climate, faces—time to sort herself out, as it were—would do her a world of good.

Winnie had looked up from the typewriter she had placed on a card table up against what had become her favorite window. "You don't understand," she said. "I don't want time— I don't want space—I don't want *flesh*. I don't want anything new, anything else." And as though some shameful family secret were about to be unwrapped and poked at, she had risen and slid the Indian shutters from behind the paneling and across the sash, leaving only the private lantern of the fire to light the room.

"Oh, Winnie," Helen said, turning her back to her so Winnie could not see her take a handkerchief from her purse, "I just don't know what to say to you, don't know what to do about you, you've become so . . . black."

Recluse, hermit, eccentric, they were all terms we could use in speaking of her. Surely hers had become a life of eating out of cans, sleeping in her clothes, of living in a world narrowing from an unlit, unheated house into a single silent room.

Sometimes she would walk the four miles to Roscoe's store to do her shopping, where if you met her she would give you that insipid smile that was her defense against having to speak. Then she would walk the four miles back. Roscoe figured it was because her car wouldn't start, or because she had forgotten to register it or even that she owned the thing. Most of the time, though, he delivered her groceries himself. "You know, sometimes I get fooled," he said one evening. "When I drive out the Old Crown Road to the Hoitt place, I get to thinking it's twenty, thirty years ago. I used to make the same deliveries for old Mamie when she lived out there. Sometimes I think it's Mamie that's living there, still living there. Because Winnie sure isn't living her life much different from the way Mamie took to living hers."

Old Mrs. Bob Cressman was also known to confuse Winnie with Mamie, although at other times she seemed to know perfectly well who was living in the old Hoitt place, and who Winnie really was, and that she could confuse the two. Her mind had begun to wander, both her son and grandson said. Once she talked old Bob himself into driving her out to the Hoitt place. They needed that woman's support, she said. Bob waited in the car while she, cane in hand, stumped up to the door. When Winnie answered and did not invite her in, she stood in the doorway and railed against the flock of newcomers who were moving into town and trying to take it over, trying to change it. And by that she did not mean all the new people, just those professional and white-collar people and retired military people who wanted such things as zoning laws and more tax money for the schools. Her husband was coming out of retirement to run again for selectman after all these years. He would appreciate her vote. And old Bob leaned out his rolled-down window, smiled up at her, and waved.

Then, shaking with her old age, Mrs. Cressman took Winnie by the arm. She spoke with a kind of final effort and show of pain. "There's not so many of us old-timers left anymore, is there?" And seeing that Winnie looked confused, that she did not know whom she could be referring to, she said, "Now, Mamie—" And then, catching her mistake, "Winnie, I mean—I mean like Bob—and me—and you!"

A NOTE ON THE TYPE

THIS BOOK is set in Electra, a Linotype face designed by W. A. Dwiggins (1880–1956), who was responsible for so much that is good in contemporary book design. Although much of his early work was in advertising and he was the author of the standard volume *Layout in Advertising*, Mr. Dwiggins later devoted his prolific talents to book typography and type design and worked with great distinction in both fields. In addition to his designs for Electra, he created the Metro, Caledonia, and Eldorado series of type faces, as well as a number of experimental cuttings that have never been issued commercially.

Electra cannot be classified as either modern or old-style. It is not based on any historical model, nor does it echo a particular period or style. It avoids the extreme contrast between thick and thin elements that marks most modern faces and attempts to give a feeling of fluidity, power, and speed.

Composed, printed, and bound by
The Haddon Craftsmen, Inc.,
Scranton, Pennsylvania

Design by Gwen Townsend

6208 ✓

Date Due

JUL 1 4 1976 SEP 1 9 1987		
AUG 1 1 1976 NOV 2 7 1987		
AUG 1 1 1976 MAR 1 2 1988		
AUG 2 5 1976 AUG 0 6 1980		
SEP 1 0 1976 SEP 2 6 1982		
SEP 2 9 1976 FEB 0 4 2000		
OCT 1 5 1976		
NOV 0 5 1976		
DEC 2 2 1976		
JAN 4 1976		
MAR 1 5 1977		
MAR 3 1 1979		
MAR 11 '83		
APR 2 '83		
FEB 24 '84		
JAN 3 0 1987		

BRO DART   CAT. NO. 23 233   PRINTED IN U.S.A.